Ready or not

Other books by Mary Stolz

TO TELL YOUR LOVE

THE ORGANDY CUPCAKES

THE SEA GULLS WOKE ME

THE LEFTOVER ELF

Ready or not

by MARY STOLZ

Harper & Brothers NEW YORK

READY OR NOT

E-D   OCLC#302824

The lines from *The Wasteland*, by T. S.
Eliot, on page 145, are used by permission
of Harcourt, Brace and Company, Inc.,
publishers.

.

Library of Congress catalog card number: 52-7877

For EILEEN, MY SISTER

and PEG, DEAR COZ

Ready or not

Chapter One

They were moving again.

Mr. Connor announced at dinner, in the faintly sullen voice of a man who doesn't like what he's about to say any more than his hearers will, but is determined not to let it be known, that he'd found just the apartment.

"What?" Morgan's fork clattered against her plate as she turned toward her father.

He immediately took refuge in rebuke. "It seems to me, Morgan, that after sixteen years you could think of something to say besides what. If you'd listen to people . . ." He broke off, realizing that pretense of a normal fatherly reproof would not be allowed. He'd tossed this apartment into the middle of their meal and side issues were now out of the question. Sighing heavily, he repeated that he thought they'd find it just the apartment.

"We'll find it just what apartment?" Morgan's voice was carefully restrained. "Pop, are you saying that we have to move again?"

Mr. Connor started to shake his head, then nodded it and shrugged. He glanced hopefully at his son and his other daughter. They were younger than Morgan and might conceivably enjoy the prospect of yet another move. Morgan, he knew, wanted to go somewhere and scream right this minute. He wouldn't have minded going along. But prices kept going up, and he hadn't got the raise this time either. Each time they moved it was to something cheaper still. Up went everything and down went they.

Julie leaned an elbow beside her plate, nestled her chin on the fist and said with her jaw clopping up and down that as far as she was concerned she thought it was a slick idea. "And you don't have to pay attention to *some* people," she added, loudly loyal to her father, but avoiding Morgan's glance. In weak moments, when she was ill, or afraid to go to school, Julie found her sister nearly all that her mother might have been. There was the added advantage of being able, on occasion, to be as disrespectful as any young sister has the right to be. Julie was not a girl to forego advantages.

"Well," Ned said cheerfully, "when do we start packing?"

"Why do we ever unpack?" Morgan muttered. She started to stack dishes without getting up from her chair, then remembered what she'd decided about keeping the home gracious, and rose. We will not, she had resolved, when they moved to this apartment slightly over a year ago, put catsup bottles or wrapped loaves of bread on the table. We will remove the dishes of one course before we serve the next. This was simple, as they never had meals of more than two courses (Julie and Ned would have been surprised to hear them called "courses" anyway) but the principle was important. As the apartments in which they lived grew cheaper and gloomier, the importance of keeping them clean and gracious increased. Of keeping Ned and Julie aware of courtesy and things like . . . oh well, things like not having catsup on the table in a bottle. They showed no signs at all of caring. "Will you please take your elbows off the table?" she snapped.

Julie removed her arm with elaborate gestures. "Surely. Let's keep the elbows polite, even if the tongues aren't."

2

"Stow it," Ned said. He did not expect Julie to listen to him, and she didn't. She was thirteen, four years older than he was, and they got along pretty well, but for all the attention she'd pay to his words he might as well speak Chinese. "Julie," he said, "if I woke you up in the middle of the night yelling *Fire,* what would you do?"

"Look to see if there was one, of course."

"Don't you ever believe anything I say?"

"Not without checking."

"You realize you could lose your life in this fire?"

"There're fire escapes, aren't there?"

"Yeah, but this blaze is out of control."

"Then what are you hollering for? You're going to lose your life too."

"That's why I'm hollering."

Morgan began to laugh. "Where is this apartment, Pop?" she asked, acutely aware that the time had passed when she could reach over to tousle Ned's hair. Or, if she and Ned were alone, she could. But Julie was growing up, and demonstrations of love by members of her family were embarrassing to her. Morgan tried to remember it.

"Not far away," her father said. "In that development, over on the river."

Slowly Morgan turned from the sideboard to face him. She said in a tone of disbelief, "You mean . . . that housing development?" She ran at him, forgetting all Julie's preferences for dignified aloofness, and clasped her arms around his neck. "Oh, Pop, Pop . . . how absolutely wonderful. How did you do it? Why didn't you tell me? Oh my gosh . . . oh lovely, lovely . . . It'll be clean. And practically new!" She whirled around. "What a glorious thing. My cup runneth over. . . ."

"Your head runneth over," Julie frowned.

"You're pleased?" Mr. Connor said cautiously. "As a matter of fact, it wasn't easy to get the place."

"Of course it wasn't easy. Pleased? Well, naturally I'm pleased. Those places are clean, and they have windows that open on the street, and they—"

"It's clean here, isn't it?" Mr. Connor looked around the dark kitchen in which they sat.

Morgan laughed again. "Is it? Perhaps. It's cleaned. But there's a difference. How can we afford it?"

"It's cheaper than this place. Why do you think we're moving?" her father asked curtly. "This is a better neighborhood."

"Oh, neighborhood," Morgan said with divine indifference. "Who cares about that?"

"Pop does," Julie put in, feeling enough time had passed with no word from her. But neither Morgan nor Mr. Connor listened. Morgan had drifted away to newly painted walls and outside rooms. Mr. Connor had drifted back to Sarah, who, if she had lived, would have recognized the hurt in his voice, would have known that a low pay envelope trailing lamely behind prices meant more than fewer clothes, a cheaper apartment. But that was nothing the kids could understand. Morgan was wonderful, and she wanted things nice. She liked to be lazy, but still she put catsup in a little blue bowl (and a messy business it was, getting the stuff out of a bottle—he wondered if she ever tried to put it back in) and she taught the children manners. She hated the windows on the gray court. Well, a girl does what she can, a man does what he must, and Sarah had been gone a long time now.

"When are we moving?" Morgan asked.

"First of September. At least . . . well, yes, the first. They're painting the apartment, and all. That's when they said it would be ready."

"Painting the apartment and all," Morgan repeated dreamily. "What do you suppose 'and all' means?"

"September gives us practically a month," Julie said, beginning to wonder if she'd miss her friends. Life, to Julie, was a seesaw. There she sat at one end, with most of the world at the other, going up and down, up and down, never sure how she got on nor how to get off. Morgan just ambled along on a level, with a little rise here and there to make things interesting, and a gentle, unemotional gait to keep her from getting tired. I wouldn't want to be like that, Julie told herself. But the statement carried little conviction. Julie was given to bursts of generosity and confidences, followed by periods of sullenness during which she felt she'd been gulled in some way. She went into friendships quickly, tired of them quickly. Now she decided it was just as well they were moving. Everyone was getting sort of impossible lately. Mag Lewis, who had begun to prance and giggle and act a perfect fool whenever a boy was near. Or Deborah, who had been her very *best* friend, but hadn't invited her over to listen to records for almost a week. I won't even tell them till just before we go, she decided. And then I'll just say, oh, I *hardly* thought you'd be interested. Or, perhaps it would be best to act as if she'd quite forgotten, in all the excitement, to inform casual acquaintances. "I think I'll go in and start packing," she said.

"I think you'll sit and finish your dinner," Morgan corrected.

Ned leaned across the table toward his father. "There wouldn't, by any chance, be two bedrooms in this place? Yeah, I knew there wouldn't. Well, that's all right, Pop. Just thought I'd ask." He swung back into place, toyed with his pudding, and sighed.

Morgan, looking at his arms that were long and thin, the face that now showed no little boy roundness but a light

5

forecast of the face he would wear in five, in ten years—longish, with tight skin over the bones—realized that of course he didn't wish any longer to sleep in a room with his sisters. The one bedroom, with the double bed and the cot by the window that Ned used. When he was little, he'd been happy in there with them. He'd lie in the dark and call to them in whispers. "You asleep, Morgy? You sleeping yet?" "Not yet. I'd like to." "Oh, all right, Morgy. I just wanted to know." "Know what?" "Just know," he'd say cozily, happy to be safe and near his sisters. But now he was nine, and he'd want a room of his own (that, of course, was impossible) or at least to share a room with Pop. Pop slept on the couch in the living room. He had slept on it for years, and it was just a couch. In the newspapers you saw couches that opened up to become double beds, twin beds, that converted to this and that by day and night. If they'd had one like that, Ned could have slept in the living room too. Theirs refused to be anything but its narrow self, slack with years, covered with green frieze that rasped through the sheets, inhospitable even to Pop's thinness.

"Why am I the only person in this family who isn't thin?" she said. Pop looked up, surprised at this turn in the conversation. "Mother was thin," Morgan continued. "Ned and Julie are shadows. You're much too thin. What happened to me?"

"You aren't fat," her father pointed out.

"You could stop eating candy bars," Julie said.

Morgan glanced coolly at her sister. "I don't *mind* my weight at all. I'm just curious."

"Your mother's mother was an ample figure of a woman," Dan Connor said. He cast about for other examples. "And I had an aunt that no one ever spoke of as wasting away. She was a very good cook and I think was the first woman in

6

Indiana ever to send her family wash to an outside laundry. The talk was something terrible."

"And well it might be," Julie said. "Did she repent?"

"Oh no. She considered herself something of a pioneer. A spirited woman, my aunt."

Living this way, Morgan thought as the table reverted again to silence, living as they had, so huddled and without space, had helped to make Julie the sharp defensive girl she was. It had kept from them the simple right of people to be alone when they wished to be. Everyone in the family was afraid to be ill, afraid to be unhappy, for fear either of these weaknesses should spread and infect them all. If you were poor, you put cardboard in the bottoms of your shoes when they wore thin. If you were proud, you kept your feet on the floor so no one would know. If you were poor and proud you patched up your feelings too, and arranged for them not to show. Ned had asked only casually about an extra room, and had received the no quite lightly. It was important to him, but importance, too, required more space than they had.

In August the city lay down like an exhausted housewife. The air was full with the clamorous tedium of a vacation that had offered nothing but time and had offered too much of that. The dullest students were niggled by the idea that, after all, school was somewhere to *go*. They yelled more loudly, to deny this betrayal of their instincts. Other children quite frankly began to wonder what the new teachers would be like, would chemistry, or fractions, or fourth grade geography be as horrible as everyone who'd taken them assured everyone who hadn't that they would? They shrieked at each other that it was so, it was so, it would all be unbearable. The smaller, frightened children grew quieter, not telling that they were afraid of the iron stairways, the class bells, the bullies, the strangers, the tall teachers.

The loud rattle of a dying summer rang in all ears. Bells on touring ice-cream wagons began to sound thin and doomed, and the children gathered round no longer seemed gay and friendly with the drivers, nor the drivers with them. It had become a matter of hard business, this exchange of nickels and pennies for ices on sticks. Now the vendors and buyers were tiring of each other, the wares were no more delightful than any other habit, though once in a while some child denied would feel a flash of the old rapture and scream for pistachio with the ardor of June.

Morgan sat on the brownstone steps, watching Julie and Mag and Deborah play hopscotch. Briefly, she thought it might be fun to play too. She used to play with Kitty Mc-Mahon, who had moved to Jersey with her family. Funny, she thought, half watching the chalked boxes, the hopping feet (Julie needs socks, the mother part of her mind registered) and half seeing Kitty McMahon's bright little fox face laughing at her from the far reaches of Jersey, funny how much you can care for someone, and then forget. She hadn't forgotten Kitty, really. But all these distances lay between them, and they rarely wrote, and weeks passed when Kitty was never in her mind at all. Morgan looked up and down the street, at the children playing, or standing with unoccupied eyes and slack hands, or leafing through comics with the stern attentiveness they bring to this task; at the large, sweating, aproned women sitting on folding chairs, as though it were a boardwalk they faced and not a tar-bubbled street. Nearly every window incased a housewife leaning on a pillow, a shirt-sleeved man yawning and scratching his chest, a dog peering between plants in red pots or striated brown and green jardinieres. The development they were going to move into was tremendous, a red brick city on the

East River. Morgan had walked over to look one day. Beautiful tall buildings on the river, they were.

They found that three large safety pins strung together worked best for hopscotch. Bottle tops slid, small rocks had edges that would unpredictably tip them over the chalked blocks, and in either case the player was out. Mag Lewis kept glancing up at Marty Banks' window, because sometimes in the afternoon he lounged there, blowing softly on his clarinet. Today she had joined the hopscotch game with an air of amused ineptness that should certainly inform any watcher that she played from boredom, on a whim . . .

"For the love of mud, Mag, if you're playing, *play*," Julie said loudly. "We didn't draw this hopscotch in the sky." Deborah laughed, and Julie went on, encouraged, "Anyway, Marty Banks is *not* home. I saw him go out ages ago."

The three safety pins jingled in Mag's hand. She thought of throwing them in Julie's face, but was afraid of what coals of fire might be heaped on her already burning head. She looked down, praying that no one had heard. There was such a lot of noise on the street that perhaps awful Julie's awful voice had not been noticed. She pitched the pins into box six, hopped after them in apathetic retrieval, thinking, anyway Julie will be gone soon. Julie hadn't told her, but had told Deborah in strict secrecy, and in still stricter secrecy, Deborah had told Mag, that the Connors were not long for this street. Well, they can't move too soon for me, Mag thought. Then she noticed Marty coming up the street, and it was too late to get out of the game. Mag glared at Julie, who'd suggested it, and Marty eased up to Morgan without a glance at the hopscotch players.

"Hi, Morg," he said, settling back on the steps as though they were cushioned.

"Do you have to call me that?" she asked, though other people did and she didn't mind at all. "It sounds like a place to die."

"I didn't name you."

"There are these small blessings."

"What's eating you, sugar?"

"Nothing is. I just don't like to be called Morg. Or sugar either, for that matter."

"Pretty particular, aren't you?"

"You bet I am."

Marty debated a moment, decided to ignore that. "Want to go to a movie Friday night?"

"No thank you."

Marty took out a pack of cigarettes, lit one, leaned back blowing smoke first through his nose, then in a long, fast, irritated breath from his mouth. "This is all because of the other night, I suppose?"

"Suppose away. I don't care."

"Look, Morg . . . I mean, Morgan . . . you're sixteen years old. How long do you intend to wait before you kiss a guy? Maybe you don't know what you're missing, eh?"

For the first time since he'd sat down, Morgan turned to face him. A grimy T-shirt, old brown pants, white shoes. Black glistening hair, brown skin, eyes that slid beneath thick lashes. She thought a sunning lizard would resemble Marty. "What gives you the idea," she asked slowly, "that just because I won't kiss you, I never kissed anyone?"

They stared at each other for an uncomfortable second. Then Marty flipped his cigarette toward the gutter. "Have it your way," he said, getting up. He was attempting to look scornful, which he was not, rather than angry and ashamed, which he was. "So long, *Morg*," he said as he walked away.

"Oh, honestly, this is so much *fun* . . ." Mag's lilting laugh came from the street. "I just haven't played it in years . . ."

"What do you mean?" Julie began. "We . . ."

"In simply the longest *time* . . ." Mag's desperate gay voice climbed over Julie's.

Marty was across the street and away. Morgan continued to watch the children and the street. A few houses down, Ned and some other boys were building a wagon out of an old doll carriage and a wooden crate. They'd barely begun work but were already fiercely arguing over who got the first ride. That is, they all argued except Ned, who continued to pore over the wheels with loving attention and his own prize—a screwdriver with several concealed heads (adhesive tape around the broken handle), which enabled him to deal with almost any size screw. He was alone in a world of wheels and tools, and when the wagon was made, it was probable he wouldn't want a ride at all.

Morgan, looking at her brother, at her sister, decided they were well occupied for a while. She got up, dusting casually at her skirt, and turned into the house. In the entrance of the old apartment building (grimy, once-white, octagonal tiles that had never been a good fit, and walls painted brown to hide the squalor of years) she paused at the tier of scratched brass mailboxes, each surmounted by a squat button for announcing arrivals, and peered into the dark slot of the Connor box. It seemed empty. She pushed through the door and began to mount the thin steep stairs, not touching the rail nor looking at the treads. She mounted as though to a scaffold, head up, arms hanging.

Her father, descending, had this impression. "You look like Mary Stuart preparing to die well."

Morgan was pleased. "Mary Queen of Scots? She was pretty, wasn't she?"

"I don't know. They've been viewed from a bias for so long, these dead queens. Even Elizabeth has somehow emerged as a redhead. California version."

"Well, she did have red hair, didn't she?" Morgan asked, a bit vexed. She loved the movies, and her life had a celluloid gloss that blurred and softened its outlines. Through chaste pulp love stories, the cinema's impossible beauties, columns which aspired to provide physical perfection, Morgan pursued a dream of herself—lovely, beloved. Her father had a ruthless attitude toward the glamor she attached to history or literature. He said that Abraham Lincoln had, in all probability, been barely acquainted with Ann Rutledge. He said that the Brontë sisters did not resemble three young ladies in the movies. He said that the great sirens of history had been loved for their minds, Morgan, their minds. The body was beautiful if the mind was. Morgan didn't believe what he said. She went on changing her hair-do, almost her personality, after each movie, then subsiding into her own rather sweetly indolent one as the picture lost its outline.

Now, on the stairway, she and her father edged past each other, smiling a little, but moving on. Mr. Connor carried a scraped blue dinner pail in a knuckly white hand. There was a book in the pail, squashing his sandwiches. His bent head concluded the stooped line of his back, his blue suit was too large, as though he had bought it to grow into.

In the street, he waved to his daughter Julie and turned east toward his job in a subway station. When we move, he thought, I'll be the same distance away, only on the other side. He'd fallen into the habit of saying When we move. When they moved. Well, he'd had many opportunities to say it. They moved about the city like Arabs, from this place to that. Arabs, it seemed, managed more easily.

He walked along, thinking of Morgan. He had named her. "What sort of name is Morgan?" she'd asked him once. "People don't get named Morgan."

"You're named for Morgan le Fay, sister of Arthur."

"Arthur who?"

12

"King Arthur."

"Oh. Well, that's nice. Only it's sort of silly, don't you think? Morgan le Fay Connor . . . of Dump Street."

"As opposed to Easy Street?"

"I guess so."

"You don't have to live on Dump Street all your life," he'd answered, hurt.

As so often happened, Morgan heard the words and missed the tone. "No," she said softly. "I don't." But he had named her, and surely the magical-mystical gleam of such a name as Morgan would some day penetrate her being?

Morgan went upstairs, to the fourth floor and their apartment. She thought she should have been nicer to her father. Said something more, perhaps, or inquired further into the olden queens. Only she never did know what to say to him that wouldn't start talk about things she didn't understand, explanations of things she didn't care for. He's lonesome, she thought sadly. He wants to talk to someone. He wants to tell someone that Edwin Arlington Robinson once worked in a subway too. But there wasn't anyone to listen to that. Ask the next fifty people you met who Edwin Arlington Robinson was, and they'd tell you to look in a phone book.

By mid-afternoon, the sun had left the Connors' apartment. (In winter, coming home from school, Morgan found the shadowed stillness very cold, though there was always plenty of heat shimmering from silver-painted radiators.) The soft gloom was inviting. The stillness, touched by the clock's chatter, was peaceful. There was nothing to do but set the kitchen table, put macaroni and cheese, already prepared, in the oven, open a can of fruit. She could do that later. Now she had a couple of hours all her own, if the children stayed downstairs.

She stood in the room where the oak and green frieze living-room furniture squatted on thin linoleum (a design of

13

flowers, pocked with scratches and worn spots) and began to cry. In a moment, hot tears were tickling her cheeks, running into the corners of her mouth. She walked to the bedroom, fell on Ned's cot by the window, and tumbled with her tears like a stick in the surf, crying for the things she wanted but would probably never have, for the mother she missed and sometimes couldn't picture, for Julie's torn socks and Ned's broken screw driver, for her father who had no one to talk to.

Then, when the passion had leaked away, she rolled to her back and lay staring through eyes that took no picture. Her breath fled in gusts through the still heat, and the heavy pulsing of her blood gave her a sort of headache. But she lay, tear-dampened, sweat-dampened, relaxed, believing that now everything would be easier, that it was possible to go on for a while in the dreamy luxury of just-after-crying, not being touched or hurt at all.

That business of Marty could be forgotten now. She shouldn't have gone out with him in the first place. She wasn't a child, and it was silly to think that someone who looked and talked like Marty would take her to a movie and then take her nicely home. She should have known that the fumbling hard hands and the persistent mouth would be at her. She squeezed her arms together against the remembrance. Well, that was over. And he hadn't really kissed her. Only her cheek. The fight against him had been less awful than giving in would have been, but it had been bad enough. Scuffling in the darkened hallway, trying not to make a noise. But that was all right now. Because soon they were moving away.

After crying, she felt this limpness, this languor touched faintly with shame. Suppose one of the kids should come up? She stirred uneasily, dropped one leg beside the cot, her foot touching the floor. How long had she been doing this, stealing off to cry? A year? Longer than that? Since her mother died, perhaps. She remembered liking to be near her mother's dresses that hung in the closet, when she'd been a little girl. There'd been an old blue coat that even in summer had a fresh fall smell . . .

On the ledge beneath the window pigeons strutted and spoke in low bubbling tones. Morgan sat on the side of Ned's cot, feeling the wash of dizzy blackness that followed when she lay down on hot afternoons. Her skirt was stuck to her legs, and sweat tickled her neck. She pushed to her feet and went in to fill the bathtub, glancing at the clock in the living room. Not quite four. There was still a lot of time. There was the trickle of water sliding into the tub, the tick of the clock, voices outside and the traffic that purred past, making the apartment even stiller.

The bathroom had a small window with a frost-glass pane that slanted outward when opened. It gave upon an air shaft, sooty, dark gray, chilly on the hottest day. Pop had once written a poem about it and sent it to *The New Yorker*. They returned it immediately. Pop, who said he wasn't disappointed, had printed it in large black capitals and pasted it on the frosted glass.

> The city buildings,
> Like giants' teeth,
> Have cavities in them
> That plunge to hard-boned floors.
> No cosmic dentist could fill them
> But it might be good to pull the teeth out.

The paper on which it was written was wrinkled and yellowish now. Visitors sometimes read it and came out looking surprised. Pop read a lot, and cared terribly about the way of the world. But he didn't seem to *mind* much. A roof, a meal, a book . . . he said he needed only those. And if the meal wasn't too good, and his job kept him underground from three till midnight, and even if he'd ever thought that things might be different, there was nothing in what he said or the way he acted now to show that he cared.

Morgan, after a long time, let the water out. It swirled away reluctantly, making a series of rings down the side. When at length it had seeped out, she leaned over the old claw-footed tub and scrubbed till she was almost as hot as when she'd got in.

She took her discarded clothes from the floor and put them on, went into the kitchen and set the table. Then for an hour she read in her magazine a succession of stories about pretty poor girls with high moral standards who withstood confusion and heartbreak and, ultimately, were made happy.

Chapter Two

Whenever they moved, they stored the packing barrels in the latest basement, along with the large black trunk that was one of the earliest things in Morgan's memory. (Where was that? Some apartment long ago. The trunk had stood open in the bedroom, and the brand-new baby had slept in a shelf arrangement that suspended near the top. Slept, or cried. "Why does she cry so much?" Morgan had yelled angrily. "Why doesn't that Julie stop it?" "Because she's a baby," her mother had said. "You cried like that when you were a baby too." "No. I did not. Is she going to stay? How long is she going to stay?" "Forever. She's ours." "Not mine," Morgan wailed. "I don't want her." "All right, then. I'll take your share." Fear and despair increased in Morgan. "No, no, no," she sobbed. "I'll take my part. I *will*.") And then, when the time arrived that must see them packing again, Mr. Connor went down to the basement to arrange for having the barrels and trunk taken upstairs. This time he said that he and Ned would get the things up between them. "No sense tipping that janitor a quarter to do something we can manage ourselves."

From the first floor a flight of cement steps dropped steeply to the cave of still air and shadows where behind a series of doors was stored the material of living that the tenants could neither throw away nor, for the time being, use. A monstrous furnace hulked in a corner, black and dirty, with asbestos-wrapped arms plunging into the ceiling. It was chill, a little damp, and there was no motion at all. Mr. Connor, descending the stairs with Ned, thought that the inside of a hollow stone would be like this. "There's an elevator, where we're moving," he said to his son.

"That's nice. Except we're only on the second floor."

"Ride it anyway." Mr. Connor thought a while, turning keys over on the large ring the janitor had given him to open the trunkroom. "If you can run it alone," he added, thinking of Morgan, who tended to be nervous about Ned.

"Oh, I probably can."

"This must be the room." Dan paused before door No. 4, consulted the tag on key number four and nodded. "I thought so."

Ned was not impressed by this display of memory. "Seems like we only finished getting the stuff put in here," he said, but without ill-feeling. Ned was prepared to move every month, if necessary. He liked exploring the new apartments, didn't mind saying good-by to the old, was at home anywhere.

The trunkroom contained, besides trunks, barrels, crates, huge old suitcases, unused doll and baby carriages. All were filmed with dust and had the inert deserted air of human belongings that have been put aside. "It's odd," said Mr. Connor, "how completely people's things need people in order to be things at all. If you see an old branch lying in the forest, or a shell tossed up on the beach, you don't feel they've been forsaken by the tree, or the ocean. They're part of nature and complete in themselves. But a trunk in a storeroom has been abandoned, and it can't be itself till someone comes and takes it out of the storeroom. Isn't that so?"

Ned, who was used to his father's habit of talking his

thoughts, sometimes didn't bother to answer the question generally tacked on the end. He was often uncertain of his father's meaning, always sure that no matter what he said the low musings would continue. This time, looking around the silent trunkroom, he understood and agreed. "Spooky," he said. And then, "I hope the trunk is empty, because it's going to be sort of heavy if it isn't. Or even if it is." He started walking through tiers of trunks. "It's back here somewhere, Pop. I can remember."

Mr. Connor looked at the slim boy's figure sauntering along and thought, he really is very young. He looked like all city boys about his age. This part of the city, Mr. Connor amended. Faces begrimed, hair a little too long, shirts tattered. Swaggering and sure of themselves and older than their ages. Ned, at nine, was harder and just as capable as Mr. Connor in the Indiana town had been in his early teens. Probably I never did catch up with him, Mr. Connor thought.

"Here it is, Pop." Ned lifted on tiptoe to grasp a thick shabby leather handle of their black trunk. Dan hurried over, wishing he'd asked the janitor to help, but aware that the suggestion was now out of the question. "We'll get this up and then come back for the barrels, okay?" Ned asked.

Very young and thin. But self-reliant. Relaxed.

Morgan said to dump the trunk in the living room and she'd start packing while they went for the barrels. "Come on, Julie," she said. "You were all set to pack a month ago, so suppose we get at it now."

"Okay, okay. Did I say I wouldn't?"

Morgan pushed her hair back. "No. But you haven't done anything, either. Look, honey, go in and get all your clothes and mine out of the closet and then Pop's and Ned's, and pile them in the bottom of that thing." She looked at the trunk. "You used to sleep in that, did you know?"

"You tell me every time it comes up from a basement."

"Do I? Oh, well . . . Get the stuff spread around the bottom, and then I can put the clock and pictures and things like that in between layers of clothes and sheets. Oh, and bring in the towels and linen and pile them on the couch here. You know what I mean."

Julie leaned toward her and murmured, "Yes, but I want to hear you *say* it, dear."

Morgan giggled, going to the kitchen where she had already begun to take pots and dishes out of the closets. "Julie," she called. "You'd better get a little box and empty the medicine chest, too. Use paper so the bottles won't break."

"If you give me much more to do, *I'll* break," Julie said from their bedroom. "I'll die of overexertion. And if I do die," she added, "I'll come back and haunt you. Not in my own shape, either."

"It's good enough for haunting. Here's a box that might do."

Julie came in for the box. "You know, Morgy, I don't think this is quite as much fun as it was last time."

Morgan slumped to a chair. She'd been up since six. She'd done a washing, made potato salad and meatloaf for tomorrow, when the movers were coming and eating would be rather uncertain, packed her father's books, and a few boxes of assorted belongings that, as in the past, she'd been tempted to throw away, and, as in the past, had finally retained. "I haven't thought it was fun for ages."

"Why do we do it? I mean, there are people who've lived here for ages. I know a girl who was actually born on this street." Julie said this with the air of a bird watcher who's discovered a new species.

"I'm glad I wasn't," Morgan muttered.

"Well, still—"

"We move because Pop has to support us and supporting four people on what he makes is hard."

"Then we should stay where we are. It costs money to move."

"The other apartment costs less. Only don't say anything about it. Anyway, this time I'm glad. Julie, it'll be fun to live over by the river, in a practically brand-new apartment, won't it?"

"Oh, sure. I don't mind leaving. Even Deborah's beginning to get on my nerves."

"I thought you two had made up."

"We have. But making up with Deborah reminds me of the way Ned puts a clock together . . . all the pieces left over that you don't know what to do with."

"Making up with anyone is like that."

"I suppose so. Maybe it'd be better not to know anyone in the first place."

"Oh, go do your packing," Morgan said with a smile.

Still Julie lingered. "Morgan, do you think that if . . . if mother were alive, we'd be straying around this way?"

"Pop would still be earning the money. And it still wouldn't be enough."

"Maybe," Julie said. "I mean, maybe he'd have a different job by now. A woman makes a lot of difference to a man," she said severely. "Do you suppose we could get a kitten?"

"When?" Morgan asked.

"In this other place. I've always wanted a kitten."

"We'll see," Morgan said gently. It was obvious why Julie had spoken of their mother. She always did when she wanted something badly. To soften me up, Morgan thought as Julie went off with the little box. And yet, wasn't that right? The way it should be? Sarah Connor had died when her younger daughter was ten, but years later just the recollection that she'd been there was help that Julie needed and took. A kitten might be fun. . . .

It was beginning to get light when the alarm rang beside Morgan in the morning. The clock, with its large practical face, its uncompromising voice was part of the family. Morgan hushed its cry, and lay back thinking, here it is, another moving day. She could recall lying here that first night, a little over a year ago, and hoping that perhaps this time they'd stay a while. Not forever. The thought of staying in such a place forever was unspeakable. But, for a while, just not to hear the moving men clumping up the stairs, not to see the meek furniture herded into the street and exposed to the passing eye. Not, oh not for a while, to pull the wedged, newspaper-covered dishes out of the familiar barrels, still slightly damp and odorous from a recent basement. Not to go through the first uncomfortable days of entering strange groceries, unfamiliar drugstores, of walking on alien streets where no face or corner was known, where nothing, because it was familiar, could be ignored.

And here it was, all to do again.

She nudged Julie, curled and warm beside her. "Julie, wake up." Patting one thin warm shoulder that shrugged under her touch. "Wake up."

"Wake up why? What're you talking about?" Julie mumbled, cringing closer into herself.

"We have to get up. The movers said they'd be here at seven."

Julie turned a slow sleepy head toward her sister. "I'll bet you anything they don't get here till noon."

"But they said they would."

"They *said* the last time. But we moved after dinner, didn't we?" Julie rubbed her eyes and sat up. "I suppose we might as well. It'd be just like them to get here on time. Ned! *Ned*."

"Huh?" There was a stirring on the cot by the window and Ned emerged from the covers, alert and fully conscious. "Hey yeah, it's today, isn't it?"

And so it was, today. Not the sort of today when you realized, incredulously, that it was Christmas again, or your birthday, or the day you were going up to the Paramount to see a live movie actor, but the today you'd known before when everything suspended on the wait for the furniture van. It was not true, but it seemed that this day came more often than the others, than Christmas, or birthdays.

Outside the air was gray. Dark gray, thin, a little cool, because summer, too, was moving. Down the street the wheels of a milk wagon rolled roundly, the brakes cried out, the bottles rang against each other as the milkman swung from his seat to the sidewalk. Now and then the feet of some early riser hurried by, loud in the stillness of the hour.

Ned gathered his clothes and went to the bathroom to wash and dress. He flicked on the overhead light as he left and in the hard illumination Julie and Morgan hunched a little, as though the room were already unfamiliar, not theirs, and they felt uncomfortable sitting in their nightclothes in a strange room.

They dressed quickly, and stripped the beds, folding blankets and linen, packing them away in the bottom bureau drawer.

"Go tell Pop to get up," Morgan asked as Ned emerged blinking and stretching, redolent of toothpaste. "And Ned, ask if he'll rope up that dresser, will you?"

"I can do that."

"Can you? Maybe Pop'd better, because if it all came loose . . ."

"Oh no," Julie moaned. "I'd never survive that."

"Neither would the movers, I guess," Morgan said, recalling without pleasure movers of the past. Husky, uncommunicative men who insisted on precision in packing and, though they had never done this, seemed to Morgan quite capable of leaving half your furniture behind if it were not packed to suit them. They did not like books to be put in boxes, pots to be left out of them. They were willing to assemble your beds in the new place, but grumbled to find them intact in the old. They wanted to find bureaus with wedged drawers (bits of cardboard for that) and a good lashing of rope. They arrived within two or three hours either side of the time set and expected an alert preparedness the moment their heavy shoes were at the door. They were critical, unreasonable, and, for the hours when you were depending upon them, all-powerful. Morgan regarded them with nervous awe and never called the same ones twice, for fear of having unwittingly violated some established rule the last time.

The room, curtainless, furnished only with boxes, bare bedsteads supporting thin mattresses, and the as yet unroped bureau, looked queerly large. Her heels on the hardwood floor seemed to echo, and her voice when she tried to hum sounded like a voice in a tunnel. I didn't want to, anyway, she thought.

Morning was filling the street outside. Traffic of footsteps and tires increased, a pastel light spread over the city. There were voices now. Downstairs a child began to cry, and upstairs a radio was suddenly loud with news and dance music.

"I hope," Mr. Connor said, coming in with a length of rope, "that in this brave new flat of ours there will be neighbors who don't play jazz in the morning." He rubbed a hand over his head distractedly. "It's like eating candy before breakfast. It's . . . it's perverted."

"I know, Pop," Morgan said. She turned off the light.

"Maybe, if you tried, you could get different hours. Work during the day, I mean. Then it wouldn't be so bad."

"Maybe I can," he said wearily.

"I haven't washed yet, Pop," she told him. "If you want to get that dresser done, then maybe Ned could help you take the bed down and fold the cot. I'll get breakfast." She turned to go, hesitated, and looked back. "Do you think there's anything uglier than mattress ticking?"

Her father almost smiled. "Now that you mention it, no. Well—" He advanced on the bureau, leaned his arms on it and began to laugh. "Morgan," he said, shaking his head and gesturing with the rope, "Morgan, is it possible that we are moving? Again? Is this the next time, or the last time, or what are we doing anyway?" He straightened, sighed, jockeyed the dresser away from the wall. "A city is the most restless place in the world. A city must be like those things you see through microscopes. You know, drops of water, or plague germs, or whatever. Everything scampering around, bumping into everything else, always on the move, on the move. Like us. Back in Indiana we never moved at all. You lived where you were supposed to live and I guess nobody but fruit pickers and race horses drifted around the way we do now. Don't you think that'd be dull, Morgan? Always living in the same old place?"

Morgan shrugged and didn't answer. She left him tying a lot of knots that no one would be able to untie this evening.

The kitchen, like the bathroom, opened on the airshaft and so it was always necessary to have the light on here. In the development (every room an outside room) they would be able to eat in the morning sun, for their apartment faced east, to the river, to the sun rising. And now, quite unpreparedly, Morgan felt the singing rise of delight, the lightening expectation of newness and wonder that took her with the same caprice and suddenness as did, at other times, the rushing tears. She had merely glanced at the icebox, think-ing that the hunk of ice remaining would have to be put in the sink before they left, and happiness rollicked through her like a breeze tossing branches. Almost, she lifted on tiptoe to meet the thought—*there is something wonderful. I'm ready*, she answered silently. *I'm ready.*

"I suppose it's cold cereal," Julie said, staring at the empty closets. Four soup dishes, two glasses, two cups and saucers had been held back from the barrel, for this last breakfast. Julie began to quarter oranges, which they would eat, the stinging juice squirting on their chins, over the sink. "It's a funny thing about cold cereal that they can make it dif-ferent shapes and colors but they can't ever make it taste different."

"Different from what?"

"From cold cereal." She spilled some from a large box into each of the soup plates. "Did you pack the sugar?"

"I guess I did."

"Anywhere I can get at it?"

"I don't know. In that box there." Morgan waved vaguely, as though afraid a gesture might brush away her happiness. This sort of transport never seemed to be within her, but outside, and unsubstantial. "There's an electric icebox over there," she said.

Julie looked at the water pan beneath their small icebox and said, "Well, I think it's a good thing Pop didn't get his raise. Everything's turning out better than if he did."

"You'd think so," Morgan said without conviction. There was something wrong in Julie's reasoning, though what she said was true enough. "Maybe Pop would rather empty the water pan." And not have the sun in the morning, she thought, agreeing with Julie but reluctant to say so.

"Do you think he'll take the poem? It's still stuck to the window."

"The poem? Oh, in the bathroom. Maybe he's going to leave it for the next people."

"That'll be a surprise for them," Julie giggled. "They'll think there were crazy people here." She looked aimlessly about the bare, baldly lighted kitchen. It was so empty, so peeled-looking. The metal soap dish that hung over the sink looked odd without the usual bar of yellow soap clinging to its precarious slope. The closet shelves behind solid doors were swept clean. Morgan always cleaned apartments they were leaving. She did it in a virtuous way, as though she heard the voices of the new tenants. "Oh, but what a *difference*," they'd be saying. "How wonderful to come into a place where people have been *clean*. And *thoughtful*." They couldn't say enough to express their approval. Morgan, apparently, couldn't clean too much to win it. She followed the movers out with the dust mop, the last piece of equipment used, the last in the truck.

As if by design, the cereal box had contained just enough to fill the four soup plates. Julie shook it to be sure, but it was quite empty. She dumped it in a cardboard box with a few other bits of rubbish. She poured two glasses of milk, put the coffee cups beside the two other dishes. There was no cloth on the white kitchen table, and no silver other than a spoon apiece. There was no other emptiness like this.

Mr. Connor came in with Ned and they sat at the table, the crunch and swallow of their eating loud because no one spoke. Morgan thought, Now, at any moment, wonders will begin to arrive . . .

The movers were on time, and she was too occupied to notice at what point all her lifting elation flowed away. Emotion was always like that. She sprang to meet it, forgot, and some time later would realize with surprise that it had gone and she had not known its going.

After the men had descended to the van, taking with them

the last-minute mop trailing a drift of gray dust that in her hurry she hadn't managed to shake free through the kitchen window, Morgan walked around the dismantled rooms. Living room, kitchen, bedroom, even the bath. She didn't particularly want to. She did not feel moved in any way at the reminders—the scar in the linoleum where Julie had dropped the iron, a familiar stain on the bedroom wall that Ned claimed looked like an Indian. She went quickly, dutifully, prompted by an impulse that said it would be insensitive to leave without a backward glance. Deliberately, as though there were watchers, she ran a finger lightly round the Indian stain, tracing it. She hadn't been to all those movies for nothing.

At the door leading out, she turned again. Well, there it was, and that was that. Naked, shadowy rooms. Part of her life, she supposed. She was saying good-by to part of her life. Abruptly, she pulled the door to and ran downstairs. She had said good-by to a part of her life in just this way too often. The appropriate sentiment would not be summoned.

The morning sun was still flooding the new apartment when Julie and Morgan turned the key, opened the door, and stepped in. They stood wordless in a little space called the foyer (the renting agent had pronounced it fwa-yay) and stared at their home. The windows had been cleaned, though there was still cloudy powder at the corners of the panes. They were closed, and the sun coming through was hot and bright on new paint, varnished floors. The living room looked enormous, and there were three double floor plugs in the baseboards. They hurried to the windows.

"Oh Julie," Morgan wailed. "Julie, we can't *see* it. We can only see a piece of the river from here."

"Because we're only on the second floor, I guess." Down in the street mothers were lined up with their baby carriages, it being a fine day. They shoved the carriages away, yanked them back, with the violent motion Julie had often noticed in all but very young mothers of very young babies. It seemed as though these others, older, with more children to watch and rear, released a certain resentment by changing the rocking motion from something gentle to something nearly fierce. Bounce, bounce, bounce, the buggies were thrust off. Bang, bang, bang, they were hauled back. The babies seemed to sleep well. Children on tricycles pedaled furiously along the sidewalk, endangering, but never halting for, pedestrians, who automatically side-stepped as the three-wheeled cyclones advanced upon them. A group of girls played jacks on the sidewalk, some boys played stick-ball in the street. On the sidewalk where the development stood there was a thin tree planted in a patch of grass every twenty feet, and a strip of grass, inadequately protected by wire, ran along the wall. Across the street, stretching as far as they could see in either direction, were tenement buildings, which might some day be displaced like the ones where the development now stood, but meanwhile were insolently clinging to the old ways. The windows sprouted pillows and blankets, metal boxes to hold food, potted plants. Stores ran along at street level. A dingy drugstore at the corner. Why did drugstores always get the corners? A cleaner and dyer, a grocery with vegetables and hanging cheeses displayed outside, a hardware store with nearly opaque windows. She could see a section of wooden pier, a strip of piles, a glimpse of brown water. That was all that was visible from their apartment on the river.

The kitchen was narrow and tiny, with metal closets and red sideboards. The sink, the stove, the wonderful electric icebox were alabaster white.

"We'll never get the table in here," Morgan said, moving quickly, as though something might escape her if she lingered.

"Who cares? We'll put it in the living room. I'd like to eat in the living room," Julie said excitedly.

29

"What luck," Morgan breathed, "to have it facing east." She examined the buff walls of the living room, the white woodwork. They went into the little hall, to the bathroom.

The sinks, the bathtub, were not quite clean. There was a coating of dust on them, and dried scouring powder. "If they'd hurry with the things," Morgan said, "I could start cleaning." She wheeled, after a long glance at the square light bedroom. "Is that icebox thing going?"

Julie put her ear next to the refrigerator. "It's purring." She opened it. The interior was cold and clean and looked tremendous. There were three ice trays in a compartment near the top. "Aren't we supposed to fill those with water?" she asked, pulling them out. "Isn't it beautiful, Morgy? Did you throw out the ice pick? How long do you suppose it takes to make ice cubes?"

Morgan put the meatloaf and potato salad she'd carried with her on one of the racks. "Don't they look funny? Julie, you'll have to go to the store. We haven't anything at all, really."

Julie set her mouth. "I won't. I will not always be the first one who has to go to the store. I hate it."

"But I have to take care of things up here." Morgan didn't want to be the first one either, but this rebellion of Julie's was new. Always before she'd gone for the new supplies. Reluctantly, but without argument.

"I don't see why I can't take care of things up here," Julie said now, looking defiant and rather triumphant, sensing Morgan's hesitation. "I've *always* shopped before," she repeated pressingly.

"I know," Morgan said. She lifted her shoulders a little. "All right. When the movers come up, you'll know where to have things put?"

"Well, I don't see why not. We've got the same number of

30

rooms and the same furniture. I'll just have the table put out there." She waved away from the kitchen.

Morgan nodded as they walked back to the large living room. "You know something, Julie?"

"What?"

"We could . . ." She looked around happily. "We could put that cot of Ned's in here, couldn't we? Over there, by that wall. And then the couch could go here, and Pop and Ned could have this for their bedroom at night."

"Gosh, Ned'd be crazy about that." Julie looked as pleased as Morgan. "Sure we can. And then we can have a room of our own, too." She stopped. "What about sleeping? Do we have to go to bed when Ned does? After all . . ."

Morgan interrupted. "We shall have a sitting room," she said gaily. "We'll retire early, to our sitting room, when Ned goes to bed."

"What will we be sitting on, the floor?"

"If we put the cot in the living room, that'll be something extra in here, so we could take one of the chairs for our room, and alternate sitting on it. I mean, you could use it one night and then me, and the other one could sit on the bed. With the light between us." Why do I have to do all this explaining? she thought. "Sometimes I think you're an awful pill, Julie."

"So do I," Julie said unexpectedly. "I think it's a nice idea, Morgy." She continued tremulously, "It really isn't an awfully nice neighborhood." She was beginning to miss the streets she knew. And to miss Mag and Deborah too. The three of them had had a highly emotional leave-taking which had contained (like all partings except those of small children) elements of relief. But now she was suddenly conscious of having truly left them behind. She would be going to a different school in a few days. No matter where they moved, it always put Julie in a new school district, but Morgan, because she was in high school, hadn't had to change. It was something she'd rather not have remembered. Having remembered, she had to talk of it. "I don't see why I can't go over to my old school." Her voice was piteous, and her stomach, which always failed her in a crisis, felt heavy. "Morgy, couldn't you talk to the principal, or something? Couldn't you?"

Morgan sighed. "No, Julie. It wouldn't do any good anyway."

Julie didn't answer. Morgan went out, closing the door carefully, thinking that perhaps she should have said more. But it just didn't seem bearable to have one of those spells of Julie's to cope with today. Not bearable, and not fair. She wondered what had happened to her own wild happiness of the morning.

With a sense of shock, almost of humiliation, Morgan recognized their furniture on the sidewalk. Pop was talking to one of the movers, and Ned was in the back of the van, getting in the way, but being jollied by a huge fellow who rolled a barrel forward from the black rear. Brown padded blankets hung like tapestries along the sides of the van, muffling sound, protecting their scratched old chairs and tables.

Morgan stood there, wishing they wouldn't just pile the poor stuff in the street. Why didn't they begin carting it up? It seemed so defenseless out here in the daylight, and upstairs there was the security of walls and doors. She looked at the bedstead, the lamps, the rolled up mattresses and boxes of pans, wondering why they seemed so much shabbier in the sun, so much the target of the sly curious eyes of children. The women with the baby carriages went on talking to each other, but looked intently at the pieces of furniture emerging from the van. They memorized the green frieze sofa, nodded knowingly as a green frieze armchair followed. They all had such matching pieces, but theirs were smugly away, sitting

32

where they belonged against the many walls of many living rooms. These women were respectable and free, for the moment, not burdened with private belongings spread all over the street.

Morgan went quickly across the street, disassociating herself from the mattresses, the cardboard cartons of cornstarch and pepper, from her father and her brother.

Julie, upstairs, walked from room to room in the light air, wondering what the new school would be like.

Chapter Three

"Since both your schools are so close," Morgan said on the morning of the first day, "why don't you meet and have lunch together?" She was at the sideboard, packing sandwiches in brown paper bags. Three bags, each containing two sandwiches, a chocolate cupcake filled with a blanched creamy substance, an apple and a napkin. They each had a nickel for milk, and Morgan, who had to ride the subway, money for carfare. She made her suggestion, turned to find her brother and sister regarding her with horror.

"Honestly, Morgan, you act like you'd never been young at all," Julie said. "We'd be ruined."

Ned sank back with relief. For a frightened moment he'd thought Julie might agree. She'd been carrying on so about having to go to a different school that there was no telling what she'd do. Reassured, he continued to eat toast and jam.

Morgan poured coffee for her father, for herself, checked the lunch bags once again and sat down. "Julie, I wish you'd eat." She watched as her sister pushed a listless spoon through shredded wheat. "You can't get through the day with no food."

"I can't eat," Julie said flatly. "There's no point in trying to make me, because I can't." She looked trim and pretty in a plaid skirt, navy-blue sweater, a narrow navy ribbon through her light hair. "Morgy, I don't feel very good."

Ned got up, took a bag from the sideboard. "I think I'll go now," he said.

Morgan looked desperately from Julie to her brother, wondering which to speak to first. As Ned was already on his way to the door, she called, "Are you sure you know the way?"

"Well of course. It's only four blocks." He sounded very reasonable, almost as if he were teasing Julie, only Ned so rarely teased that Morgan couldn't be sure. "So long, Pop," Ned said. "Bye, everyone." He was gone.

Mr. Connor reached over and patted Julie's hand. "You really don't feel well?" he asked dubiously.

Julie shook her head.

"You know, baby," Dan continued, "if you don't go today, you'll have to go tomorrow, or the next day. You can't just stop school."

"And if you go later," Morgan said, "it'll be harder yet, because then you'll be the only new one. This way, all of you will be there together not knowing anyone—"

"How can you say that?" Julie interrupted in a high voice. "Everyone will know each other from last year. And I'll be all *alone*."

"But you've said that every time we've changed," Morgan sighed. "Every new school, and we go through this. And it isn't as if it had ever really been so bad. You make friends quicker than anyone else I know."

"I do *not*," Julie said, as though her character had been assailed. "And I'm tired of always moving around and changing things and not living like other people . . ." She broke off on an alarmed note, seeing Morgan glance quickly at their father and back to her with a hardened expression. Once again she'd been led by her own excitement into saying too much.

"You're selfish," Morgan said. "And furthermore, you're not sick. And furthermore, I'm tired of plenty myself." She got up, and, in an unaccustomed gesture, put a hand on her father's shoulder. "I have to get ready."

In the bedroom she put on the jacket to her gray, and only, suit, drew a bright red mouth with her dimestore lipstick, ran a comb through her hair. It was thick and silky, except for the ends which had been dried and split by permanents. She didn't mind that. She thought it gave her hair the cloudy look that girls in love stories had.

She returned to the kitchen, picked up her lunch, and then, aware that she couldn't possibly leave like this, that the thought of Julie would be with her all day, she said, "It may be a very nice school, honey. You can't be sure that everything's going to be awful."

Julie looked up bravely. "Okay, Morgy. I'll go. And I won't complain anymore."

Mr. Connor started to speak, hesitated, began again. "It isn't your complaining that bothers us. I mean, it does, but if it makes you feel better, go ahead. It's just that you get so . . . so hopped up," he said lamely. "You know, Julie, pretty soon you won't have any emotion left for the real problems, the way you scatter it around."

"I know this isn't a problem to you or Morgy," Julie muttered, "but it is to me."

"Well, let's not start again," Morgan said hastily. "I really have to go. Want to walk down with me?"

Julie got up. "I suppose I might as well."

When they'd gone, Dan Connor smoked a cigarette with his second cup of coffee. He did the dishes, and then lay down for an hour. He didn't get in nights till after twelve, but he always had breakfast with his children. See what I'd

36

miss if I didn't, he said to himself now. What a serious, self-important age Julie is at, he thought lazily, nearly asleep. For a moment, though, he couldn't recall what age she was.

Julie and Morgan parted at the entrance to the development.

"Well, so long," Morgan said. "Do what you can. It may be fine." Her reassurances were a little absent-minded.

"Good-by," Julie said, walking quickly away. But around the corner she slowed her steps. It was a lovely morning. Even to these mean streets fall came with its warm sun and cool breeze. Sparrows flittered in the gutters, streaked off in tiny flocks to perch on telephone wires a moment before redescending. Pigeons on pink splayed feet trudged along the street and sidewalk, lifting heavily out of the paths of cars, scarcely troubling to evade people. When she'd been smaller, Julie had thought it would be easy to catch a pigeon. They seemed so slow, so adorably stupid. She'd chased them often and vainly. So many times her hands almost closed on a fat smoky-pearl bird that she could almost feel how its wings would flutter and whistle close to her face, how its warm feathers and little rapid heart would be cupped in her palm. But the pigeons had always been able to elude her.

Her eyes, as she walked, searched passing faces, as though she expected to see someone, recognize someone, as though in all these assorted features that went by her on the street, one set would merge into smiling, loving familiarity and come toward her, and a voice would say, "*Here* you are, Julie. I've been looking for you . . ." Her glance ran from face to face, and now and then would be returned, but never with recognition, never with a loving sudden lift of the head.

"Look out, sister," a voice bellowed in her ear as she

bumped into a large stomach and was pushed aside. "Whyn't you look where you're goin'?"

"Excuse me," Julie said, but the banged pedestrian had hurried on. There were kids all around now. Yelling, pushing, screaming at each other. There was the school, uncompromising, ugly, inescapable. It stood before her, and there was only one direction left in which to go. In. All the others seemed to have someone to scream at. Julie looked at them coldly and waited for some teacher, some authority, to appear, to assign home rooms. Then, at least, she'd have a place to go.

Far down the murky, dimly lit tunnel, tremors began to foretell a coming express. Bowling thunder before it, the train came rushing, swaying jerkily, streaked past spraying sparks from bright steel wheels, raced into the black tunnel beyond and rumbled into silence. On the local platform the restless crowd pressed forward to the perilous edge, eyes fixed on blackness for signs of delivery, pushed back as a yellow eye and a tail of cars bore steadily toward them. The train arrived, waited with an air of impatience while heavy doors with thick rubber edges dragged open, a few stragglers emerged, and the anxious mob surged in.

Morgan managed to secure a straphold, and then, with the practiced air of a seasoned subway rider ignored the warm, too-close presence of people, avoided the knees of the woman beneath her, absently studied the ads above. (We take our coma seltzer When we see a football game, My wife says that it helps her, If it starts to snow or rain.) None of this made any impression on her. She was scarcely aware of having taken the ride, of mounting the dirty stairs that led up from underground. She walked one block east, two uptown, to reach the high school, looked at her passing image in shop windows, and wondered what she'd do if a handsome boy . . . Well, let's see, she thought. He'd be driving along, in a big beautiful car, and he'd splash mud on her gray suit. She glanced at the gutters, saw no water or mud. All right, he'd . . . something would come undone from his car, a screw or a bolt or something, and this thing would fly over and hit her, not awfully hard, but sort of stinging, so that she'd cry out, and he would turn, a bit angrily. But then his face would soften as she stood there, holding her hand, not blaming him. It would be better not even to notice him at first. "Oh, that *must* hurt," he'd say, looking at her with concerned brown (gray?) eyes. She'd be swaying a little, from the pain, but she'd give him a little smile and shake her head. "Now please," he'd say, "let me take you to a doctor." "That isn't necessary at all. I'll be fine, in a little while." "But I can't just go away and leave you," his deep voice would protest. "Now be sensible, I'm awfully safe, really. I'll just run you around to my doctor and he'll have this right as rain in no time . . ." His name would be Colin. Always, no matter what way he came to her, in what guise, his name was Colin.

Morgan, smiling softly, approached her school. It was larger than Julie's, just as dingy, and Morgan didn't notice what it looked like. After all, it was only school, and that was the least important part of her life.

There was a little park across the street, and at lunchtime, because the weather was so fine, Morgan and Betty Gilman and Verna Herzog walked across to eat rather than use the huge school dining room, where there were cafeteria lunches for those who could afford them, and tables and benches for everybody. The windows of this dining room were covered with metal nets, like the ones in the gym. Morgan had never been able to decide why. People threw dishes through them, perhaps? But that must have been long before Morgan's time. The dining room hadn't changed in any way, hadn't even been painted, since she had come as a freshman and had stood, appalled by its stark echoing size, holding her lunch parcel and sniffing the odor of soup and meatloaf, glimpsing the rows of salads and desserts, watching the lucky ones go down the line pushing their metal trays along, piling up the hot things and the sweet things as they went. She'd been lonely, just a little frightened, and suddenly not hungry for baloney sandwiches.

She wondered, settling on a green bench with Betty and Verna, laughing and talking loudly (so that a man who'd been sitting at the end of the bench reading a paper got up with a snort and walked away), she wondered how Julie was now. Poor baby, she thought, as Betty said in a clear voice, "Too bad about *him*, I'm sure."

"About who?"

"That fellow who decided he couldn't read his paper in such common company," Betty explained loftily.

Morgan, who hadn't noticed, shrugged a little and removed a package from her paper sack. She arranged it on her lap, spreading back the wax paper and sighing slightly when the slablike sandwich emerged. Once in a while, very very rarely, she ate in the corner drugstore at the other side of the park. That was really wonderful. The short-order cook moved as if his hinges had been oiled. He slid about, slicing buns, slipping hamburgers on the grill, off the grill, flipping toast around the sandwich spreads, sliding the dishes up the counter to the soda-fountain boy who called orders and made drinks. They worked in a smooth team, talking all the time. "What's yours? Right. *Adam and Eve on a raft!* Yours, sis? *C.R. hold the may.*" He'd take the order, translate it into slick gibberish for the short-order man. "Pie? Apple, custard, banana cream . . . Punkin? All the pies are punk in here . . .

Ha, ha. Yours, mister?" Oh, the drugstore was marvelous. I'd have a coffee frosted with a grilled cheese and tomato, she decided, biting into her cool flat sandwich.

"How'd the morning go?" Betty asked, settling back to chew and talk. "I got Mrs. Reinholt. She made us write a theme."

"Already?" Verna said. "*She* can hardly wait."

"Oh well, it doesn't make much difference, I guess. She talked a lot about the gift of gab, too."

"The gift of gab?" Morgan pulled out her second sandwich. "What did she say about it?"

"That it was a good thing to have and it doesn't mean just talking a lot." Betty pondered, added, "She knew a girl who had it and came back to the school ten years later in a Rolls-Royce. Only it's something you either have or don't have. Like good teeth, I suppose."

"Why would anyone come back here after ten years in a Rolls-Royce?" Morgan said. "Or even without one. She made it up. Anyway, why talk about it if you can't have it?"

"Search me," Betty said evasively. "It looks like a ducky English period though, for our senior year."

"My English class doesn't come till afternoon," Morgan said.

"Then maybe you'll get her too."

"Maybe. Are there any nice boys in your classes?"

Verna and Betty responded happily to the only interesting remark that had yet been made. There were only droops . . . there was a blond who . . . they all look like weeds after college men . . .

"Where'd you see any college men?" Betty demanded of Verna.

"At this place where I worked this summer. A hotel in Vermont," Verna said proudly. She was eighteen, and would be nineteen before she finished high school, but it gave her certain advantages.

"What'd you do?"

"I was a . . . a maid," she said. "Anything wrong with that?"

"How should I know?" Betty replied. "What did you have to do?"

"Oh, make beds, empty baskets, mop. Things like that."

"I wouldn't be caught dead doing things like that," Betty said.

Morgan rolled up wax paper wrappings and stuffed them in the bag. "I would. In fact I do all the time, only I don't get paid for it. Did any of the college men ask you out, Verna?"

"No. Some of them flirted," Verna said slowly. "But that's all." She added, "I'll tell you one thing. I'm not going back there next year. Bunch of snobs." She looked soberly at a squirrel bobbing past. Her long face, surrounded by a wide frame of thick hair, was pensive, remembering hurts that she would be unable not to remember for years. She'd thought it would be all right to be a maid. You could be graceful, very ladylike. People would say, "Why is that lovely girl working as a maid?" Like heck they would. That boy who had laughed and kidded with her for a few days . . . She'd got so she cleaned his room with special care. Once she'd even put flowers in it, though without a note or anything so at least she was spared the awful shame of having him know. How he'd have laughed at that. He'd laughed all the time, but in the beginning she'd thought it was wonderful. Watching him run in lightly on his sneakers from the tennis court, swinging a racket, whistling, his white T-shirt a little damp from exercise. "*Miss* Verna," he'd say, encountering her in the hall. "And how are you?" "Oh, I'm fine," she'd say. And then when he was gone she'd try to think of something funny to say next time, instead of oh, I'm fine. Only she never could. One afternoon in the quiet carpeted hallway, he'd hesitated after her reply and said, "What the heck do you do to amuse yourself? Don't you get sort of bored? Know anyone around here?" "No. No, I don't," she'd said eagerly. "I do get sort of bored. You know how it is." "Don't I, though," he'd said and gone along with that laugh of his. For a few days, whenever they'd meet, he'd ask again what she did to have fun. Encouraged, full of daring, she'd stopped him one day, ignoring in her happy confidence the look of surprise he gave at being so detained. "I'm off tomorrow," she'd said with a challenging smile. When he didn't speak, she added, "As we've been saying, it's lonesome when you don't know any-one. Except," she faltered a little, "except of course, I sort of . . . know you. In a way." Her smile and voice crumpled together. "Well," he'd said, moving away, putting distance between them, "I sure hope you find someone to help you out." And he'd gone down the hall and into his room.

On the bench, with the dry leaves hurrying past, making a little sound like rain as they twisted and ran along the park path, Verna bit her lips and felt her neck and cheeks burn. Even now, nearly two months later. She wished she hadn't said that just now about college men. It had just come out, as words always did with her. Words are the great betrayers. Fatally easy to form, permanent as death. Verna was hopelessly at the mercy of her own tongue, and nothing could save her. She set herself tests of silence, made desperate promises to her shaken pride. But the tests were failed, the promises broken, and Verna, hearing the hectic words spill out, hurrying to tell and give everything that should have been her own, would listen miserably. Why don't I stop? she wondered. Why in the world don't I *stop*?

The sun was warm on the bench and a wind that was almost warm pranced through the trees, ripping away lemon-

and cherry-colored leaves that hovered and dove and skimmed along the pavement, coming to tentative rest in the grass, against the stone pedestal of a warrior statue, in the wide gray bowl of a drinking fountain. High-school students, gamin children too young for school, men too old for work, were, with squirrels and little city birds, possessors of the park at lunchtime. Office workers in nearby buildings didn't seem to like it. It was not the sort of park where nursemaids took gently-bred children. A drab park, really, where there was too much pavement, the grass was always molting and littered, and only the trees, riotously bright, seemed unaware that this was no bit of carefully nurtured wilderness in the city, but just an overlooked piece that someone would eventually put a building on. Presently the students began to drift away in a casual but steady exodus from the park to what Mrs. Reinholt called the "Halls of Learning."

Mrs. Reinholt stood now, arms folded, at the front of her fourth English class of the day, and began to tell this group, too, about the gift of gab, something Pope and Oscar Wilde had had in high degree, and poor Thoreau, of course, not at all. Very few people in the class understood what she was getting at, and few cared. But Mrs. Reinholt had long ago decided that this school, situated where it was, would not often give her the pleasure of inquisitive, searching children. These students, brought up in want and toughness, were little apt to care for the literature she loved and pushed at them. But she knew no other way to teach. She earned her salary (leaning heavily on Milton and Shakespeare) by doing the old standard things that any principal, should he happen to stop in, could not disapprove. She read them Milton's sonnets (but not Shakespeare's), set them quizzes, encouraged creative writing once a week on themes she devised herself. And allowed herself the luxury of beginning each year's class with a little text on words. She called it the "gift of gab." That, she thought, should reach them. A slangy phraseology that would capture their imaginations. She told them of the beauty, the responsibility, the strength of words. Our great privilege, she told them, and our burden, this ability to shape sounds that had meaning. To be able to write, she said is a divine gift, one Thoreau had no less than Pope. To be able to talk, really talk, is a happy accident. We can all of us speak, but not all of us can talk, she said, drawing a distinction between the two that certainly did not persuade her hearers. But surely, she pleaded, we can do our best to cultivate to its highest potential this wonderful power of ours, this power of language. And by that she meant learn to guard against too much, as well as to attain the greatest possible degree of lively elegance, accurate expression. Read, she told them. Books are the true happiness. Read and read, ponder words and meanings. She concluded, oppressively aware that nothing had been accomplished here either. Four classes, and not one had given her that little warm current of interest she searched for, longed for.

"Now then," said Mrs. Reinholt with an air of getting down to business, of piping the tune that they would, for the rest of the year, perhaps not dance to but, at any rate, follow, "I ask that you now take fifteen minutes to write me a short theme on the subject: The Book I Most Enjoyed Reading This Summer." As she spoke, she lettered this title on the blackboard, and the students sat staring with as much happy interest as they'd have given an eye chart if she'd hung that. One boy put his head in his hands and groaned.

"Young man?"

He looked up with an expression of assumed courtesy.

"Are you ill?"

"No," he replied.

If this were a younger class, Mrs. Reinholt thought, I'd request him to rephrase that answer. An attempt to teach manners to people in their teens, however, was too exhausting to consider. She said merely, "In that case, you may write with the others," and turned her eyes away so as not to meet whatever face he chose to put on now. "Fifteen minutes," she repeated as they began, with no show of inspiration, to scribble. Most of them, she thought, probably didn't read one book this summer, far less enough to make choice difficult. Never mind, they'd dredge up a book from somewhere, and she'd have an idea what they thought about. She fixed her eyes above the bent heads and wiggled her toes in sturdy shoes. My fault, she was thinking. My fault. There should be a way of reaching them, of leading them. There should be an answer, but in twenty years of teaching, Mrs. Reinholt had not seized upon it. She looked over the heads of her fourth class and wondered what to have for dinner.

In all her little speech, she had not mentioned any girl who returned in triumph and a Rolls-Royce to this shabby school. Such a story would not have occurred to her, nor such a reward for the strong understanding of words. Betty Gilman, however, had been for many years a wholehearted liar. She lied when she felt it was necessary and lied when she knew it wasn't. This particular embroidery had been woven by chance on the park bench at noon, through idleness, through not really remembering what Mrs. Reinholt had said, through simply wanting to talk about a Rolls-Royce. Sometimes Betty wondered if people knew she lied, but the speculation was without nervousness or guilt. She'd never, that she knew, told a lie that hurt anyone. At any rate, never one *to* hurt. So what difference did it make if what she said was partly true or not true at all? She remembered her father, who had deserted his family years ago, saying once that if you couldn't improve a story there was no point telling it at all. Betty had taken this paternal folly more seriously than even he might have wished. And he had been a liar too.

Morgan chewed on her pencil and finally wrote. "The

book that I read and enjoyed most this summer was a book by J. Farrell called *Studs Lonigan*. It had real characters in it and good writing. Some of it was pretty nasty but so is some of life, so who can argue with a writer about that? I guess he gave a true picture of what he was writing about and that is the reason I enjoyed the book." She stopped, not being able to think of additional reasons. It was the only book she'd read in the summer, and she hadn't enjoyed it at all. Marty had loaned it to her, and reading it was one of the reasons she'd begun to feel so—so sort of crawly around him. Still, she'd read, in rapt fascination, every word. You didn't have to like a book in order to read it, she thought. But Morgan was too conventional to think of putting an idea like that in a school theme. If the theme given implied that the book had to be one you'd enjoyed, then you gave reasons for enjoyment. If she'd been able to think of another book, she might have used it. But the pressure of fifteen minutes drove concentration from her mind, leaving only the truth and Studs Lonigan to work with.

She put her pencil down and was tempted to put her head on the desk too. Her eyelids felt thick and dragged down heavily. This always happened in the afternoon at school. I could sleep better here than I could in bed, she thought languidly.

Suddenly, with a panicked start, she heard the voice of Mrs. Reinholt. It stabbed into her near sleep like an angry shout. Actually Mrs. Reinholt was merely asking for the papers. Morgan shook her head and wondered how she'd get through another hour.

Julie, at dinner, talked steadily, warding off threats of interruption by raising and speeding her voice. She talked around her boiled ham and cabbage, spitting sometimes, ignoring it, rushing on . . . "the rooms 'er like great bleak caves, Morgy, and practically no sunlight in the one I'm in on account of being practically smack up against a huge tall building. I do think it would be rather nice to build schools only in penthouses, don't you? Or out in the country so we'd have to ride for hours to get to them, and hours to get back. There's a pretty nice girl sits next to me, name is Anna Marie, and we ate our lunch together. She doesn't like the school either, so we had a good time . . ."

"Is she new, too?" Morgan interrupted.

"Yes, she . . ."

"Well, didn't I tell you?" Morgan insisted. "I did tell you there'd be other new people and you'd meet them."

Julie stopped eating for a moment and looked at her sister with exasperation. "That's just so *silly*, Morg. You couldn't really have known, and it might have been unkind to give me hope. Then what if I'd gone and no one had spoken to me or anything? It seems to me . . ."

Morgan began to laugh. "I'm sure it does, Julie. Anyway, your day wasn't so awful, and if I can give you another unkind hope, it'll probably be fine at the new school." She turned to Ned, who'd been unnaturally quiet ever since she'd come home and found him sitting alone in the living room. "How about you, honey? Did you have a—" She broke off. "What's wrong, Neddy?"

He blinked at her several times, opened his mouth, and then shook his head.

"You haven't eaten," Morgan said.

Ned's voice was loud when he spoke. "I saw a puppy run over today. At first I thought it had a red flower in its mouth, but then I saw it was all . . . all blood and—"

Julie jumped up. "Stop that!" She turned and cried loudly to Morgan, "How can you let him talk this way, Morgy? Make him cut it out!"

"You be still," Morgan snapped. "I mean it, just keep still." She went around the table, and kneeled next to Ned. "Honey, I'm sorry you saw the puppy. It's . . . it's awful for you . . ."

"Awful for the puppy," Ned mumbled thickly.

"Yes, awful for him too. But darling, you're just going— going to have to face things like that," she said slowly. "I don't mean that you'll see it again. Probably you won't. But it'll be happening, Ned. Terrible things do happen, and we have to learn to know it." She cuddled his head against her, and he seemed to welcome it. He didn't cry, but his breath came and went shakily. And Julie, who loved animals, stood against the door, telling herself that she had only yelled that way because of the puppy. She hadn't thought of Ned's part at all. Morgan held the thin boy close. How soft his cheek was, how fresh and warm the smell of him. Nine was really awfully young. They forgot, with Ned, how young it was, because he was usually so cocky, so able to care for himself. She held him tight and mourned, not the puppy's death, but Ned's seeing it. In a little while she let her arms slacken, still watching him carefully. He's handsomer than the rest of us, she thought. The black hair and blue eyes, the dimple in his cheek, the smile that darts and flickers as he talks, the drowning sadness of his eyes when he's hurt . . .

"Don't you want your dinner at all, dear?" she asked gently.

Ned exhaled a great sigh and moved out of her arms. He eyed the ham and cabbage, picked up his fork, and began to eat slowly, without speaking.

That evening, for the first time, he was not happy about his cot in the living room. When the girls had gone into their "sitting room" he sat stiffly on the edge of the cot. His pajamas were too small, so that his wrists and ankles looked stretched. His gaze was on the window that looked, with the lamp on inside, like a black mirror. He was not looking at

49

the window, it was just a place to fix his eyes because he was afraid to close them and go to sleep.

"Ned?"

He looked pitifully, gratefully at Morgan in the doorway. She wore a frayed green bathrobe, her hair was up in bobby pins, there was a blob of calamine lotion on her chin. She looked beautiful.

"Ned, Julie and I were wondering if it would disturb you to have us read in here tonight? The light is getting bad in our room. Probably the bulb's going to blow out or something."

"Oh, *sure*," he breathed. "That'd be fine."

Morgan, calling Julie, realized that this time he hadn't even cared about face-saving, about his boy's dignity. This must be the worst, the very worst thing that's ever happened to him, she thought. She had a feeling of pride in him, because he was taking it well.

She and Julie settled down, one on their father's couch, one in the armchair. Ned turned his back to them, away from the light, and prepared to sleep. For a time there was silence, except for a slight hiss from the radiator, a movement of feet in the apartment upstairs, the sound of intermittent traffic below. Morgan turned the pages of her magazine, Julie those of her book, very carefully.

"Morgy?" Ned turned under the blanket.

"Yes, honey? You really should sleep."

"I know. Morgan, do you suppose a puppy has a soul? I mean what could a puppy do wrong that he couldn't have a soul?"

"I don't see . . ." Morgan began.

"Sure they do," Julie put in. "Why shouldn't they?"

Ned smiled at them both. "That's what I kept telling my-self," he said, and turned away from the light again. " 'Night," he said, and in a little while was really asleep.

Chapter Four

In the other apartments the Connors, like their neighbors, had hung their wash on lines that stretched over alleyways from building to building. Or, when they lived on a top floor, the roof. It was pleasant, when the weather was good, to stand on the soft tarry surface, pulling clothes from the creaking wicker basket, shaking them out, hanging them absently while your gaze wandered over other rooftops set like boxes on different levels. Some were close together, with only a low wall for separation, and others had black alley crevasses between. All had a boxlike structure that housed the stairs. Ned, when he was little, had thought they were tall doghouses, even after Morgan pointed out that there was one on their own roof and it only concealed the stairs. All three of them liked to lean at the roof's edge, looking down to where squat traffic slid along, and people looked so inferior. "Look," Julie would cry with delight, "there's silly Mrs. Hooley strutting around like she was somebody." And they'd all regard the insignificance of Mrs. Hooley who, on a level, could be terrifying. Once Julie and Ned had brought a paper bag and a bottle of water up, with designs of dropping a water bomb on the street. But, the bag filled and beginning to darken, swaying riskily in Julie's grasp, her courage failed. "You do it," she said, thrusting the bag at Ned. He retreated. "Uh huh, *I* won't." "Well, whose idea was this?" Julie demanded. Ned said he didn't think it had been his. The bag swelled and sagged with its weight of water, suddenly shredded down, splashing their feet and leaving a soaking bit of paper in Julie's hand. Ned had studied the wreckage without regret. "We might have been arrested anyway," he said thoughtfully.

In the winter, hanging the clothes had been an icy aching task, whether on the roof or across the alley. Their clothes and linen stiffened into frozen attitudes which made it almost impossible to drag them back through the window or fold them in the basket. Ned, who had only to watch, adored the rigid defense his clothes put up against Morgan, who clutched at them with stinging fingers. Still, she'd laugh at her brother, whirling around the room, his pajamas wooden in his arms.

But the roof, in summer, was to the city people their "out of doors," their garden retreat (without flowers). Here, on the hot evenings, they brought their canvas chairs and lay under the stars. Here the fumes of traffic couldn't reach them, the purr of traffic was their night chorus. North, the rose haze of neon fogged the air. South, the always lighted Battery buildings stood tall against the sky. And on the roof low voices murmured in what could have been darkness on a country lawn.

The development, unbelievably, had top-floor apartments with narrow gritty terraces. These were referred to as penthouses and used up all the roof. To offset this deprivation (in the washing way) automatic laundry machines were provided in the basement, where laundry could be washed for a small sum, and racks in the kitchens furnished lines for drying. The racks were on pulleys and could be lowered and heightened. They hung over sink and stove and were inadequate, so that only a small wash could be done at a time.

"Well, anyway," Julie said, "you don't have to wash the stuff in a tub anymore."

"No, I guess not," Morgan agreed. The washboard and the old set tubs had not been easy. "But the blasted basement's so far away, and I have to go so often."

"I'll do it," Julie offered.

Morgan refused that. "You won't wander around these cellars by yourself, Julie. Understand?"

"Okay. Why not?"

Morgan looked weary. "Just don't. It's . . . well, just don't."

The basement in the development might have been laid out by Daedalus. It was wide and winding, endless in length because it turned on itself, studded with doors to trunk-rooms, package rooms, furnace rooms, exits and entrances. It was a subterranean world of doors and gray tunneling. Morgan disliked it. When she went down in the green metal box of an elevator, and walked the unfamiliar distance to the laundry room (signs and arrows on cement walls leading her steps), she held her basket tightly, like a shield, and looked over her shoulder fearfully till the steamy safety of the laundry room and solid women was reached. She wouldn't let Julie or Ned in the basement at all.

"I don't care," she complained to Ned one day, pulling the rack with its burden of sheets as high as she could and still finding it interfered with the sink and stove, "I don't care what the conveniences are. I miss a roof."

"Me too," Ned said agreeably. "Remember, Morgy, how the tar would bubble up and stink so good?"

"Smell," Morgan corrected absently.

"Did it ever." Her brother sighed in loving remembrance of sticky fingers in the tar bubbles. "Just the same, I like it better here. Could I bring a friend of mine to visit?"

"Well sure, honey. Some one from school?" She bent down and reached in a bin for potatoes. The sheets dripped quietly on her neck. "Would you rather have rice than potatoes?"

"No, it's a guy I met in the playground. Rice would be okay."

"That's good, because there aren't any potatoes. Bring him any time you want. If I'm home, that is." Ned was a little too inventive to be left alone in an apartment with his friends. Once he and two of the "guys" he knew had decided to be chemists with ink and pancake syrup. It had been one of the few times Morgan had been grateful for linoleum on the floor rather than the rug she craved. Another time they'd made a railroad train with every movable piece of furniture in the apartment. Morgan had come home to find a line of chairs and lamps and tables trailing from room to room and four boys engaged in driving this contrivance to Texas. "Ned," she shouted, trying to push the door in against an armchair, "Ned, what are you doing?" "Look out, Morgy, that's the tender. Toot, toot!" "Toot, toot, my foot," she yelled. "You get this tender and all the rest of the furni—the train—back where it belongs." "Okay, okay," he said patiently, "you just wait out there in the hall and we'll steam back to the round-house. Toot!"

"Oh, sure," he said now. "I want you to meet him anyway."

Morgan, washing rice, turned her smile away from him. He was so formal sometimes. So dear.

Dan Connor thought if a person fell asleep and then woke days later, he would always be able to tell if he'd wakened on Sunday. The weekdays had a sort of jumbled similarity, though Monday had a moodiness and Saturday a loutish quality that gave them distinctness. But Sunday could only be Sunday. An empty, drawnout peace, rather like a stifled yawn, going on and on, never coming to a climax. He didn't like Sunday, and even its being his day off made him no more lenient toward it. A day of drugged late sleeping, rumpled afternoon beds. Of cooking odors and scattered newspapers. But most of all a day of waiting for the point, though you knew perfectly well there was none.

"Oh damn," he said one Sunday in October. *"Damn."* He let the *Times* slip toward the floor, his limp hand still holding a few pages. The paper was just another part of too much. Too many sections, columns, too many cautiously worded bursts of optimism, too many menacing words of pessimism. "There's going to be another world war in my lifetime," he said, and waited for Morgan to ask why, how did he know, when . . . to ask him something. But she was hovering over the stove where onions sputtered in the frying pan. He got up and went to the kitchen door. "We'll have another world war," he said to his daughter.

Morgan looked around. "Oh gosh, do you think so?"

Dan waved his hand impatiently. "Is that all you've got to say?"

"Well—" She poured tomato sauce on the onions, lit a flame beneath a large pot of water, turned to get a box of spaghetti from the closet. "I hope we don't. On account of the Russians, you mean?"

"That, and so much more." He shook the newspaper, as though its terrible messages would sprinkle on her.

"Hungry?" she asked, stirring the spaghetti sauce. It was warm out, and the kitchen window was open, but still the odors hung heavily.

"Sort of." He leaned against the door jamb, watching his daughter, wondering what went on in her dreamy mind, thinking of his wife and a love long ago that had brought him to this Sunday, this dinner, these problems uncoped with and unshared. To his *Times* and Morgan's *News* scattered on the floor in separate disintegration. To Morgan cooking dinner and himself in the doorway and no words between them.

Sometimes, when he encountered one of his children, he had difficulty believing in them. He would stare, for a moment, without comprehension at the moving figure which might never have been save for the chance that took him down one street rather than another, eighteen years ago in an Indiana town.

"Want to call the children and tell them to wash?" Morgan said.

He nodded.

On a late September Sunday, eighteen years ago, he had strolled, goalless, from his boarding house. He'd been twenty-five and without family. Employed as a stitcher in a slipper factory, he had money in the bank because there was nothing to spend it on, aside from his books, and went forth on Sundays because there was nothing else to do. A man can't read *always*. Autumn, by the calendar, had come. But summer filled the yellow-hazed air. Now and then a stray harbinger of coming breezes would swirl a fountain of parrot-colored leaves along the walks, strike with spicy fragrance across his face, and retreat, leaving the sun still hotter and more golden. Summer, reluctant to leave, lingered over piles of smoking foliage in streets and yards, warmed the last late slender wasps giddily clinging to fallen apples. The streets had a timeless quality at this hour, this season. A languid suspension in which even the leaves that detached themselves and spiraled away from the living branch seemed to move without motion. A spiny chestnut burr clicked on the walk at his feet, halved open to reveal its brown fruit. He scooped it up, coddling and rolling the polished heart between his palms. He walked on, past well-kept, middle-class homes on whose porches upright women and blue-serged men exchanged muted views, rocked gently. Children, subdued for Sunday, sat on the steps.

Suddenly, almost between one step and the next, all the somnolent charm of the town was gone for Dan. That gentle ignorance of worlds outside its limits made it like an ancient cat lying in the sun, sure of being fed and indifferent to the rest. I'll have to go away, he thought. I'll have to go somewhere and find out if I'm alive. Here, under this sleepy town's wing, a man could lie down and never notice death coming on or life leaving.

He tossed away his chestnut and walked faster. He could go East. What was it that kept the East pulsing? The docks? The waterways to Europe, the tide sucking and filling, the trains pushing in and out on steel elbows? Was it the amalgam of tongues and gods and disbeliefs? He swerved, taking a street that would lead back to his boarding house and his suitcase.

Therefore Morgan and Julie and Ned were now alive, and Sarah, whom he might not have known, was dead forever.

He was halfway down the street, that long-ago Sunday, noticing its gradual decline in atmosphere from the avenue he'd just left. Lawns that were smaller. Fences, where there were any, of wood rather than gleaming black-painted iron. Narrower porches on houses set nearer together. Still, a nice street. Not timid, nowhere near being slovenly. A conventional street that knew its place and, what's more, liked it. Wouldn't be anything else if asked.

"Hello! Dan . . . hello!"

He turned toward a brown-shingled house as Tad Walsh, who also worked in the slipper factory, came down the steps to greet him, draw him toward the porch. "Come and meet my cousin from New York," Tad said. Like many words that change the course of life, these were said casually. They went up the steps, and Sarah, slim and cool and very lovely, smiled at Dan and put out her hand.

So Morgan and Julie and Ned had their problems, Dan his, and Sarah none. Turning the corner that day he sowed the seed of Morgan's inability to cope with geometry, Julie's hyperesthetic conflict with life, Ned's poised and mechanistic mind. He planted this apartment in his future, and this spaghetti dinner.

But then, if not that accidental turning, perhaps another would have served to ends not very different. Each day he and his children and every mortal soul made some irrevocable choice that set another wheel turning within the larger wheels. The benefit conferred was not to recognize the choice as final.

"The spaghetti's good," said Ned.

"Very," said his father.

The telephone was an extravagance, but they'd always had one. Julie's tendency to feel it was free, and Ned's to forget it altogether had to be checked. ("Julie, you aren't in that girl's living room, you're on the phone and you've been on it nearly an hour . . ." Or, "Ned, if you aren't coming right home from school, will you *please* phone from whosever house you go to?") Dan felt safer knowing the kids could, if they had to, get in touch with him. So they afforded it, and possibly in doing so went without something else, though Morgan couldn't imagine what that might be. They never seemed to buy anything but food, and, once in a while, with extreme caution, clothing.

Betty Gilman did not have a phone, so she went to a drugstore to call Morgan. "Hi, Morgy? Oh, it's you, Julie. Get her for me, will you?" She waited a second, eyeing the boy behind the cigar counter. Cute. "Morgan? Look, could you

58

come over tonight? Oh, nothing . . . just sit around and talk, or something. It's an awfully nice night, and maybe we could take a walk . . . Well, a movie if I can get the money . . . See you about eight, huh? Yeah . . . Well, g'by. Say, there's an awfully cute boy here, you ought to see him . . . Okay, about eight."

"I'm going out," Morgan said, hanging up.

"Where?" Julie, at the table that doubled as a desk, was doing arithmetic. She did it easily, almost without paying attention, an accomplishment which filled Morgan with admiration and awe. She looked up, nibbling on her pencil. "Tell Ned he can't go out, will you? If you don't tell him I can't manage him at all. When'll you be back?"

"By eleven, anyway. I'm going to Betty's."

"That birdbrain," Julie said scornfully, turning to her homework again.

"I wish you wouldn't talk about my friends that way," Morgan requested without heat. Julie was contemptuous of so many people and so many things that no one could take time to resent her remarks. "Ned—" she began.

He was lying on the couch with *The Adventures of Reddy Fox*. "Yup," he said, not looking up. "I heard her. I wasn't going no place."

"I wasn't going *any* place."

"Thought you said you were." He kept his head down, grinning.

Morgan laughed and Julie snorted.

Ned and I have the same sort of minds, Morgan thought, going down to the street. We both laugh at jokes and love movies and wiggle through school any old which way (except, she thought, Ned seemed to wiggle more successfully). Julie despised jokes and she was so good at school that if Morgan had had a different temperament, she might have been envious. She thought Julie must be like Pop. And yet, for all his

59

bookish restless brain, poor Pop hadn't got much of anywhere. Shoving change at people's hands every night in a subway booth. That wasn't very far to go with good brains. Sometimes she wondered how he must feel, never having anyone to talk to about the things he loved . . . his books, his grand ideas. How he felt about never "rising in the world" as the magazines said. He might have talked to Julie, if she hadn't been so immersed in herself. He might have found a friend somewhere to smoke a pipe with in the evening and gravely discuss the important matters . . . if he didn't have to work at night. And I can't talk to him, she thought, walking slowly toward Betty's, five blocks away. Pop and I can only talk about groceries and moving and whether the kids are staying healthy.

In this neighborhood, the shops did not close at five or six. They lighted their windows and welcomed customers till nearly ten at night. Grocers stood at their doors with folded arms, aprons rumpled from the long day, nodding to a passing customer, following another into the shop, exchanging views with next door merchants. Barbers sheared their patrons in bright white shops that, in the evening dark, looked almost like stages. The brilliant barber poles whirled, the drugstores blazed with light, and along the street the pushcart merchants set forth their wares and sometimes chanted them. One green cart had lettered on its side, "You Can Purchase No Cheaper Cravat," and "Nick's Haberdashery." Nick, proprietor of the pushcart, called to Morgan as she passed, "Like da nice tie for your Pop, girly? For your fella?" Morgan grinned and shook her head. "Pop's got one." "Ah . . . and your fella?" "Oh, he's too young for ties," she called back and left him smiling.

The evening was dark, but not black; the air gingery with delicatessen aromas, with the salt pungency of the river, with the cool tart taste of autumn. Morgan breathed deeply, wishing . . . Well, she'd be going along, like now, and suddenly a young man, obviously not of this neighborhood, would put out his hand to detain her, with beautifully polite hesitation. "I'm terribly sorry to seem rude," he'd say, "and if you wish, just walk on and I'll quite understand . . ." She'd pause, not really waiting, but courteous, a little curious perhaps. "Yes?" she'd murmur, "I don't think . . ." "Oh no," he'd say, with a quick white smile, "we haven't met . . . not yet, that is. It's just that . . . This is difficult to say . . . My name's Colin— (Colin what? Oh well, Colin something.) I'm down here scouting a location for our new production. I haven't picked the star yet, because I never seem to find quite the right person. A young girl, a beautiful one, one who looks as though she might live in a place like this . . ." He'd sweep his hand about. "But not be *of* it. You see what I mean?" "Well, I think I do," she'd say softly, lowering her eyes. "I think I understand what you mean. But why are you . . ."

"Hiya, duchess." She automatically turned her head and then flushed because she had. The boy who called leaned against a street lamp. He was smoking, and like so many of the boys who smoked in the streets at night and called to strange girls, he looked coarse and hard and handsome. His eyes wanted a lot and believed nothing, and they looked straight in hers with a glint of laughter because she'd turned at his whistle. "You want company?" His smooth bogus voice accompanied a slight forward motion.

Morgan ducked her head and hurried. She heard his laugh, his called, "Don't worry, baby, I'm not gonna follow you," and went the next block almost running. She hoped Betty would want to go to the movies, that she would not want just to walk around, the way she often did, strolling past the boys, locked in words and giggles (too many words, too shrill giggles), exchanging hot glances and, now and then, flip, fast comments. Not that Betty ever let herself get picked up, but she liked to go around teasing and running. Well, no one was forcing her to walk with Betty, nor even to see Betty at all. It's awful, she thought, the way we act. Kitty, too, though Kitty had been so gay, so—what word?—so wholesome, probably. With Kitty, flirting had been different somehow. She flirted better than she breathed, and with the same naturalness. But Kitty would never walk around with Betty after dark. And Kitty wouldn't drift along doing something she didn't like simply because she couldn't think of anything else to do. Morgan turned into Betty's building. You get used to people, she thought. Used to people and unwilling to spend every night at home with Julie and Ned, listening to the radio, reading. . . .

The Gilmans lived in a railroad flat, one room opening on the next in a string of identical shapes. It saved the builders three-and-a-half feet of hall space, and, if it produced ugliness, that was nothing the builders brooded upon.

Betty was at the door before Morgan could touch the bell. "Where've you been?" she asked impatiently, not waiting for an answer. "Don't say anything about going out till Angie's gone, will you?" The words were whispered. Beyond, Morgan heard the clink of china and rush of tap water in the kitchen. Mrs. Gilman, then, was still home. In a chair beside one of the windows, with the radio going softly in her ear, sat old Mrs. Metzger, Angie's mother. She smiled uncertainly at Morgan, her filmed eyes too unreliable for her to identify the caller.

"Hello, Mrs. Metzger," Morgan said, going closer. "How are you?"

"Well, thank you. That's Morgan. How are you dear?" Mrs. Metzger always said, "Well, thank you," when you asked how she felt, though everybody knew she was almost blind and had arthritis in her knees so that she only walked with help from Betty or Angie. Yet she seemed well. She sat by her little radio, listening to drama and dance music, and she smiled happily when people came in.

The Gilmans had a thin flowery rug on their floor, and furniture covers of zebra-striped cotton. Mrs. Gilman had made them. She was a seamstress on Seventh Avenue, and young. There were red satin cushions scattered around the room. One was on the floor, and Morgan started to pick it up.

"Don't," Betty said. "I put it there on purpose."

"Why?"

"Because it's casual. Didn't you see the cushion on the floor in that movie?"

"But I guess the floor was clean. Anyway, it was a much bigger cushion. I think it wasn't a cushion at all. Just shaped like one."

"You don't *have* to talk that way, do you?" Betty asked coldly.

"What way? Oh, about being clean? Well, nobody's floor is, really."

There were ecru-lace curtains at the windows, so dusty that it was difficult to breathe if you stood close to them, and signed photographs of movie stars in ten-cent store frames on the tables. Betty sent for them, and hers was the only apartment Morgan had ever seen where they weren't banished to the bedroom.

"Can you go to the movies?" Morgan asked.

"Hush," Betty said fiercely, with a quick glance at her grandmother. "I told you to wait."

Mrs. Gilman came out of the kitchen, turning her head to fasten a dangling earring, smiling at both girls. Her lips were very scarlet, her figure thin, almost gaunt. "Hi, there, Morg," she said. "What do you think of this girl here, letting her poor old mother slave in the kitchen while *she* entertains friends in the parlor?" She flitted across the room in her girl-ish tight-waisted dress, took a cigarette from a glass dish that had a cluster of rosebuds for a handle, and patted her mother's tangled gray curls. Mrs. Metzger paid no attention. Lighting her cigarette, Mrs. Gilman dropped to a chair, arms outspread, still smiling. "Tell you what, girls, I think you'd better cut out this walking the streets at night."

Morgan started, and Betty said, "Hey, for Pete's sake, Angie."

"Oh, don't get so huffy. I didn't mean anything. I'm talking about how it looks to other people. Two big girls swaying along looking at the boys. Now, I ask you . . ."

Well, Morgan thought miserably, her throat hot, her hands moist, I'm glad somebody said it. Someone should have, if we couldn't figure it out ourselves. She looked from Betty to Angie. Very alike they were. Thin, with glittering crusts, like the dangling earrings at Angie's ears. When she first met Angie, she'd been fascinated by what seemed to her glamour, by the rows of perfumes on the fluffy (slightly grimy) dressing table, by the stories of models on Seventh Avenue. Angie could be awfully funny. Once she'd told them about the time one of the girls modeled a black velvet gown at a fashion show in a swank hotel. "And she started up the platform steps in this full-skirted glory—about eighteen yards around —and what did she do but walk up the front of the skirt, till she was *right* on her knees." She put a hand over her mouth and laughed pealingly. "*What* a fox paws, as they say uptown." "What did she *do*, Angie?" "Oh, she was a grand girl . . . just wriggled a bit and walked back down till she could stand up again. Things didn't bother her." Angie sighed with the pleasure of having laughed so well. Oh, Angie had a lot of spirit and she had something else, too . . . she took her pay as a seamstress, worked hard, and didn't seem to mind how much more the women around her, the models and the others, had. She was practical and honest, though she ran around a lot and didn't seem to care that Betty lied. Morgan no longer thought that Angie was glamorous, but she liked her. She liked old Mrs. Metzger, who sat so pleasantly ignoring people. And Betty? Well, you could never be sure about Betty, never tell what or who Betty was.

"You understand?" Angie was saying to her daughter.

"Oh sure," Betty said easily. Angie looked at her sharply, then shrugged. "You're a big girl, now, Bets. I tell you these things for your own good, but I can't follow you around and check up."

"I know you can't." Betty's voice had no inflection at all.

Angie sprang lightly to her feet as the doorbell rang. "Think it over," she said. "That'll be Bert. Have a good time, girls. Make fudge or something. 'By, Mom." She grabbed up a light short coat, opened the door to her date, and was gone.

Betty stood at the window, watching till her mother and the man turned the corner. "Okay, Gram," she said, turning back, "time to get you to bed."

Old Mrs. Metzger looked up. "But it's early, Betty," she said, with a note in her voice that seemed to recognize the futility of protest. "I don't want to go to bed. I want to hear that mystery play. I want to very much."

"Sorry. Mom said to get you right to bed, soon as she left."

Morgan opened her mouth to protest, but a glance at Mrs. Metzger's face, defeated and quite helpless, silenced her. All three of them knew the lie was there, not one lifted a finger to point at it.

"Good night, Morgan," the frail unhappy voice said, as Betty's firm hands led the way to bed.

"Good night, Mrs. Metzger," she said softly, and felt like crying. What was the old lady to do now? Lie in her bed in the dark, not able to sleep for a long time, because old people slept so little, not able to hear her radio, or talk to anyone, or get up without some other arms, some other strength, to help her? Morgan sat in a zebra-striped chair, staring at the floor, till Betty came back.

"C'mon," Betty said.

"Where?"

"Oh . . . out."

"Don't you think that was a filthy thing to do, really?"

"What? What are you talking about?"

"You don't even know?"

Betty shook her head, honestly curious.

"Your grandmother. She didn't want to go to bed. Why *couldn't* she sit and listen to her mystery program for a while?"

"Listen, Morgy, you don't understand at all. If I left her, we'd have to be back practically right away. She doesn't sleep well, and it is early, but she gets tired if you leave her sitting in the chair. Once she even fell off. If I didn't put her lying down now, and get her ready, she'd be in an awful state in a little while. At least this way, she's safe . . ."

"But she's lying in the dark in there, wide awake and all alone," Morgan cried out.

"Hush." Betty looked at Morgan, then away. "I don't *care.* Angie knew I wanted to go out tonight, but that didn't bother her, did it? Am I supposed to stay home all the time, taking care of Gram? Don't I ever get to go out or do anything? How would you like it?" She was breathing quickly, squeezing her hands together.

Morgan sighed and shook her head. "I suppose I wouldn't. But it seems . . . sad."

"Well, so do a lot of things," Betty said quietly. "We've all got our sad, sad troubles." And after a short silence, "Want to see a movie? I guess Angie's put the kibosh on our walks, for a while, anyway."

"She's put the kibosh on for good, as far as I'm concerned," Morgan muttered.

"What's the *matter* with you?"

"I don't know. Maybe I do. I just don't like that walking around, that's all."

"No? I haven't noticed you not liking it."

"You haven't?"

They looked at each other warily, knowing that something resembling friendship, that had, at any rate, the security of habit, could now be very easily discarded. If neither of them made a move to save it, this relationship that had, whatever its value, lasted more than three years was ended.

They waited, and then Betty said, "John Wayne's at the Lyceum."

So they went to see John Wayne, and for the first time Morgan couldn't give him all her yearning attention. Sometimes you save things not because you want so much to keep them, but because you're afraid of what will be left if you let them go. Afraid of empty places that might not get filled. Afraid of meeting as strangers eyes that were once familiar. You go on, safe with the known, thinking that it wasn't what you'd hoped for, but thinking, too, that what you'd hoped for might not exist at all. Betty and Morgan were neither daring nor rich enough to gamble.

Chapter Five

"Morgy, this guy's invited me to dinner."

Ned, coming in from the playground, another of the development's facets, was red-cheeked from the chilly late November air.

Morgan, because Julie was out, pulled him close. "Let me feel your face," she said, putting hers against his brilliantly cold one. "Lovely. Like snow." Like cold velvet. Before Ned was born, her mother had said, "We're going to have a baby, Morgan." Morgan had begun to love him then. Julie had come as a stunning and unwelcome surprise, but Ned was a baby that "we" were going to have. Oh, how I love you, she thought, letting him go because he squirmed in her arms, how I love you, darling. "What guy?"

"That one that I told you, that I met in the playground."

"Oh. That was ages ago. Where's he been. I thought you were going to have him up here."

"Well, I am. I don't see him much, because he's pretty busy."

"So are you."

"Morg, it isn't the same thing. This guy goes to college, and he works in the playground to—"

"He *what*?" Morgan interrupted.

68

"Works in the playground week ends and some afternoons for the dough, and—"

"The money. I thought you were talking about a little boy."

"I don't play with little boys," Ned said.

"Oh. Well, I meant . . ." She smiled and stopped speaking.

"I know what you meant. Can I?"

"Have dinner with him?" Morgan shook her head. "Now, don't blow up. I have to know more about him first, and so does Pop. I mean, honey, we just can't let you go off to some stranger's house, can we?"

"He's not a stranger. I've known him for months."

"*I* haven't."

"But he isn't asking you," Ned said furiously. "Honest, Morgy, you aren't being fair. I don't meet everyone you go out with, do I?"

"You . . . I'm not nine years old." She knew it would make him angrier, but could not help laughing. "Ned, hold on. You bring your friend up here and let me or Pop meet him first. Then if—I mean, then you'll probably be able to have dinner with him. Why in the world does he want you for dinner?" she added curiously.

Ned took off his coat, turned back to his sister with dignity. "Because he likes me. That's why."

"Yes, but dinner . . . it just seems funny." She picked up his jacket, hung it in the closet. "Does he live here?"

"Yeah. In Building F." The buildings went all the way down to J. "His mother is real nice."

"You mean you've already been to their apartment?"

"Well, sure. Lots of times."

"But you never told me."

"You never asked."

Morgan walked over to him quickly. "Ned Connor, you *know* you aren't supposed to go in people's homes that I don't know. How many times have I told you . . ." She stopped and slumped to the couch. "It's too much for me. It really and truly is. How am I supposed to bring you up? Nothing I say makes the least bit of difference, nothing I ask . . ."

Ned, nervous and subdued, sat beside her. "I'm sorry, Morgy. I forgot."

"No, you did *not* forget," she said sharply. "You disobeyed. And I've asked and asked . . ."

"I won't do it any more, honest." His voice was low and unhappy. "Tom isn't like just anybody. I never went in no one else's house without telling you." He waited for her to say "anyone else's," and when she didn't, put his hand on her shoulder and shook her gently. "Don't be mad, Morgy."

"Oh . . . mad. What's that got to do with it? Look, Ned, I'm doing the best I can with you and Julie, but you just can't do . . . put things over on me like this." She got up and moved away from him. "Don't you understand? I'm not a mother. I can't figure things out all the time. I can only trust you to do what I ask, what Pop asks. It's too hard for me, I tell you. It's too *hard*." I'm going too far, she thought, I shouldn't be talking to him like this, and glanced over to realize that she really had said too much. His face looked peaked and too still. Shaken, she rushed over and, with her arms around him, tried to take her words back, out of his mind. "Baby, I didn't really mean it. I adore taking care of you. I don't know what in the world I'd do without you, Ned. It's just that . . . oh, try to understand, won't you? It's not that I'm trying to be nosy or strict. . . ."

Suddenly he patted her hand. "I know, Morgy," he said with his darting smile.

Morgan leaned against the wall weakly, as though she'd won a fearful battle. He really does know, she thought. Ned

70

understands things. But I must never, never . . . "Will you bring him up here sometime?"

"Sure," said Ned. "How about tonight?"

When, that evening, Tom Miller rang their doorbell and Ned answered it, Morgan's first thought was, well, he ought to be all right. Her second, slower and more amazed (she had never basically believed Ned could like someone who was not all right) was that if Verna or Betty could see what little brothers brought home, they'd both be screaming for one.

Tom was tawny and tall, with a faintly Slavic face. High cheekbones and long eyes made him look amused, and a little secretive. He wore a plaid wool shirt and gray flannel pants. They were good clothes, Morgan thought, thinking of Ned's corduroy pants that were thin at the knees and seat. Before Tom spoke a word she began to resent him. Is he by any chance being charitable to Ned? she wondered. Bestowing kindness on a neglected little boy?

"Ned, dear," she said, "you really shouldn't wear those old things around when you have company." Ned looked at her in undisguised surprise, and Morgan couldn't help spoiling her effect by laughing. That sounded like Betty, she thought.

"You certainly shouldn't," Tom said seriously to Ned. "Especially since I got all dressed up in my best."

"Oh well," Morgan said, still laughing. "Sit down, won't you. I'm sorry my father isn't here to meet you, and I'm sorry to make such a fuss about letting Ned have dinner with you. I . . ."

"I don't mind," Tom said. "Glad to meet Ned's sister, anyway. He and I supervise the playground together, you know. And this dinner is his reward. We're going to eat only the things we want. That right, Ned?"

"Mmm," Ned said, with a warning glance at Tom and a significant motion toward Morgan. Obviously he had no wish to describe the menu to outsiders. One of the truths Ned lived by was the superiority of sugar over other forms of food. He was constantly engaged in defending this theory against the meat-and-vegetable one, constantly resorting to tricks and duplicity for the sake of another spoon of sugar, another bar of chocolate. At this moment he had hidden in the closet, in the toe of one of his sneakers, a licorice witch left over from Halloween. The broom was chewed off and the witch was sticky. She was even a little smelly from her hiding place. But she represented Ned's reserves. This dinner promised replenishment and Ned had no intention of sharing it, even verbally, with Morgan, who seemed to think that prunes and carrots were the point.

"Supervise the playground, how?" Morgan was saying.

"That's my job," Tom Miller said proudly. "I go to Columbia, and I have this job in the playground here, week ends and some afternoons. Ned's my assistant."

Ned smiled brightly. "I blow the whistle, Morgy."

"That's quite a responsibility."

"Oh yes," he nodded. "It's louder than a cop's whistle."

"Policeman," Morgan said.

Ned ignored that. "And I tell kids, here there, you can't do that."

"Do what?"

"Whatever I want them to stop doing."

Morgan put her hands to her face. "Oh, *Neddy*. Do they stop?"

"Not unless Tom says it too," Ned said without embarrassment. "Still, I *do* blow the whistle."

"I'll bet you're the toast of the playground," his sister said.

"He's okay," Tom said. "Got good wind. That whistle probably stops traffic in the Bronx when Ned blows it."

Ned, vindicated, surveyed Morgan with good will. "Now, is it all right about dinner?" he asked, feeling the purpose of this meeting was too slowly arrived at.

72

"Of course," Morgan said, as though there had never been any question at all. It was a measure of Ned's affection that although Morgan, like other adults, often betrayed him with this sort of inconsistency, he never betrayed her by pointing it out.

"Well then," Tom said, "let's say Friday. All right?" Morgan nodded. "That's the night my parents eat out, and my brother's never home to speak of at all, so Ned and I will have the kitchen to ourselves. Which is the way we plan it." He added, "We'd ask you, only—" Ned's alarm was pathetic "—only it's a thing just between the two of us," Tom said quickly. He looked at Ned. "Manners, boy. You know."

Morgan resented that, and was about to say something, but Ned forestalled her.

"Tom lives in one of those penthouses, isn't he lucky?" he said, shoving his hands in his pockets, slumping in the chair and banging his heels on the floor.

Tom grinned. "He makes it sound like doormen and Fifth Avenue."

"All I know is they use up the roof, and I miss the roof," Morgan said coolly. "What's penthousey about them? Do you have gardens or something?"

"Heck, no. A glass door leading on to a square foot of brick and fresh air."

"Still," Morgan said, "it's better than none at all. I don't mind for now, because it's so cold, but I'll mind next summer. And anyway, those rack things they have in the kitchen are good for about three socks and a washrag and then they're full up." Tom looked confused. "For washings. Doesn't your mother hang her wash on them?"

"I guess she has someone in to do it," Tom said uncertainly.

"Oh. The pleasures of the rich," Morgan said, aware of how boorish that was, but still smarting at Tom's correction of Ned.

Tom flushed. "We're not rich," he mumbled. "No one who lives in this place is rich."

But there are all the different degrees, Morgan thought. She was conscious of the change from friendliness to faint hostility between her and Tom Miller. It was her own fault. But somehow, she thought wearily, I just don't care. He's Ned's friend, not mine. I was only checking. And I hate hanging the wash in the kitchen. But why was it that the boys she made up in her mind were the only ones she felt happy with? Once she'd practically told Marty Banks that she kissed other people than him. It wasn't so. His unsuccessful kiss was the only one she'd ever known. His sudden, horrifying kiss in the hallway at night. . . .

Tom Miller stood up. "See you tomorrow afternoon, Ned," he said. "Uh . . . it's been nice meeting you, Miss—that is, Morgan." He put out his hand.

Morgan, rising, took it briefly. "I'm glad. You make Ned happy," she said. There should be something to add, but whatever it was eluded her. She closed the door after him and smiled at Ned, who had missed the final undercurrents and was perfectly content.

In a little while, Julie, who had been at Anna Marie's doing homework, came in, pinched with cold. "Could we have some cocoa, Morgan?" she said, shedding her heavy, fuzzy coat. (She'd thought, when they bought it, that it looked sort of like fur, but no more. It looked like something Ned might have made out of mops.) She rubbed her reddened hands together. "Could we?"

Morgan nodded. "With water."

"That's all right."

"Are there any marshmallows?" Ned asked.

There were. They had cocoa and marshmallows, and then Ned went to bed. In their room, Morgan and Julie prepared for the night. Julie, who finished first, settled in the armchair

with the *Idylls of the King*. Morgan sat at a dressing table Ned
had made out of two orange crates and a board. It was covered with thin chintz and had been inspired by Angie Gilman a long time ago. Angie had even given her the pretty
good mirror into which she now peered, patting on cold
cream. Cold cream and calamine lotion were the wonder
workers, the magic. She did not use them every night (you
don't make a habit of magic), but now and then she sat at the
mirror, smoothing the thick cool substance over her cheeks,
surveying with pleasure the little Woolworth bottles of scent,
the minute lipsticks, the small flat powder boxes that were
hers. Dreamily she massaged while Gene Kelly, John Wayne,
Ned and Kitty McMahon smiled from tiny pictures stuck in
the mirror's frame. She would sleep with this oily enchant-
ment on her face and, in the morning, know she was lovelier.
Because Morgan wasn't fooled for a moment by Mrs. Reinholt who said happiness was in books and words, by her
father who said it was in books and character. Morgan knew
that happiness would be found in beauty.

Until the first of December, Julie spent her thirty-five
cents a week allowance on liverwurst. In December, she put
it in a box for Christmas money. Thirty-five cents on each of
her family was what she spent. Ned, who would have spent
much more, usually arrived at shopping time with nothing at
all. His money, unsubstantial as foam, passed from him to
the hands of candy-store proprietors with scarcely time to
touch it in between. On Friday morning his allowance was
coin. By Friday evening it was gumdrops or peashooters, balloons or tiny cars to garage beneath his pillow, licorice sticks
or colored candies stuck to strips of paper. Sometimes he
bought his father a ten-cent cigar, or something for Morgan
—a ten-cent pin with blue glass stone, a key ring shaped like

a heart. His offerings at Christmas were schoolmade or hand-made products accompanied by long explanations and promises of handsome things for future years. He would begin saving his money immediately. He would save all year and buy them whatever they wanted. (Obviously, a year's accumulated allowance would buy anything.) He would go forth and spend no more. No words of Morgan's could convince him that this was unnecessary, and no sincerity of resolution ever saw a penny saved.

In the final week of November, Julie made what would be her last purchase of liverwurst till after Christmas. The butcher shop, when she hurried in, was almost as cold as outdoors. There was a sharp odor from sawdust on the floor. The butcher wore an old derby, a heavy jacket over his stained apron. From behind a not immaculately clean counter his gelid face studied her without optimism. There was nothing personal in this. He was simply not an optimistic butcher. Julie, unlike Morgan, was never friendly with tradespeople. Years of being overlooked while adults who had followed her in were dealt with first had taught her to regard them as unfriendly, if not actually hostile. So, though every Friday for nearly three months had seen these two meet at three-fifteen for a transaction unaltered in any detail, the butcher now looked up and said, "What'll it be?", quite as if he had no idea, and Julie said, "I'll take thirty-five cents worth of liver-wurst, please," as though she had strayed into his shop by accident with no clear intention of what to buy.

"You want it sliced?"

"Please."

"Cheaper if you don't," he said, reaching into the case and pulling out the long pale roll. Julie didn't answer, and he began to run his swift honed knife through the soft meat. She watched silently, counting the slices. She felt slightly guilty about not taking it whole, but the feel of the meat was unpleasant, and, sliced, she at least didn't have to get it under her fingernails pulling it apart.

"There y'are, girlie, thirty-five cents." He pushed the white package at her and drew the money away. Joyless and practical, their encounter was at an end.

In the street, Julie pulled her fuzzy coat tighter, wondering why the liverwurst should be cheaper unsliced. It weighed the same. Because he had to use his knife, perhaps? Because it took half a minute of his time? She turned into an alleyway of iron air, walked till she reached a length of connecting alleys that lay between two blocks of buildings. There was a tall gray fence down the middle, separating the property of one block from the other. All windows, all dark cellar doors were closed. There was nothing in the alleys but ashcans and Julie. And, presently, the cats.

She walked along slowly. "Kitty?" she called, "*here*kitty-kittykitty . . ." Her voice was high and sweet and loving. It lured the cats from boxes and doorways where they curled out of the cold. There was a scrabbling on the other side of the fence and a big fawn-colored tom appeared. He leaped lightly to Julie's feet and lifted his broad blunt face, eager, hungry, but controlled. Julie opened her package with stiff fingers and peeled thick yellowish skin from a piece of liverwurst. She broke it quickly, and put it on the ground, using part of the paper for a dish. He pulled it off the paper, turned his head slightly, and began to eat. Seven more thin quick cats had joined him before the last of the liverwurst was shredded and laid on the paper. Julie watched them, her gaze fond and brooding. When they'd finished, they walked curling around her ankles. Some of them cried anxiously and nosed at the paper till she crumpled it. Stooping down, she patted their small heads, ran her hands along fur that, for all their washing, never was anything but rough and a little gritty. For a while, for the liverwurst, they remained, then

77

drifted away on their light-footed errands. The big tom followed her part way down the alley before he leaped over the fence. Julie put the paper in a garbage pail and started home. She wondered why it never made her feel better, feeding them. She came away each week only aware that they were still hungry, still prowling, still cold.

At home she found Morgan and Verna practicing dancing. The small radio whined and tinkled. It moaned of love, lost, lost . . . Morgan and Verna soberly, inexpertly, fitted their steps together, stumbled when Julie appeared at the door.

"Hi, Jule," Verna said.

Julie said, "Hi, *Vern,*" but Verna didn't notice. The two girls made an abortive movement toward a continuation of the dance, abandoned it when their knees clashed. The radio lamented a little longer, then pleaded the cause of a cleaning product, returned to the music and yearned for something— or someone—else.

"That crumby music," Julie said. "And I don't think you can learn to dance with another girl."

"We don't expect to learn," Morgan said lazily. "We already know how, I guess. We're just trying it out."

"Why?"

"Why not?"

Julie shrugged. "I have homework to do, so I suppose I better do it in the bedroom."

Morgan said she thought that would be a good idea. "I'll turn the radio low, so it won't bother you. Ned's having dinner with that Tom Miller, so Verna's going to eat here." Julie gave them a nod that might have meant anything and went into the bedroom, closing the door.

Verna looked after her doubtfully. "I wonder what it's like to be that sure of yourself."

"She isn't, really," Morgan said. "But I know what you

78

mean. She sort of unnerves me sometimes too. She's at a difficult age."

"What age isn't?"

Morgan tried to think of an untroubled age. Not hers or Verna's. Not her father's or Angie's. Not old Mrs. Metzger's. "I guess a baby . . ."

"That's not an age, it's a condition."

"Ned seems all right," Morgan said slowly, wondering how much of Ned's all rightness was real. There were the nights he couldn't sleep well, when he cried out in fear, and either she or her father put on the lights and talked to him, trying to wake him out of his terrible dreams. He seemed to forget, in the day, these cluttered terrors of the night, but the fact that they were unremembered didn't mean they did not exist.

"You want to dance any more?" Verna asked.

"You mean will you have the next stumble with me?" Morgan laughed. "Do you think we'll ever manage?"

"You can always pretend it was someone behind you, bumping," Verna said reassuringly. "Those restaurants are always awfully crowded."

"Maybe you should have asked Betty. I'm scared of blind dates."

"I didn't want Betty. Besides, he isn't exactly a blind date. I mean, I know him, even if you don't. And I wouldn't stick you with anyone too bad."

"What do you mean, *too* bad?"

"Well, my gosh, Morgan, do you expect Prince Aladdin?"

"Aladdin?" Morgan said. "Aladdin wasn't a prince."

"Neither is this fellow," Verna said sulkily.

"Then I won't go out with him. I don't mean I wanted him to be a prince, but you're beginning to sound too . . . skittish about him."

"I am *not* being skittish. I'm pointing out that people in our social circle can't turn up movie stars. He's a nice enough guy. What are you fussing about anyway? We don't have so many dates that you can afford to get on your high horse and ride away."

"That's cute," Morgan giggled, and Verna smiled again. "I don't have any dates at all, to speak of," Morgan went on. "Only I could, you know, if it were just a case of taking anything that came along."

"Oh, baloney. Let's forget the whole thing."

"What does he look like?"

"I told you. Just . . . in between. He's tall, and all-right-looking and isn't a wolf. After all, we're only going to a restaurant and dance. It isn't a marriage I'm arranging."

"Well, I'll go. Only maybe he'd have liked Betty better." She thought a moment. "She probably has a date anyway."

"Betty," Verna said firmly, "would spend the whole evening talking about her wealthy relatives in Virginia, and how boring it is to have nothing to do next year but pack her trunks and go to Vassar . . . I don't want Betty."

"What are you going to do next year?" Morgan asked.

"Get a job, I suppose. If I can find one. What would you think I'd do?"

"Go to Vassar, maybe," Morgan said, intending a joke. But Verna said softly, "I'd love to go to college." She sighed and ran her palm along the chair arm.

"You would?" Morgan looked surprised. Verna did study hard, but somehow college was nothing Morgan had ever associated with any of them. There were some kids at the school who were destined for universities and colleges, and they were apart, marked in some way. Verna had upon her the mark of job hunting, just as Morgan assumed she and Betty had. She wished she hadn't thought of it just now, but the end seemed rather clear-cut, and all the dreaming she'd ever done, all the dreaming she'd do in the future, wouldn't alter it. She'd take a job somewhere and go on dreaming of something different. This cold unexpected moment of clarity stabbed at the dusky softness of her mind like a harsh light. She shuddered away from it. "Why?" she asked Verna hastily, wanting to talk and answer. Wanting not, just now, to think.

"So I could meet some nice boys," Verna said simply.

"I don't suppose going to college makes them nice," Morgan said without assurance. Actually, she supposed just that.

"It doesn't make all of them nice," Verna said bitterly. "But somehow I can't help feeling it would help in most cases."

"Do you think you could go?"

"No. No, I know perfectly well I can't."

"But maybe you . . ."

"No." There was a flat hostility in Verna's voice that Morgan recognized had nothing to do with her. It was Verna's acceptance of a role she didn't want in the world she never made.

"Should we practice dancing some more?" Morgan asked after a while.

Verna shook her head. "I don't care if I trample the dope's feet or not. Let's get dinner."

"What was all that dancing about anyway?" asked Julie, coming out of the bedroom when the odor of food had reached her.

"Verna and I are going on a blind date tomorrow," Morgan said. "At least, I'm going blind. Verna knows them. They live in her apartment building."

"Where are you going?"

Morgan named a restaurant.

"I thought you ate pancakes there," Julie said.

"In the basement of the one at Times Square there's a band and a place to dance," Morgan explained. "And green tile walls and a fountain in the middle."

"Sounds like an aquarium."

"I can think of worse places to dance," Morgan said without rancor.

Verna was setting the table and Julie offered to help. "Wonder what Ned's having for dinner?" she mused.

Morgan laughed. "I can't bear to think."

"Pie, probably," Julie said.

"And sweet pickles."

"And doughnuts."

"And pie. For dessert."

"No, candy for dessert. Pie for dinner."

"What did you have for dinner, darling?"

Ned blinked, sleek and languid with contentment. Tom had returned him at ten-thirty, shortly after Verna had left and Julie had gone to bed. He hadn't come in, just winked at Morgan, handed her a drowsy brother, and departed.

Ned yawned at her question, began to pull his sweater off. "Chicken," he said.

"Chicken?"

"Mmm. Fried."

"What else?"

Ned sat on his cot, prepared by Morgan for his sleep, and gave her a dreamy smile. "Oh, chicken . . . and potato chips, and . . . celery and hot rolls . . . and tomato juice and chocolate eclairs . . ."

"Who selected the dinner?" Morgan asked in amazement.

"I did, Morgy. Tom said I could have anything I wanted. That's what I wanted."

Morgan shook her head. I'll never understand children, she thought. Never. She had to rouse Ned, who was falling asleep with his shoes and pants on.

Dan Connor, coming in shortly after midnight, found a note from his elder daughter. "Ned," it read, "had his dinner out tonight. He did *not* eat syrup in a spun-sugar basket. He chose a perfectly good meal. What do you think of that?"

Dan hesitated, smiled, took up a pencil and wrote, "Train a child up in the way he should go, and he will not depart from it."

The table was set for breakfast as, in the evening, it always was. Dan slipped the note under Morgan's plate, thinking that a word of praise to Morgan from her father was long overdue.

Chapter Six

Verna and Morgan sat with stiff backs on a sofa in the Herzog's living room, waiting for the hoarse buzz of the doorbell to announce that their dates had arrived. Verna's voice reeled into the silence like thread spinning from a spool—thin, swift, and, so far, unchecked.

Mrs. Herzog, in a wash of yellow lamplight, rocked and knitted. Her gray-brown hair was braided round her placid face, her glasses hung low on her nose. She looked peaceful, provident, humorous, like a cover on the *Saturday Evening Post*. But she blinked a lot, and shot quick glances at her husband whenever it seemed he might stir and speak. He, a large man with a still-featured veinous face, sat in an overstuffed chair. His hands were on his thighs, as though at any moment he planned to rise and leave, and his eyes were on Verna. As though, Morgan thought nervously, he was deciding when to say shut up.

He lifted a big freckled hand to the chair arm in an impatient gesture, and Verna's voice snapped off.

"Where's your sister?" Mr. Herzog said to Verna.

"How should I know, Pa?"

"How shouldn't you know? Don't you people keep track of each other?"

Mrs. Herzog's lids lifted and descended rapidly. She rested her knitting in her lap. "Emma's resting," she said.

"Resting?" he repeated, as though unable to believe his ears. "Resting from what, if I may be so bold as to ask?"

Oh boy, Morgan thought, I hope those fellows get here pretty soon.

Mrs. Herzog was explaining that Emma had worked overtime at the beauty parlor. "She had a late perm to do."

"Too bad someone in that beauty parlor don't do a little overtime on Emma," Mr. Herzog said. "She could use it."

Morgan quivered inside. Emma was homely, with the sort of homeliness that you knew no effort could alter. She was not like the girls in movies who wore glasses and flat heels and for the first part of the picture drooped unnoticed, only to shed these drawbacks and emerge, radiantly beautiful, to stun the hero into love forever after. Emma was just hopeless. Sallow, skinny, and twenty-six.

Morgan looked at Emma's father. You ape, she said silently, without altering her expression. They all had their ways of dealing with him. Methods of walking warily around his temper, as though it were a quiescent snake that might ripple and strike, but, on the other hand, might continue to lie sluggishly inert. Ways of stiff naturalness, of delicate sensibility to the direction of his mood. They were all, Verna, Emma, and Mrs. Herzog, watchful but not really alarmed. Years of living with him had taught them that even considered as a snake he was prone to rattle but reluctant, perhaps slightly afraid, to strike. Behold the bully, all grown up.

He rose. "Well, it's pretty dull around here. Guess I'll go see George for a while." Unexpectedly, he nodded at the two girls on the sofa. "Have a good time." He went out. The door closing behind him was like a moon pulling tides of peace into the room. Mrs. Herzog resumed her knitting, Verna leaned back easily to talk again, from a room down the hall, Emma's radio began to play.

"You know," Mrs. Herzog said, "a man could get way with anything, just saying he guessed he'd go see George. I'll bet men all over the country are saying it right this minute. It's such a reasonable thing to do, don't you think?" Her voice was relaxed, chatty.

"Well, you certainly could never prove that anybody *wasn't* going to see George," Verna said. They laughed, and Emma came in to join them, and it was like a little holiday. The doorbell rang twice before they heard it.

Morgan, half-attending the departure of Mr. Herzog, and the resultant brightening of the atmosphere, still had remained in a fantasy projection of the evening to come. Rationally, she knew that this unknown boy would probably be just what Verna claimed he was. An in-between. The world was full of those, and often they were nice enough to know, to talk to. Morgan didn't expect much, and in that was rarely disappointed. On the other hand, she didn't want much from the people she knew. To the ones she dreamed were given all the cherished qualities, all the endearing responses that she needed. The difficulty lay in her tendency to confuse the dreamed with the real but not yet met.

He might, this Roy Austin, be . . . Well, he'd be not too tall, with a compact graceful build, so that when he walked he was all of a piece, not gangling around with extra arms and flaring ears. His voice would be rich and never loud, and when they met, he'd smile slowly, as though he'd come to the end of a search. "Hello," he'd say, low beneath the other voices in the room. "Hello—Morgan." She'd put her hand out, her eyes on his face, and not speak for a moment. Just smile slightly, the way he did, to let him know she, too, was thinking that at last they'd met . . . she, too, was experiencing alarm that one of them might have refused this date, might have been busy, or just not interested. But they'd be there, together, looking in each other's eyes while the voices swirled around them. And then— Well, *then* was harder. It was always this way. She'd define for herself a boy, a meeting, a vibrant realization. But after that the picture clouded. Nothing presented itself as a way to go on. When it was a boy she might actually meet, not a movie producer she knew perfectly well she would not, it was impossible to think her way past the meeting. With the movie producer, she could go on in loving and clear detail, through the conversations, the screen tests, the ultimate adoration of the public and Cary Grant. But a boy . . . The rich voice, the clasped hands, seemed to lead only to a moment in the future when they would kiss. And the kiss summoned up Marty and the darkened hallway. So she went back to the beginning. He'd be graceful, and low-voiced. . . .

When the doorbell had rung twice, Verna heard it. She went down the long hallway. There was the sound of the door opening, of the mingling voices, Verna's abruptly high and arch, as it became around boys, and neither of the answering ones deep and rich. Easily distinguishable as male voices, but that was all. There were the footsteps approaching. Mrs. Herzog knitted, Emma turned the pages of a magazine. But they were safe. They didn't have to meet a stranger and try to be the sort of blind date anyone would be overjoyed to have. She had a moment yet, before the advancing three converged upon her, to wish that she were Emma . . . homely, uninterested, safe.

Then they were there.

Slightly blinded by nervousness, Morgan could distinguish only two lank boys, dressed in fairly flashy best, thrusting their hands at her. She didn't know which was Roy Austin, the handclasps were brief and scarcely tender, no one said, "Hello—Morgan." One of them said hi and the other nodded, looking over her head, something he could do easily. He was over six feet and his arms and legs were like twine. He, it developed, was Roy Austin. The other was Pete, for

Verna. Morgan never found out what his last name was. Pete was not very tall, not in the least graceful. He fidgeted. He put his hands in his pockets and jingled coins. He took a comb from his pants pocket, ran it through his hair, returned it to his vest pocket. He jutted his jaw and grinned and said he had news for them—tempus was fugiting.

In the buses (one uptown, one a transfer crosstown) the four were separated. Morgan and Roy Austin sat tensely together, looking with elaborate interest at the passing scene, their fellow passengers, the floor. Roy swallowed loudly and flung his long thin hands about as though they were unexpected encumbrances that he hadn't quite decided what to do with. Morgan looked surreptitiously at his window reflection. He had yellow hair, a gently sloping chin, and a peering expression.

"Well, here we are," said Roy.

"Where?" she asked, startled. "It's time to get off?"

"No, no. Not yet. In a couple blocks. I just meant—here we are."

"Oh." She turned to him, but his face was too close, and she looked away. "Yes. Here we are."

"Cold tonight."

"Isn't it, though? Winter is practically upon us."

"Sure is. Hate to see the warm weather go. Don't know why it is, but that's the way I am, a real water baby."

"You like to swim?"

"Like it? Tell you something it's the only thing keeps me sane."

"It is?" Morgan said with mild wonder. "Have you . . . I mean, are there a lot of problems in your life?"

"Who hasn't got problems? But I just like to swim."

"That's nice."

There was silence. Then, "Well, let's get out of this fire

trap," Roy said. He lifted his twining length into the air and preceded Morgan down the aisle.

The four of them stood on the corner of Forty-second Street and Seventh Avenue, shivering in the night air, looking at each other cautiously. Downtown, the streets looked canyon-like, dark and scarcely peopled, except where the lurid lights of the Metropolitan Opera House announced the presence of an art Morgan and Verna and the two boys were almost unaware of. From Forty-second uptown, as far as they could see, night was nearly vanquished. Sliding, glittering, twisting, winking, blaring Broadway drove away the dark, drove away the stillness, eclipsed the character of night from these blocks and substituted its own daft personality in shards of color, brittle minglings of music and voices, mutable throngs of human beings who here had found escape from the final human fear, which is to be alone, and in the dark.

"Man, the joint is jumpin'," said Pete, snapping his fingers so that they made a tune. "Maybe we shoulda gone down to hear Ray."

"Ray?" Verna said, smiling. Morgan realized that Verna had been smiling ceaselessly since they got off the bus. She looked vivacious, and slightly strained already. She wouldn't meet Morgan's eye. Why? These boys were all right. They were trying to be friendly, to have a good time. Morgan hadn't indicated in any way at all that she didn't think the occasion was fine, and the way it turned out, if badly, would hardly be Verna's fault. But nervous sponsorship was apparent in Verna's laughter following Pete's every remark. She was gay and delighted. She was having a *fine* time.

"Sure. *The* Ray," Jack said. "He's playing at the Stat."

That's a hotel, Morgan thought nervously. She hoped they wouldn't decide to go there. None of them would know how to go to a hotel dancing room (ballroom?). Didn't tables have to be reserved? And didn't you have to know headwaiters and things? They'd just make fools of themselves, going to a place like that.

"I don't want to go down there," Roy said loudly, and Morgan realized he was uneasy too. "It's too . . . it's too cold. Let's beat it on over and warm up, hey?"

Pete looked relieved and said that'd be better probably, it *was* pretty cold, and the girls were probably sick of riding buses by now. Fuss on a bus, eh?

"Oh, *Pete*," Verna giggled. She thought he was terribly funny. A riot.

Rumble of music and voices and shuffling feet came up the stairs to meet them as they descended to the dancing lower level of the restaurant. The six-piece orchestra was mounted on a dais, and the tables, equipped with napery slightly soiled and large ash trays, were closely crowded. In the center of the floor, revolving round an infirm fountain, the dancers moved in restricted rhythm.

"How delightful," Verna said, as they sat at a table granted them. No one replied. They sat, looking around, and were grateful when a waitress came to take their orders. The boys said they'd have beer. They let the girls order for themselves. Two orangeades. The waitress stuck the order pad in her apron pocket and left.

"Well," said Pete. "Dig the femmes . . . orangeade, no less." He told a joke about the three college men in a bar, two of whom ordered cokes and the third water, "because he had to *drive*." This was received in silence. Pete spun the ash tray with one finger, tapped his foot in time to the music. "Dance?" he said to Verna.

"*Love* to," she replied.

They rose and thrust themselves upon the field.

Roy shook his head and lit a cigarette. "Funny thing about me," he said, and paused.

"Yes?"

"Yeah. I just can't stand dancing. I've always been like that. Don't know why it is, but there you are."

Where? Morgan wondered. This was supposed to be a date *for* dancing. "Perhaps because you like to swim so much," she suggested, relieved at not having to get close to him as, if they danced, she would. He was apparently content—eager— to take the burden of conversation practically unassisted. It made him easy to talk to.

"That could be it," he approved. "I got my mind on a new sort of dive. My own version of the one-and-a-half gainer." Roy's brow furrowed, showing how clearly his mind was on this, not on that.

"Could you have a version? I mean, either it is a one-and-a-half gainer, or it isn't. I should think, anyway." What did she know about it?

"Well, now, that's just where you'd be wrong . . ." Roy leaned forward, eyeing her intently. He was going to explain, so pretty soon she *would* know. Five minutes later, he was saying, "So there you are. Not exactly a one-and-a-half, but almost. See?"

"Oh, yes. Yes, I do."

Roy leaned back again. He lit another cigarette. "Ever been over to the St. George?"

Morgan shook her head.

"Tell you what. Let's you and me go over there next week, okay?"

"But . . . what is it?"

"What is it? It's just the best darn swimming pool in the city, that's what it is." He fanned smoke away from his face. "Got mirrors everywhere. You'll love it."

No I won't, she assured herself.

"Pick you up Saturday, Friday, any time you say," Roy was telling her.

The idea of going anywhere at all with this lank blond

crane, much less to a pool where he'd be mirrored all over the place, and she beside him, was inconceivable. "I can't swim," she said hastily.

For a moment he looked as though she'd announced she couldn't breathe. "Can't . . ." He deliberated. "Really?"

"No."

He blinked and rubbed the back of his neck. "I could teach you . . . I suppose."

"I'm allergic to chlorine." How many ways could you refuse without saying you didn't want to?

"That makes it hard," he said, without noticeable regret.

Makes it impossible. "I'm afraid so," she admitted. She pulled orangeade through colored straws and wondered when Verna and Pete would return. She wondered, suddenly, how Ned and Julie were. I wish I were home, she thought. I wish I were home reading a magazine. But the evening was not half over, and she was spending the night with Verna. I'll be going on through this night forever, she thought. I'll never be home, and free of all this, away from Roy Austin and jolly Pete and Verna being vivacious. I'll be sitting here forever, talking and understanding why he doesn't dance and how he dives. . . .

Pete and Verna returned. "It was *delightful*," Verna was saying. Pete hummed, sliding on easy hips . . . "We'll be there de da da . . ." He was graceful, in a fashion, when he danced. "Dance?" he said to Morgan.

"Oh, I'd *love* to."

"Well?" Verna said.

They were back in the Herzog apartment, in the bathroom. Morgan was washing her face. It was one o'clock, and Mr. Herzog was snoring, and they knew that the night was bitter cold outside. The bathroom radiator hissed sweetly.

Morgan lifted her shoulders, the washrag over her face.

"We had fun, didn't we?" Verna demanded.

"Oh, sure."

"Then what's the matter?"

"Nothing, Verna. I'm tired."

Verna sank to the edge of the bathtub. "I know what you're thinking. But gosh, Morgan, you have to go out once in a while, don't you? I like to have dates."

"Me too. It's just . . ."

"Yes. But it's *always* just . . ." Verna turned her head, eyes down, and sighed. "Sometimes I wish I could die. I look ahead and I can't see anything but dopes like that, and Pa raising the roof over nothing, and Emma crying . . ."

"I cry sometimes," Morgan said nervously, after a long pause, as though it might help Emma. Or Verna, perhaps. "I don't know why."

"You do?" Verna said in soft surprise. "Aren't girls funny?" She smiled suddenly. "Anyway, we can tell Betty on Monday that we went dancing."

"My little brother knows a nice boy. His name is Tom Miller."

Verna giggled. "Tell him to look me up when he's older," she said. "Move over so I can brush my teeth."

They went on talking, in whispers, after they got to bed. Verna fell asleep in the middle of a sentence. For a while, Morgan tried to think about Colin, but he evaded her, and she too fell asleep. Except for that one attempt, they had made no mention of the evening past. The worst that could be said was that it was dull; the best, that it was over. Verna would go on seeing Pete, if he asked, because he was better than nothing. Morgan would not see Roy, because he hadn't asked again, and she considered him worse than nothing.

In the Herzog apartment, black and too hot, there was no

sound except Mr. Herzog's bearish snore and the restless turning of Emma in her sleep.

The hands thrust quarters, dimes, dollars, over the satin-slick funnel of wood. Dan returned change, answered an occasional question as to how the shuttle could be reached, where Ninety-sixth Street was located. He rested his chin on his left hand, and read by the insufficient light of his cage. A whale-oil lamp might have burned this dimly, the words he saw might have been written by such a lamp.

"God help thee, old man, thy thoughts have created a creature in thee; and he whose intense thinking thus makes him a Prometheus; a vulture feeds upon that heart for ever; that vulture the very creature he creates."

The station was a catacomb of still, refrigerated air, threaded with steel, strung with iron. It was dark, and only a random passenger walked the stone length, footsteps echoing, waiting for the far-away rumble that would promise relief, that would bring the train, a patient drab, sliding breathily beside the platform. Passengers were borne away, the station clock moved past nine, past ten.

Dan read, and made change, and read again.

"Thy thoughts have created a creature in thee. . . ." What dark creature sat in him, made of his despairs, his thoughts? Shaped of his aloneness, and his desire to be alone; of his unknowing of his children, his reluctance to know them. Sarah should not have done this, should not have left him with the three beloved strangers. A roof, a meal, a book . . . enough for Dan. But how was he to tell what was enough for *them*? What they needed, were afraid of, wished but never asked of him? Morgan, with her medieval name, her blurred and dreamy ways, her instinctive precision as a mother. Morgan who was doing Sarah's job, and pretty much all of Dan's.

94

What did Morgan le Fay Connor of Dump Street want? Not to live on Dump Street all her life. Well, she liked the new apartment, and Dan had got that. But the lines of communication were down between them. Whether Morgan would have them up, he didn't even know. For himself . . . well, for himself, he wanted nothing except that state most impossible of attainment, changelessness. To be, like those small articulations in amber, finally fixed and unreachable.

Ned had been six when Sarah died, Julie ten, Morgan thirteen. Julie and Ned wept and remained children, Morgan wept and grew up, Dan pulled misery around him like a protecting jacket and never noticed he was losing his job till it was gone. Sarah lost forever, ninety dollars in the bank, no job, three children. Well, he had a job now. And inertia was lighter to wear than misery.

The station clock moved forward. He read, and made change, and once during the evening recalled that tonight Morgan was dancing somewhere with a "blind date." He thought how daring young people were—risking hours on the unknown.

Chapter Seven

They told you in school that all people were created equal, but Ned thought it didn't take much looking around to discover it wasn't so. And it seemed sometimes that the unequaler you were, the better things worked out. There were kids a few blocks away so unequal they got sent to camp two weeks in the summer.

"Are we underprivileged?" he asked Morgan.

"What are you talking about?"

"About underprivileged. I could go to summer camp, maybe, if we were. Enough."

Julie looked at her brother without kindness. "You don't have any pride, do you?"

"You mean if I could take my pick between pride and two weeks in the country, which would I take?"

"Don't answer," Julie said, walking away.

Ned turned back to Morgan. "Maybe I don't," he said, not regretfully.

"Oh well. One man's pride is another man's—" She hesitated.

"Summer camp?" Ned suggested.

Morgan smiled, and then said, "Not in your case, honey. We're not poor, really. Not enough to get benefits. We have a decent home, and enough food and clothes. There's an awful difference between being us with nothing extra and nothing left over and being poor."

Ned nodded. "I thought so. Maybe I wouldn't like camp anyway."

"Maybe you'd get poison ivy."

"Yeah. Or drowned. Could you come to see me in a play?"

"Darling! A play? When? You didn't tell me."

"I'm telling you now. I'm a Wise Man. Do you know the names of the three Wise Men?" Morgan shook her head. "Well, I do. Melchior, Gaspar and Balthasar."

"Ned, you're marvelous. I'll bet you're the only person on this block knows that."

Ned thought this was probably so. "The play's next Wednesday. Can you come?"

"Wednesday? Well, Wednesday's a school . . . Oh, I'll play hooky. Pop can write a note saying I got a terrible stomach ache all of a sudden."

"I must say," Julie called out harshly, "you certainly set him nice examples. Don't think for a minute that I care, because I don't. I'm just saying."

Morgan sighed unhappily. While she wondered what to answer, the phone rang. It was Mrs. Miller, inviting the three of them to her apartment to eat doughnuts. "I made mounds of them today, Morgan, and you kids'll simply have to help me out. I thought since it was Saturday you could let the homework go and just sit around gorging for a while."

Morgan said they'd love to and hung up. The Connors, even Dan, had got to know the Millers, though between Morgan and Tom there remained a sort of tension that was not unfriendly, but wary. They seldom spoke to each other directly. Morgan wondered what they'd say if they were ever alone together. But then, that was not likely. Where Tom was, people were. He wasn't hearty, or loud, did not have that explosive attractiveness that some of the best-liked boys at school had. He was warm, with a bright vigor that people liked to see, liked to be near. He had, Morgan admitted, an easy rhythm, moved as though he were all one flowing piece. A pulse began to tap at her throat and she tried not to know why. Tom liked Ned and took the rest of the Connors with him. Besides, there were college girls . . .

"Am I invited too?" Julie asked.

"Of course. Why do you talk like that?" Morgan said irritably. Colin was going, fading away. It was Tom's fault. She was losing Colin, Julie was always getting hurt, and there was never a moment's peace. "You're invited. But for heaven's sake, try to be agreeable, will you?"

"Oh sure. *I* should try to be agreeable. Nobody else. Just me, me, me. Julie be agreeable, be a nice girl, don't bother people. Do this do that don't be such a nuisance . . ."

"Do you think you aren't?" Morgan said loudly. "Do you think you're a nice sweet easy person that anyone could get along with?"

"No. I *don't* think I am," Julie said, walking on hard angry feet toward the bedroom. "And I'm not going with you. Not tonight or any other night, anywhere." She started to pull the door shut. "You—you fat marshmallow!"

"Just because you've got the door handle doesn't mean you can have the last word," Morgan yelled, starting after her.

"Oh doesn't it?" Julie said. She slammed the door as Morgan reached it. There was silence. Julie, breathing heavily, stood in the unlighted bedroom. Morgan, in the little hall, hesitated, half turned away, turned back again. Ned chewed his fingernails, saying nothing.

I don't want her to speak to me, Julie thought. I don't care about anything, not about anything at all. But she listened for Morgan's footsteps, listened to know what would happen now. If Morgan didn't come, didn't call, if she and Ned simply left for the Millers . . . What would Julie do then? I'd have to run away, she thought strangely. I couldn't stay here, all alone, with everyone angry. She didn't cry, but began to tremble and had to lean against the wall to stop it. When Morgan's tap came at the door it was a moment before Julie could answer.

"Julie? May I come in?"

Julie took a deep breath. "Sure. Come on," she said.

Morgan opened the door, walked to the lamp and turned it on. "I'm sorry," she said, not looking at her sister. "I shouldn't yell, and I shouldn't get angry. I'm sorry, really."

Because she did something she didn't want to do, Julie thought listlessly. It was awful that you couldn't make even someone who loved you (Morgan did love her) really *care* what you were feeling. They either did or they didn't. "I'm sorry too," she said.

"Well . . ." Morgan picked up her hairbrush. "We should go pretty soon."

Julie nodded. "I'll wash my face." She went in to the bathroom, avoiding Ned's eye.

Tom Miller was, as all the Connors had noticed, bright and warm. His mother was like a great blazing fire. Deep voice, enormous frame, a crackling vitality that, in an hour, left Dan Connor exhausted. ("Oh, admirable," he'd said in answer to a question from Morgan. "Admirable. Sort of wearing, though." He'd yawned at the mere recollection. He was grateful to the Millers for their interest in his children, but he did not envy Mr. Miller his wife, and he regarded Tom with that faint contempt the physically soft man has for athletes.)

Mr. Miller opened to them. "Good evening, Connors all," he said. "How do you like the first snowfall?"

"Snow?" Ned yelled. "We didn't know it was snowing. We came through the basement." He ran toward the window.

"I thought you didn't like the basement?" Tom said.

"I don't," Morgan answered. "Only it's cold out. And three of us together seemed safe enough."

Mrs. Miller came out of the kitchen. "I hope you're all hungry. I have enough doughnuts here to feed an army." Mrs. Miller didn't believe in searching for words.

"Can I go out on the terrace?" Ned asked.

Mr. Miller thought he could. "Come on, girls. The first snowfall of the year. Let's all look at it."

They crowded onto the tiny terrace, into the cold blanched air. Snow spun and spiraled, falling more densely even as they watched. Julie leaned over, watching roofs on the building across the street whiten thinly. It's going to stick, she thought happily. Ned said it. "It's going to stick," he shouted. "We can have snowmen and snowforts."

Morgan shivered and went back into the apartment. "Beautiful," she said as the others followed her in. "But cold."

"Beautiful things are so often cold," Julie said. Morgan just managed not to sigh.

"Julie," Mrs. Miller said, "how about helping me in the kitchen?" Julie started slightly. The sudden selection of her name reminded her of those terrible games they played at school, where leaders selected their teams. Julie was uncertain how the choice of leaders was arrived at. She'd never been one herself. But knew, far too well, the tense, falsely indifferent attitude of waiting to be chosen. The thinking that at any moment, the magic word Julie would come, the sudden realization that of course it wouldn't . . . she'd be the leftover, the unwanted, the fiery-faced unchosen one assigned willy-nilly to either team when all the other choices had been made. She hadn't, actually, ever been the last. Not adept at games, she still had the advantage of long legs, and apart from catching balls, running seemed to be the essence of recess periods. Mrs. Miller's request gave her the same momentary surprise that, no matter how anxiously awaited, her own name called in the schoolyard did. She rose happily and followed the big woman.

Ned, who was helping or hindering Mr. Miller in the construction of a clipper-ship model, coaxed for a few minutes work.

"It's in the bedroom," Mr. Miller explained to Morgan. "I work on an old table they won't let me bring in the living room. Would you excuse us? That is, unless you'd like to come along?"

Morgan shook her head. "Thanks. I'm fine here." She was peacefully fitted into a huge armchair with a finish smooth to the touch, quite unlike the frieze at home.

So, briefly, she and Tom were alone.

Outside, the snow fell, palely visible through dark shining windows. Within, silence fell, soft as the snow, with something of its coolness. Morgan's gaze moved about, lighting on the fine old rug, the smooth auburn finish of mahogany furniture, the things of wood and bright brass that Mr. Miller had bought years ago when he worked for the Near East Foundation. Enormous brass trays with Persian inscriptions, brass candelabra, little carved figures of stone and wood. The room was richly, deeply colored. It was worn, but the wear came from age, not flimsiness.

"Ned tells me you go dancing a lot," Tom said. "You like to dance?"

"Isn't he funny," she said with surprise. "I've been once in the last six months."

"Where'd you go?"

"To the . . ." For a moment, she knew the temptations Betty had. It would be fun to say, to the Stat, wouldn't it? A restaurant didn't seem a glamorous admission. But she couldn't quite picture herself saying the Stat, like Pete. And anyway . . . oh well, anyway . . . She told him where they'd gone. "I don't suppose you've ever been there?"

"There are lots of places I've never been, so don't hold it against me."

Suddenly Morgan laughed. "You haven't missed the opportunity of a lifetime, I assure you."

"That bad?"

"Oh no," she said, a little giddily, "not bad at all, really. But I was on a blind date and he didn't like me." Saying this made her feel quite superior to Roy and the entire evening. Tom grinned, and she went on happily, "If I'd grown a fishtail and swum into the fountain, he might have."

"You couldn't dance with a fishtail."

"He didn't dance anyway," she said triumphantly, and they yelled with laughter. Oh, it was a wonderful feeling, laughing with Tom. It was being special, and luckier than anyone else. It was being happy. When Mrs. Miller came in with a tray of cider mugs, followed by Julie with a platter of doughnuts, Morgan and Tom were still finding things funny. As he got up to help his mother, Tom's eyes fixed for a moment on Morgan's and he smiled again. A different smile this time, no longer amused at her silly date, a smile just for her. So that's it, Morgan thought, floating into the sort of happiness she'd always imagined with Colin. This was what it was like to love without the help of a dream. I'm in love, she thought. I can only sit here nibbling doughnuts, but I've just fallen in love. She took deep silent breaths and looked at the floor, so no one should guess.

Mrs. Miller patted Julie's hand, sank into a chair. "My, it's good to have girls around the house. Not, of course, Neddy, that you aren't a treasure, but you know how it is. Or I guess you don't, really, but *I* do." She patted her large bosom. Ned seemed not at all hurt. His eyes kept straying to the bedroom door where the unfinished clipper ship offered so much. "Boys are wonderful," Mrs. Miller went on, "but I never had any girls, more's the pity."

"Where's your other son?" Julie asked in a voice so tender that Morgan winced. She could see Julie preparing to slip into the role of "Mrs. Miller's little girl." "Doesn't he ever come to see you?"

"With great regularity," Mrs. Miller said. "He has a room in Washington Heights, to be near his job—he's on a newspaper, you know—but he's over here often enough. Too often, if you ask me. Geoff's in love, and I think love is dandy, but I don't want it underfoot all the time."

"Too bad about you," Tom said affectionately.

Morgan drank her cider nervously. It couldn't be that Mrs. Miller was warning her? But that was silly.

Mrs. Miller, who was not clairvoyant, sailed on with a wink at Tom, "Your brother is the languishing type, you know what I mean? That's what I don't want underfoot. Once he gets some girl for good, I'll be more than satisfied."

Later, Tom walked the three of them back through the basement. Julie was frankly tired, and Ned, vigorously protesting wakefulness, could scarcely keep his eyes open.

"I think the Millers keep your brother up too late," Tom said.

"No you don't," Ned said, lifting his lids heavily. "No you don't, Tom."

"He can sleep late in the morning," Morgan said as they reached the apartment. She looked around a little shyly. "It's been very nice."

Tom leaned, elbow on the door jamb, head against his hand. "I have an idea, sort of."

"Have you?"

"Yup. Have you got some heavy clothes? Boots, or something?"

Morgan nodded slowly. "I have boots. Why?" she asked, thinking she knew but afraid to be sure.

"Well, I thought that if you wanted to, you could get into some warm things and then come up with me while I got some, and we could take a walk in the snow. Do you like walking in the snow?"

"Oh, I love to," Morgan said, thankful that Julie couldn't hear through the closed bedroom door. "Or, I'll tell you . . . I'll get ready, and you go up and get your things, and then I'll meet you by the gate." Her voice was high with excitement, and she lowered it to say, "All right?" Now it sounded growly. She flushed and turned away.

"See you in ten minutes," Tom agreed. He sounded perfectly normal. But then, Morgan thought with unwelcome clarity, he wasn't feeling the strange, sweet, riotous emotion that she was. He just wanted to walk in the snow and thought it would be fun to have her for company.

She hurried into the bedroom. "Julie," she said to her sister, who was standing at the window, forehead on the cold pane, "Julie, I'm going for a walk with Tom. Not for long." She waited, expecting some outburst of elaborate unconcern. But Julie murmured something noncommittal and continued to stare at the crinoline night. Morgan pulled out a pair of boots, sat on the floor to tug them on. "I wish I had a nice jacket," she said mournfully. "I'll just have to put on a sweater and wear my coat." A beautiful red wool jacket would be so fine, and maybe a pair of fur mittens, like Betty's. How could you get a boy to like you if you went around dressed like something that had fallen off the hanger? She pulled on brown cotton gloves, put a kerchief on her hair, stood at the mirror to apply lipstick, and wished she looked delicate, like, again, Betty. Betty had smooth dark hair, small lovely features, little bones. Morgan had hair that was thick and glossy, like the mane of a toast-colored horse. Her face, with its definite jawline, broad forehead, wide-spaced eyes, had a bright bold attractiveness that she failed to see. She did not resemble anyone in the movies, as Betty, and Verna, could be fancied to. She didn't look like the women in the cigarette ads, nor the girls in the love-story magazines. *They* either had golden, flaming, or blue-black curls, possessed cameo features, and were, without exception, slender and willowy. She didn't look like any one but herself, and it was discouraging.

Tom was waiting by the closed iron gates of the development. He wore a wonderful thick leather jacket, boots that clasped his trousers tightly round the ankle, and no hat. He came toward her through the falling snow, and Morgan realized that she liked everything about him. His voice, his gait, the remembered look of his smooth muscular arm. Colin had never been a figure for her, she had never known what his gestures would be, what he would wear. He'd been a response, a dream person who assumed many forms but had none of his own. Tom was real. He was here, and his jacket was leather, his eyes brown, his voice quick and firm.

He said, putting his key in the smaller door that fitted in the large gate, "I hate these things."

"What things?"

"These blasted gates. Who are they keeping out?"

"Why, I don't know," Morgan said with surprise. She'd never thought of the gates one way or the other. They swung back by day, were locked at night, and you had to have a key to go through the door if you came in after nine. "Strange people, perhaps?"

"Who's strange? Is there anybody so valuable in there—" he asked, waving a hand back toward the red-brick buildings they were leaving, "that they have to be protected?"

"I don't know," Morgan said again. "If there is," she added

thoughtfully, "it's not the Connors. We'd be more likely to get locked out than in. I'm terribly glad to live here."

Tom looked at her sideways with an odd expression—gentle, and even, she decided hesitantly, protective. She yielded to the warm delight of being so looked at, and walked along smiling softly to herself.

For a while nothing more was said. The snow, with soft inexorable accuracy, was finding, filling, covering every crevice, every plane, every step and sill and doorway. The alleys, the doors that were deeply recessed, were whitened only part way, making their untouched reaches blacker than ever. Now the street lay whitely muffled and still. Occasionally there was the flat clapping of chained tires on a cruising automobile. Headlight beams, restless with wild tossing flakes, would glide slowly past and away. Down the street a man walked his dog, their footprints shuffling and mixing. But there were not many people. Numberless windows alight, few adventurers. Where the street lamps glowed, snow seemed to drive rapidly, in bright, beaded sheets, but when it passed the areas of lamplight, it hesitated, slowed, drifted about idly. It settled in soft mounds on hydrants and window sills, sifted airily against Morgan's face, and Tom's.

It wasn't cold, but cool, vibrant, delicate. "It's marvelous," Morgan said, breathing deeply. "I'll bet even your old gates will have peaks of snow."

"I guess I sounded pretty silly. But I burn at things like that. Locking gates so everyone will know the development is sacred to people who can pay the rent. It's symbolic of the sort of thing that goes on all over the world. In this case it's just sort of ludicrous, since probably half the people who are locked out have more money than the ones who get all the protection. Mr. Rasche, the grocer, lives over his store and it's no palace, and he could buy us all. But . . . generally. You know?" He spoke with the utter outrage at injustice that only young people can summon.

"My father says he recognized the world's wrongs and settled down to live with them long ago."

"That's a criminal attitude."

"Such a silly thing to say about my father," Morgan answered softly. "I'm sort of mixed up. I thought you were a phys. ed. major?"

"Heck no. Economics. But even that's not the point. A phys. ed. major can be just as conscious of things as anyone else. It's *caring* about it, don't you see, Morgan?"

Morgan, aware only of his voice saying her name, nodded fervently.

"People have *got* to care," he said firmly. "There's something wrong when you see little kids that don't have enough to eat or wear, and old people staring all day at the floor because they've got nothing else to do, and young people scared of what they'll have to do."

"Well yes, there's something wrong, all right," Morgan said slowly. "But suppose there isn't any answer?" This wasn't at all what she'd expected them to be saying as they walked in the snow. But where Tom led, she was willing to follow. She was even prepared to make an effort at understanding, as she had never been with her father.

"Oh, there's an answer. Make no mistake, there's always an answer. Not that I've got it. But it's there."

"Answers aren't necessarily cures." Her voice was low.

"How do you mean?"

"Answers don't . . . Say that I'm sick, only I don't know what with. Then say the . . . the answer's cancer. Where am I then?"

"They're working on an answer to that too."

"Yes, I do know. But it takes a long time, and what good does *my* caring do? About that, or the other? I can't change the world. And neither can you."

Tom stopped walking. He put a hand on Morgan's arm, turning her toward him. "If I thought that I wouldn't, somehow, even a little, change the world—I'd see no point in living at all." His hand fell away from her arm. Morgan could feel the light pressure still, but knew he'd been unaware of touching her. They walked on, shooting the snow in powdery wings before their feet.

"What do you want to be?" Morgan said.

"A teacher."

A teacher? Morgan would never have imagined setting out to be a teacher. It seemed a way of life that befell people, not one that was sought out. "You mean a college professor?"

He smiled. "I haven't thought that far. It just seems to me that teaching is the only way to reach people, to change them, to make them *understand*. Perhaps high school would be better. People in high school are—more flexible. Of course the real place to teach would be in the elementary grades. But the pay—"

"Isn't it funny that you're so good at sports," she mused. "Ned says you're on the track team and everything."

"Not and everything. The track team. What's funny about it? Will you tell me how this idea got around that athletes are meatheads and if you study you can't tell the difference between a lacrosse stick and a butterfly net?"

"What's a lacrosse stick?"

Tom laughed. "In other words, you study?"

"I don't study *or* know the difference."

"I see. A compromiser. Well, a lacrosse stick is—" He stopped and drew one in the soft snow with his finger. The outline didn't take very well. "The general idea, anyway," Tom said, straightening.

"Lacrosse is a game?"

"A form of murder, actually."

"Do you play?"

"I have. Running's better. You can jog along, thinking about things."

"I thought you had to run fast. You can't jog fast."

"I'm a distance runner."

"Oh. Do you always win?"

"I never win," he said cheerfully. "I bring up the rear, to be sure no one's lost."

"Let's run now," Morgan said suddenly. "Come on, Tom." And she ran down the street, snow crunching beneath her boots, snow dashing wildly in her face and eyes. Her breath felt like slivers, she was warm, and her heart beat furiously. She looked sideways, to see Tom trot idly up beside her, his arms crooked lightly.

He grinned at her. "Lift your knees. You're running like a girl," he said, with no gasping of breath.

"How should I run?" she puffed. But she watched the easy pumping of his legs, and began to lift her knees higher. "Oh gosh, I can't," she said, stopping, her breath coming in huge gulps. The snow fell between them as they stood, looking at each other and laughing.

After Morgan left, Julie went in to see that Ned was in bed. He was. He was already sound asleep. She turned off all but one dim light, and went back to get ready for bed herself. Morgan's happy, she thought, hanging her clothes more or less carefully over the back of a chair, getting into pajamas and bathrobe. She's happy, and that's nice. Was it? Well, it was probably nice for Morgan, and Julie was pretty sure that in that case it should be so for those around her. If only that kind of happiness, the kind girls got from being with boys, weren't so—private. It was as if those girls stood in a safety zone, while everyone else rushed around them and couldn't get in. Even boy-crazy Mag Lewis had had that spell of safety once in a while, though never for very long or over any but the dopiest sort of boy. Morgan wasn't boy-crazy, like her friends Betty and Verna. She didn't go around flirting with anything in pants. But still, tonight she'd escaped into that place of security where no one could follow. It made Julie a little lonesome, a little jealous. She sat in the big chair and tried to read, but it wasn't the same with Morgan gone. The room seemed stiller, and yet more unsettled, like a place that waited for another presence. She held the book on her lap and watched the white snow sift against the window.

When her father came in, she ran to meet him.

"What're you doing up?" he whispered, with a glance at Ned. He hung his damp coat in the bathroom, over the shower rod. "Where's Morgan?"

"Out walking in the snow."

"Is she crazy?" He almost forgot to keep his voice down. "What's either one of you thinking, to let her go walking around this time of night by herself?"

"She's not by herself. She's with Tom Miller."

"Oh." He hesitated in obvious surprise. "I see." They walked into the kitchen, where Julie began to heat milk for her father's before-bed cocoa. On the sideboard was a sandwich wrapped in wax paper. She put it on a plate. "Why don't you have part?" he offered.

"I'll just have cocoa, Pop."

They stood at the sideboard, swallowing the hot drinks.

"Tom's a pleasant fellow," Mr. Connor said, turning his sandwich around in absent inspection. He bit into it.

"We went up to the Millers for doughnuts tonight."

"You did? That's nice." He chewed some more. "Funny to think of Morgan walking in the snow. She's such an indoor girl, usually."

"I suppose this isn't usually," Julie shrugged.

"No. Probably not. The Millers are certainly a pervasive lot."

"Aren't they?" Julie said. Pervasive was not a familiar

word, but she knew what her father meant. "I'm glad you're home," she added softly.

"Well, so'm I, honey."

They idled through the little washing-up, exchanging slow comments. Neither admitted that they were waiting for Morgan to get home.

Morgan fell asleep with a nursery rhyme, slightly modified, in her mind. *Tom, Tom, the Millers' son,* she hummed to herself, *Tom, Tom, the Millers' son, stole my heart and away he run . . .*

Chapter Eight

Up the iron stairway went the costumed children, up and up to the lofty assembly room with its stage, its flag, its decrepit piano, its ageless musty schoolhouse odor. Child voices echoed, reverberating through the stair well. Scuffed shoes, surmounted by bright flimsy trappings—crepe paper, tinsel, brilliantly dyed cotton, cardboard crowns and papier-mâché lambs—mounted the metal treads. At the turn of each flight was a wide corridor, with ranks of classroom doors, glass upper squares pasted with Christmas cut-outs. Red paper Santas, green saw-tooth trees, bells and reindeer. Noel.

In the assembly room, a towering Christmas tree was strung with popcorn garlands, paper ornaments, silver stars. It was lighted sparsely but beautifully, and its forest breath filled the children, and the teachers, with heady excitement.

As the pupils filed in, some of them ignored the waiting rows of parents at the back of the room, but most looked eagerly for the familiar face, for assurance that this special person's part in the Christmas program would not go unnoticed. There were occasional called greetings from smaller children. The older ones contented themselves with short nods, fleeting smiles. Ned, having made sure of her, did not look at Morgan again.

Miss Applejoy, the music teacher, stood at the piano, swept the children into silence with her eyes, sat down, hands high. The principal strode onto the stage, smiling peaceably at his children, nodded to Miss Applejoy, whose hands fell upon the cracked and yellowed keys as though released from slings.

"Oh-oh, saay can you-oo seee!" the children sang, straining their young pipes, following the amiably swinging arms of the principal who had, without knowing a note of music, successfully led thousands of children through "The Star-Spangled Banner." Expectedly, most of the flute tones wavered, broke, ceased altogether at "the rocket's red glare," settled more comfortably at "proof through the night," and failed to reach the depths of "our flag was still there." The parents, the visitors, sang or hummed softly.

The singing concluded, a deep murmurous thunder ensued. Then the pupils, the teachers, the parents were seated. The principal explained that the fourth grade would present a brief Christmas pageant. He left the stage. Some of the children disappeared behind the curtains, while others, in long red robes, stood at sober attention, their eyes wandering, their hands clutching little sprigs of pine. There was a moment of utter silence, then Miss Applejoy began to play softly, with strange beauty, on the old piano. "Oh, Little Town of Bethlehem," the children sang clearly, sweetly, as the curtain drew back.

There was the stable, and there within it, Mary, in blue, bending over the cradle. Joseph, with a staff, standing beside her. Shepherds moved about, holding white lambs, and above them hung the shining star.

The children's voices hushed, and from the wings came the vibrant ringing voice of a boy, and Ned came walking with slow steps, in a robe of green, a crown of gilt, a little scarlet box held out before him.

> Myrrh is mine, its bitter perfume
> Breathes a scent of gathering gloom . . .

He sang in an unshadowed treble, a choir voice, bird's voice, the beautiful voice of a young boy. Morgan closed her eyes and felt the warm tears slide through.

The fifth grade and the sixth greeted Christmas. The audience joined in carols. The Christmas program was over. When Ned had shed his costume, he met Morgan in the hall and they started home. Outside, cold clamped immediately at their ankles, their faces. The schoolyard was sanded, and puddles, iced solid, were black irregular traceries flung over depressions in the ground. The steel of the jungle-gym glinted blue in the pale winter sunlight, the nets were off the baskets on the basketball standards, heaps of grimy snow were frozen against fence and walls.

"How'd you like it, Morgy?" Ned asked, tipping his chin into his jacket collar.

"I think it was—you were—wonderful," she said, knowing how little that said what she thought, and knowing Ned would not want more. It was the Christmas holiday, and Ned was joyous, not tender.

"Oh, swell," he replied with satisfaction, and the words that were not said, the love that was not expressed, were nothing to a boy with Christmas and two weeks of vacation ahead of him.

The stores they passed were decorated with cotton snow and folding tissue-paper bells and tiny replicas of Santa's sleigh. Groceries set forth nuts and fruitcakes twined with plush poinsettias. Clothing stores were sprinkled with glittering dust, festooned with green and scarlet streamers.

Round holly wreaths hung in the shop windows. *Christmas Greetings* the signs called in large letters as they passed. And, *Buy, Buy*, they cajoled wordlessly.

And the fragrant, cool, closely bound green trees leaned against walls and wires in the streets, filling the air with spice.

Christmas was on Monday, so that Dan would have Christmas Eve and most of the day with his children. He did not tell them that he had asked for a change to daytime hours, hoping to spend every evening with them. He and Morgan had discussed it often enough, dwelling upon the benefits they would all receive, assuring each other that the time, indeed, could not be far when they would sit down as a family to dinner, to the evening hours of radio and reading, to conversation and perhaps, now and then, a game of cards. They anticipated, vaguely but with pleasure, the outlines of a different sort of living that would emerge with shared hours. His superiors took two days to consider and informed him that "with the way things were" it would be advisable for him to continue on the present shift. Dan told himself that maybe it was best this way, that it was, perhaps, too late for the children and himself to be set down together, night after night, expecting to find new closeness, new understanding. The time no doubt had passed for him to be the sort of after-dinner father who helps his son with arithmetic, or exchanges light banter upon boys and allowances with his daughters. The time never had existed when he could have supported any of his children through the emotional conflicts that come with growing up. Dan, not through choice, had a low tolerance for emotion, either in himself or those around him. He had never thought, as Sarah had, that "a good scene clears the air." A good scene simply did not exist. There were only lacerating outbursts that produced unwise confidences, tremulous confessions, and, generally, tears. Faced even with the intimation of such passions, Dan retreated into protective silence, his eyes took an inward focus. He became, in other words, like one of the smaller animals in time of danger, very nearly unconscious. This job, these hours, gave him a sort of immunity from the world's (more particularly his children's) emotion. He felt relief at not being allowed to relinquish such immunity. The relief made him sick at his soul.

"How awfully nice," Morgan said, "that you have Christmas Eve off. It makes it so much nicer for us."

"And practically all day Christmas, too," Dan said, trying to make it sound like a week.

Ned, from the first of December, marked off days on the calendar. Each afternoon, a large triumphant cross blotted off yet another day that stood between him and joy. Today he took up his crayon and drew a mark through December twenty-third.

"There," he said. "That's done."

"The day isn't," Julie remarked.

"Well, it's as good as is," Ned replied imperturbably. "When will Morgan get back so we can go get the tree?"

"Pretty soon. She had to bring—take—her presents to Verna and Betty."

"What'd she get them?"

"A little wooden hatstand with a doll's face on it for Betty, and six love stories for Verna. She read them first."

"What sappy presents."

"What do you suggest? Roller skates?"

"What'd you get Morgy?" Ned asked persuasively. He was mad with curiosity about the forbidden bedroom closet.

"I'm not going to tell."

"Ah, Julie . . . c'mon. It won't hurt. *I'm* not going to tell."

"You bet your life you're not."

"But it's more fun. Stretches it out, you know. I'll tell what I got for her."

"I don't want you to tell. Anyway, I can guess."

Ned looked stunned. "What do you mean? *How* could you guess?"

"Because," Julie said, "you . . ." She stopped. What was it in her that wanted to torment Ned, that wanted to prod his childishness, his good humor? She wanted to say that every year brought the same things in Ned's little parcels. A calendar pasted on red drawing paper, a bit of colored rag for sticking pins in, a cardboard bookmark with a Christmas seal stuck to it. She hesitated, looking at him, and turned away.

"I what?" he persisted.

"Always want to know things," Julie said flatly. "I bet you even peek in the closet."

"I do not," Ned shrieked. "I do not, and you know it, Julie."

She did know it. Ned was quite easily honest. He'd tease and delight himself with speculations about the closet, with walking near it. He'd never open it. Oh yes, she knew. "I opened it one year," she said scornfully.

"Oh Julie, you *didn't*."

"Oh Julie, I *did*."

"But did you see everything?"

"I took it all out and looked." She sounded cold and defiant, determined to make herself and her crime fully known.

"When? When did you do that?" Ned asked with horrified curiosity.

"Oh, long ago. You were just a baby."

"Did anything happen?"

"It depends on what you mean by happen. I had a horrid Christmas, that's all. Nobody found out or anything." She was suddenly downcast, remembering her ridiculous squeals of surprise, and how hard it had been to go on pretending surprise, so that after a while her jaw had felt rigid and her head had started to ache. She remembered the way her mother had watched her. "I think Mother knew," she said.

"Mothers know everything," Ned told her sentimentally.

"I don't know about that." Julie picked up a book. "I want to read, Ned. Think of something to do."

"I'm waiting for Morgan, so we can get the tree."

"Well, wait then. Only be quiet." She studied the pages, and in a while began really to read them. Ned went into the kitchen for bread and butter, walked to the window, chewing. In the street, sunlight glistened on patches of ice, and a man, carrying an enormous tree, was followed by a little group of children. They didn't speak and they looked cold. "We won't get a big one," Ned said, but Julie didn't answer. He went on staring out the window till Morgan came in.

"Hi, everybody," she called, standing just inside the door, packages in her arms, her cheeks and eyes shining with cold. "It's simply *awful* out. Like the steppes of Amazon."

"You mean Asia," Julie said. She got up. "Want me to help?" She took some brown-paper grocery packages into the kitchen.

"What's that?" Ned said happily, gesturing toward two tissue-wrapped, seal-stickered boxes.

"They're for me, greedy. From Verna and Betty."

"Do you know what's in them?"

Morgan laughed and ran to the bedroom to put them away. "I got a turkey," she said, coming back to Julie in the kitchen. "And nuts and olives and cranberry sauce, and—"

"What are we going to cook a turkey in?" Julie interrupted. "We haven't got a roasting pan big enough for a turkey."

"Mrs. Miller is lending us one. I was up there for—for a little while, and she said she would. Tom's going to bring it down."

"Did we get Tom a present?" Ned said. "I mean, I made him one, and Mr. and Mrs. Miller. But did you two?"

"Well, I didn't," Julie said, turning the cold, bluish turkey around. "At least, not Tom. Will this fit in the icebox?"

"Take out one of the shelves," Morgan said. "Did you for Mr. and Mrs. Miller?"

"Yes." She'd borrowed from her father, and the cats would wait another week.

"That was nice of you, Julie." Morgan was darting glances at her sister, and her voice had a heady ring of delight that to Ned was the Christmas spirit finally gathering itself in their house. He regarded Morgan with a bright expectant smile, happiness swimming in him like a spangled fish in a glittering bowl. Packages continued to pour from the bags. A bottle of green olives with red centers—Christmas colors —a cellophane bag of walnuts to crack, a bunch of white thick celery, a can of cookies with their shapes drawn on the label, a huge loaf of bread (for stuffing, he thought deliriously). Everything was cold to touch, everything was brilliantly beautiful. She must have bought Julie's present, Ned thought. That's why she keeps looking at her that way. Julie didn't seem to notice as she stored food away.

The doorbell rang, and Ned ran to let Tom in.

"Here it is," he said, coming in with a huge blue roasting pan. "You could cook an ox in it." He wore his leather jacket and his ears were red from the biting air. "Hey, Julie," he said, "let's see if your bird fits."

Julie took the turkey out of the icebox. "It's awfully heavy. We'll be eating it for weeks." It fit very nicely in the borrowed roaster. "We can make turkey hash, can't we, Morgan?"

"Oh, hash, and all sorts of stuff."

"How are you people going to cook your dinner?" Julie asked Tom.

"We always have ham on Christmas. There's another pan, I guess. Listen, my mother says don't forget that you're to come up to our house after you open your presents here."

"You mean there's some for us there?" Ned burst out. He glanced at Morgan and lowered his eyes demurely, but she only smiled. "We're going out to buy our tree, Tom. Can you come too?"

"Don't see why not. Why don't we go now, before I get used to being warm?"

"All right," Morgan said. "Come on, get your things on, kids."

Ned dashed for the closet, but Julie yawned and shook her head. "I'm not going."

"You aren't? Why not?"

"You don't mind, do you, Morgy? I'm too comfortable, and I'm reading. You have Tom, now, to help you out."

"Well, of course. I just thought you liked to."

"I do, in a way. Only not now. It's too cold."

Morgan started to say something else, changed her mind. "All right. We'll be back in about an hour, I guess."

Julie nodded. "I'll finish putting this stuff away."

A little uncertainly, with backward glances, Morgan and Tom and Ned left for the tree buying. But once outside, in the splintery air, they forgot Julie and began to run, holding hands and laughing till the breath was like nettles in their lungs.

"You got Julie's present, didn't you?" Ned asked Morgan when they'd stopped, gasping and almost warm. "Didn't you? Where is it? You didn't bring it in, unless one of those presents from Betty or Verna wasn't from them . . ."

"Little big eyes," Morgan said. "You just keep still about what you think, Neddy. I'll take care of Julie's present, and you're to be as surprised as anyone else, see?"

"Yes, but—"

"No buts. Hush. Don't say another word."

"But I only . . ."

"Ah-*ah*," Tom said warningly. "Another word and I'll bop you one."

Ned laughed and began to jig up and down. "C'mon. Let's run again," he called, spying lines of Christmas trees outside the stores. "Hurry *up*." The words plumed whitely from his lips and he ran, lifting his knees high, as Tom had taught him to.

Tom put a base on their little fat springy tree. "Don't you think your father would rather do it?" he asked. But they didn't, so he hammered as Ned held the tree braced, and then they put it upright, tenderly moving its branches down, inhaling deeply its resinous ether.

While they'd been gone, Julie had got from its place of storage their box of Christmas ornaments. An old cardboard box, scuffed and bound with twine, it had come out every year that Julie or Ned could remember, rich with the familiar treasure, more bewitching than pirate chests, stranger than Pandora's box. *Was* there something they'd forgotten? Would the bird with tail of ivory floss glow quite so purple and red as they remembered? And had they—oh had they— broken anything? Had some amber ball, some crimson heart, been put carelessly away last year to lie these many months crushed in its bed of tissue? Gently they took the wrappings from the frangible radiant globes, the ruby, the emerald, the night blue with frosted stripes.

Tom draped the single string of lights carefully over the tree's forward branches. It was placed in a corner, so that the back branches, when they were finished, remained almost untouched, while the façade was massed with tinsel, with little glowing bulbs, with rich-hued ornaments. Nothing was broken, the bird gleamed fiery colors, the star with its ring of tarnished tinsel poised at the tree's tip.

All evening, after Tom had gone, they listened to the radio playing carols. They heard a play, *Our Lady's Juggler*, read by a resonant British voice. They heard a woman read from the Bible. ". . . and the angel of the Lord said unto them, Be not afraid, for behold, I bring you glad tidings. . . ."

Julie read *The Christmas Carol* to herself. Ned lay dreaming on the couch, hands under his head. Morgan listened to the singing, hearing Ned's voice in the school auditorium, and Tom's in the cold bright air. When Dan came in, he had packages to hide in the closet, and the four Connors had cocoa together.

It was Christmas Eve, after dinner. Ned was in the bedroom, with the door open, wrapping his gifts. His tongue tipped out at the corner of his mouth as he worked with seals and red tissue paper, as he wrote on the little tags. Caroling filled the apartment, and Ned thought it was nice to hear his father's low voice now and then through the music.

"I'm going out for a bit." That was Julie. Ned looked up from the intricacies of her present. Why would she be going out tonight?

"Julie, where would you go tonight?" Morgan said. "It's Christmas Eve."

"That's why. I'm going over to the church for a little bit."

"The church?" Morgan repeated. "Well . . . that's nice." She seemed rather at a loss.

"They put the baby in the cradle tonight," Julie explained. "I've been watching them move the shepherds and the Magi closer and closer. Tonight the baby goes in and I want to see it."

"I didn't know you were doing that."

"How could you?" There was the sound of the closet door

opening as Julie got her coat. "I didn't tell you." A pause. "Would anyone like to come?"

"Gosh, Julie, it's cold out," Morgan said. Her voice was regretful, but lazy and warm too. Ned could see she didn't want to go out at all. And his father's gentle, "I could, I suppose," didn't sound convincing to Ned, or to Julie either, apparently, for she said quickly, "Oh you shouldn't anyway, Pop. It's good for you to stay in when you can. I won't be gone long."

"I'll go with you," Ned called. He shoved his two unwrapped gifts under Morgan's pillow and went into the living room. "Don't look under your pillow, Morgy. I'll finish when we get back."

"You really want to come?" Julie asked.

"Sure. I'd like to go in a church."

"It's good to go to church on Christmas," Dan mused. "The Birth seems to have got trampled in the market place."

"What?" Morgan said.

"Christmas. The merchants' bonanza. Another hundred years of this and they won't remember who the Christ Child was."

"Let's go, huh?" Ned said.

A dry snow was falling through darkness as they hurried down the street. Wind-blown flurries of white swirled over cold sidewalks, and the two children looked a bit enviously at yellow windows where wreaths were hung and behind which warmth was stored. Ned shoved his hands in his sleeves and darted a glance up at Julie. She was blinking her eyes against the winter air and did not return his look.

The church was two blocks away, on a corner. Its windows were luminous with color and they seemed, from a distance, through the snow, to float like great stiff tapestries. Nearer, gray stone walls took on substance and the large carved doors swung open as a group of people came out, shivering as they passed from the thick, faintly incensed warmth into the freezing night.

"Take your hat off," Julie whispered as they entered.

"Oh sure." He snatched at it, stuffing it in his pocket. "What do we do now?"

"We just wait a minute. Till those people near the crèche are gone."

"What's a crèche?"

"The stable, with Mary and Joseph and the cattle."

"I know. Like we had at school."

"They've been moving everything closer, the Wise Men and all. Tonight Jesus gets put in the cradle."

"Is He in already?"

"I'm not sure. We'll see."

The church was musky, candlelit, soft and mysterious with shadowed places. Ned glanced up at the ceiling, which was lost in darkness. He was surprised to find that the windows seemed, from inside, unlighted. That was because the night pressed at them out there, but somehow he'd imagined that church windows would shine from both sides. It made the almost white light about the stable seem brighter, having the walls so dark, so without substance. As they stood behind the rows of wooden pews, an organ began to play *Adeste Fideles*.

Julie shivered a little and lifted her head. She walked softly toward the side aisle and down to the stable, Ned following.

The little figures of the Magi, mounted on camels, were at the stable entrance. ("That was me. I mean I was him," Ned said, pointing.) Angels were clustered overhead. Joseph and Mary and the shepherds were within, with a cow and two lambs close to the cradle. But the baby did not lie in the plaster straw.

"He isn't there," Ned said unhappily.

Julie didn't answer. She looked over the snow-powdered

crèche, noting the change in position of each figure. Then she sighed. "I can't understand. When does He go in?" she whispered.

"Just before Mass," said a woman's voice, and they turned to an old shawled person who had moved up beside them without a sound.

"What mass?" Julie asked.

"Midnight. But the singing starts at eleven, and just before the singing, the nuns put the Baby in."

"I see. Thank you," Julie said. She was relieved that the woman went on then, to kneel at the altar. She didn't like to talk to people in a church where they belonged, for fear they'd know she did not. Of course, that old lady must know anyway, since she and her brother had been so ignorant about the crèche. She looked at Ned, who whispered loudly, "But that's more than two hours away, Julie. We can't wait."

"No, I suppose not." They continued to study the stable, the Christmas host. Julie said, "Ned, let's sit in one of the pews there, all right?"

"What for?"

"Listen to the music, maybe."

Ned hesitated. "Okay, Julie. It's nice here, isn't it?"

"Yes. I like a church." They slid self-consciously into a nearby pew, looking first to see if anyone was watching. They didn't kneel. Just sat back rather stiffly, hands in their laps.

The organ continued to sing in the somber air. The children recognized carols, but not many of the hymns. Ned wondered if the music could be heard out on the snowy street. It didn't sound particularly loud, but it was very full and it hardly seemed that the small church could contain so rich a sound. Now and then a priest, dark-robed, silent-footed, went past. People came to kneel and pray, to see the crèche. There was, actually, a constant moving about, so quiet you had to sit still to notice. Ned shifted a little on the hard seat.

Julie fixed her eyes on the white, lace-hung altar, on the candles and the arabesques of gold. What were the mysteries there? What did it all mean . . . the music and the ivory, the gold and the shadows, the blood-colored candle cups? What did some people have that the Connors did not? (Once, long ago, she'd asked, "Did God make the world, Pop?" He'd waited to think before he answered, so carefully, "There are those who believe so." "Only you don't." "That doesn't mean very much, Julie. People far more intelligent and valuable than I believe it very deeply, and I am so easily wrong about things." "Then why don't you believe it?" An even longer pause followed, till he replied, "There's no answer. With God, each person has to find his own answer.") Pop had no answer at all. Julie hadn't found one yet. And as for Ned and Morgan—well, you didn't need answers if you weren't asking questions. Transfixed, Julie stared at the altar as though it might yield up its secret to her, if her eyes were steady. I want to be good, she thought. Most of all, over everything, I want to be good. The way saints had been good, or the Knights of Arthur's Table. She pictured them, those who had been good above any reproach, standing in fields of green, with lifted heads, square blond haircuts, armor of silver and souls like crystal. To be pure, and kind, and never wrong, she thought. Like them.

"Julie," Ned whispered. "I'm getting sore, sitting here."

At home, Dan greeted them happily, as though they'd been gone a long time. "Was it nice?" he asked.

"Neat," Ned answered. "Only Jesus wasn't in the cradle."

"That's too bad."

"He goes in about eleven o'clock. Only we couldn't wait."

"No, of course not." Dan looked at his younger daughter. "Perhaps, if you wanted to, we could walk over then, Julie?"

She shook her head. "No. No, I guess not." She lifted her gaze to Dan's and said thoughtfully, "It's funny that you can't keep a feeling, isn't it? I mean, you can feel something so much, and then in a little while all you can remember is that you did feel it."

Morgan looked at her with surprise. "I once thought that. Just that way. It was about the icebox, I think. Not that I don't still like it, but you can't go on being rapturous over an icebox, can you?"

Dan said to Julie, "Sometimes, honey, the only thing that saves us is not being able to keep a feeling. Emotions can be very strong, very exalting, very sad. But the human frame is much too frail to house one indefinitely. Like putting an eagle in a straw cage. It just won't hold. It's better to leave a door open and let the eagle go out that way."

"Or you wouldn't have any cage."

"Something like that."

Julie sighed. "Of course, this way, you don't have any eagle."

"The other way, you don't have anything at all. Besides, emotions come back. Others come." He lifted his eyebrow. "Anyway, when you're young, they do."

Morgan, detecting sadness, said quickly, "Julie, couldn't we hang some stockings? On the bookcase or something?"

So they did that, and lit the tree, and then they moved the cot into the bedroom so Ned wouldn't see them putting his presents under the Christmas tree.

On Christmas morning, Julie, opening her pen wiper from Ned, her pen-and-pencil set and the copy of Yeats from her father, her handkerchief from Anna Marie, tried not to notice that there did not seem to be a present from her sister. Oh, it'll be there, she assured herself. It's little, probably, so I haven't noticed it. She listened to Ned shriek with pleasure over the new screwdriver with alternating blades, the wool plaid shirt, the little garage with toy cars, the bathtub boat. She smiled at Morgan who was pleased with a ruffly white blouse, a pair of bedroom slippers, a scarf, an old set of crayons. ("I thought maybe you'd like them," Ned said in a dissatisfied tone. He brightened. "Anyway, next year I'll give you something real good.") Dan, earnestly delighted, received his bookmark, his volume of poetry, his tie. The pile of packages beneath the tree dwindled, and Julie began to feel a hurtful pressure in her throat. But there must be something wrong. It must have been left in the closet, she thought. Surely Morgan couldn't just forget? You don't forget your sister on Christmas. Julie had spent only a quarter on the little blue flagon of perfume, but it was the present she'd bought and wrapped and given to Morgan. Whatever Morgan spent, she'd surely just not get *anything*?

The doorbell rang.

"Merry Christmas, everyone," said Tom, coming in with a white and green hatbox held carefully before him. "Merry Christmas."

"I'm his big brother," said a voice, and a taller, older version of Tom was with them.

"Oh yeah. This is my brother, Geoff," Tom said. "These are the Connors, Geoff. Mister and Morgan, and Julie and Ned."

Geoff smiled. "I asked to come too, to meet the famous Connors."

"Are we famous?" Ned asked.

"In certain circles," Geoff told him.

"What's in that box, Tom?" Ned asked, coming closer. "What is that?"

"None of yours, young fellow." Tom stepped over and stood before Julie. "Miss Julie, greetings from your sister." And he laid the box at her feet.

Julie bit her lip and looked at Morgan. "I . . . Morgy . . ."

"Open it, darling," Morgan said.

Julie kneeled to undo the ribbon. Her hands hovered motionless as she spied the punched holes in the cover, and once more she looked up at her sister. "Is it—?" Quickly, she undid the ribbon, pulled the cover away. The kitten sat in the middle of the bottom of the box, blinking young blue eyes. Her paws were spread a little apart, her tail was a triangle of fur, and she seemed quite content in her prison. She was gray, and almost a Persian.

Julie kneeled, not speaking, not touching the kitten.

"Isn't she beautiful? Isn't she gorgeous?" Ned cried. He reached toward her. "Julie, don't you like her? Why don't you say something? *This* is what you were doing the other day, Morgy. Hiding the kitten up at Tom's, weren't you?"

"Neddy, let Julie pick her up first."

Julie reached into the box and lifted her kitten, warm and slightly purring. It fit easily in her hands, light as Anna Marie's handkerchief, soft as a ball of cotton on the branch. It licked her finger briefly, then rested its chin on her thumb.

"Where did you get her, Morgan?" Julie said in a rapt voice.

"I put in a bid for her ages ago. Before she was born."

"You did? I never knew."

"You weren't supposed to. This woman I met in the laundry room told me her cat was having kittens and did I want one. She's seven weeks old now."

"I suppose she'll miss her mother," Ned said judiciously. "We'll have to be very kind to her. Did you pay, Morgy?"

Morgan fixed her eyes on Ned, who turned his head away and said, "Oh well. Say, what are you going to name her, Julie?"

"Call her Tammany," Tom said.

Geoff shook his head. "This is a lady, Tom. Not some big dock cat. She should have a ladylike name. Mitzi, maybe."

"You could call her Dinah," Mr. Connor said. "If you promise not to disappear through the looking glass."

"Yes," Julie said. "Only I'm not at all like Alice, so I don't think I could use her cat's name." She looked at Morgan. "It's the . . . loveliest present in the world, Morgan." Ned started to pout, decided to be sensible. After all, a pen wiper was just a pen wiper, even if Julie could have been a little nicer about it. Next year he'd buy her a dog.

"Did you decide?" he said as Julie got up, holding the kitten which seemed pleased to go on nestling in her hands.

"Yes. Her name is Amy."

"Now that really is a ladylike name," Tom approved. "Suits her just right." He settled down beside Ned and the little garage. "*Say*, look at this, Geoff . . ."

"Christmas doesn't really last any longer than any other day, does it?" Ned said that night. He was in his pajamas, running an elaborate sand dumper that Mrs. Miller had given him. Julie was in the kitchen with a pan of shredded newspaper, teaching Amy to be housebroken. Morgan was slumped in a chair, doing nothing. She said, in answer to Ned's remark, that she was very glad it didn't.

"Why?" he asked indignantly.

"Because . . . It's beautiful and it's fun, but I get all worn out."

"Morgan," he told her, tipping a bucket of sand into his truck, "you're getting old, or something. Last year when I said that you said it *should* last longer, and we could take some away from the next day, remember?"

"Was that what I said? Well, I guess I am getting older. Seventeen in February."

"That's not so terribly old." He sat back, clasping his knees. "Morgy, you won't . . . get married or anything like that, will you? I mean, what would happen to *us,* if you did? And anyway, I think you'd miss us."

"Hold on. What started this?"

Ned lifted his shoulders. "I asked Geoff how old that girl is that he was going to marry—"

"*Neddy!*"

"Oh, he didn't mind. Anyway, he says he isn't going to marry her, it was a . . . a . . . well, I forget exactly, but something he's got over, so I said how old was she if he was going to marry her, and he said she was twenty-one whether he did or didn't, but he wasn't going to. They parted the best of friends," he added thoughtfully.

"He certainly seemed happy."

"He's a nice guy. Not as nice as Tom, of course."

"No," Morgan said, smiling to herself. "Not that nice." She looked at Ned. "Did you tell Tom I wanted a charm bracelet?"

"Yeah. Wasn't that all right? He asked what you wanted, so I told him."

"It was fine. I just wondered." She twisted the bracelet gently round her wrist. Not one he'd bought with all the charms attached, but a silver link chain with all different charms fastened on. Including a tiny gold track shoe that Tom had got, as he said, not for distinguished running but for perseverance. The bracelet jingled softly as she moved her arm.

"But you won't will you?" Ned persisted. "Get married?"

"Not ever, darling?"

"Well . . . not till I do. Then it'll be all right."

Morgan, about to make some light reply, saw his face and changed her mind. "I expect I won't," she told him. When he asked for unimportant things—eclairs for dessert, a movie—Ned was often hesitant. He let no doubt delay him with that which really mattered.

Chapter Nine

It rained on her birthday. When she came out of school, Morgan found the marble lobby streaked with wet dirt, acrid with the odor of damp clothing. Some provident people had provided themselves with umbrellas or rubbers that morning, but Morgan had not. She hunched in her coat at the head of the broad flight of stone stairs leading to the street and eyed the straight-falling rain discontentedly. The little park across the street looked miserably threadbare. Pedestrians went by with lowered faces. Some of them held newspapers overhead, as emergency protection. Morgan didn't have a newspaper, and, in any case, wouldn't have used one. Students, hurrying past her down the stairs, muttered at her obstruction. "Whatcha waitin' for, summertime?" said a boy who'd almost collided with her as he dashed through the doors. Reluctantly, she started down.

At the curb, a short way up the street, a little bright blue coupe glistened perkily in the rain, and as she approached the door opened and Tom jumped out.

"Morgan, hurry," he said. "Get in."

She stood, too astonished to move.

"Come on, come on. It's wet out here," he urged, and propelled her into the small front seat. He ran around and got in the other side. "There now," he said, turning to her proudly. "There. What do you think of this?"

"But . . . where did you get it?"

"It's mine. I did it with my little playground."

"What do you mean?"

"I mean I saved my money and I bought it, Morgan. Didn't you ever hear of anyone saving money before?" he grinned.

"I never knew anyone who bought a car before," she answered slowly. It seemed an incredible, a tremendous thing to have done. A whole car. "It's all yours?"

"And paid for. Also, I have a license. Isn't she beautiful?" He peered through the windshield, started the motor so the wipers would swing. There was no heater and it was cold. But not so cold as outside, and dry, with the delicious protection of a little place snugly secure from the elements. Rain beat on the roof, splashed on the blue hood. Everything, even the dashboard, was painted bright blue. Hand-painted.

"Well?" said Tom.

"I don't know what to say," Morgan answered. "I just . . . it's marvelous. I can't believe it's really yours."

"I can't myself, hardly. You're the first person to see it."

"You mean you haven't told anyone else?"

"Oh sure, I told the family. But you get the first view. And the first ride. Where do you want to go?"

"Let's—drive along the river. Would that be all right?"

"Anywhere you say." He put the car in gear, steered into the street. Morgan looked out eagerly, to see if anyone she knew would spy her here, being driven off in an automobile. Verna was absent. Betty was playing basketball. She did see a few familiar figures, but no eyes looked up from the wet streets to witness Morgan's supremacy. She sighed and turned to Tom with a smile. "I was hoping someone would see me."

"We'll give them other chances," he said. "Lucky it was raining today, so I didn't have to work."

"And I was just thinking how awful it was to rain on my birthday."

"You see. Never judge hastily. Happy birthday, Morgy." He took one hand off the steering wheel, fumbled in his pocket, and thrust a little package at her.

"Hey, watch where you're going," she cried.

Tom swerved away from the sidewalk. "Don't get nervous. I can drive fine."

"I know you can. At least, I'm sure you can. Only you ought to look." She glanced down at her present. "Shall I open it?"

"Sure." He turned east, heading for the river, giving part of his attention to the road, part to her. The present was another charm. A tiny car, which had been carefully painted blue.

"Oh, Tom, it's *darling*." She turned it around, examining its minute details. "Who painted it? You?"

"Yup."

She giggled. "You did a better job here than you did on the real thing."

"I didn't paint this," Tom said, waving a hand. "It came this way."

"Well, I'm glad it did. I like it."

"Me too. Like a bluebird. Let's call it that. Bluebird."

"All right. The first ride in Bluebird."

They'd reached the river, now. It swam along beside them, broad, brown, wrinkled and dartled with the driving rain. On its surface robust tugs nosed through the streaming veils, barges moved sluggishly. They passed a section of mud and old grass, where benches with stone standards and wooden slats gleamed wet and empty. In the summer, Tom thought, it would be nice to sit there, watching the river's traffic, peaceful in the sun or in the warm evening dark. Now it looked terribly forlorn.

"Did you ever notice," he said, "that people's places look so sad in the rain and the cold, but nature's places don't? I mean, the playground now must be so dreary, so much emptier than even an empty place should be. And those benches over there, they look more deserted than empty. Woods don't look like that, or meadows. They'd look cold on a day like this, and unpleasant. But not sad."

"Well . . . The trees and the grass don't get up and go away because it's raining. But people do, so I guess in a way their places *are* deserted."

"I'm glad I found you this afternoon. It was sort of a chance. I waited nearly an hour."

"You did, Tom? That was very nice."

Now the piers and the docks, the warehouses began. Wooden, weathered, uncompromisingly gray, they stood at the water's edge. This was no dreaming river of canoes and wild birds, no drinking place for deer, no drifting place for people. This was an artery of commerce, and these the stern bones that held it up, fed on it. Tom turned onto a vacant, two-storied pier, rumbled over the wooden floor and stopped near the edge. Rain beat against the windshield, so that the scene before them blurred. The two great bridges, Brooklyn and Williamsburg, emerged from shadows, reached through the falling rain to shadows in Brooklyn. Brooklyn buildings were outlined blottily. They could see the blue-lit windows of a factory, and two ships of war tied up at the docks.

"This is only the second time I've been in a car," Morgan said, leaning her head back against the seat. She was conscious of the cold now, of her wet ankles, and the clammy interior of the coupe. But she wouldn't mention that in Tom's moment of acquisition and pride.

"Is it?" he said. "That's odd."

"Why odd? I'll bet there are people who've never been in one at all. Why should you, in the city? Unless you want to drive to the country a lot, like your parents."

"When was the other time? That you rode in one?"

"Oh, ages ago. A friend of mine, Kitty McMahon, her family moved to Jersey and they bought a car. They took me out in it one day before they left. To Westchester. Anyway, I think you're terribly smart to have got one, Tom."

He smiled and put his arm over the back of the seat, not quite touching her head. The sudden sensibility of their nearness, their aloneness, was acknowledged by this gesture. Never before had they been alone, except for the night they walked in the snow. Never, as Morgan thought now, in a place where they could sit still, and talk, or . . . She couldn't think of anything to say, she didn't want to move, for fear he'd take away his arm. They breathed softly, staring ahead at the rain and blue dashboard. On the river a tug cried a warning.

Morgan wondered what he was thinking about, sitting so quietly, with his arm almost, but not quite, touching her. If I should lean my head back, a little bit, she thought, so that it touched his leather jacket, what would he do? He had a nice profile. A handsome, blunt nose, a mouth that was nicely shaped. A mouth for talking, and for—except he never had—for kissing. At least, he'd never kissed her. She had a moment of anguished jealousy, wondering who might have been held tight in his arms, against his chest, who might have known the softness of his mouth. Suppose she leaned her head back and he turned, so that their eyes were very close, looking over each other's faces. Her eyes would move from his long dark eyes to his mouth . . . then would his arm tighten on her shoulder, and would he bend toward her, would he kiss her?

Softly, shyly, she leaned her head back. He gave her a

quick, smiling, sideways glance, and turned back to the river.

Rather sadly, Morgan sat up.

"Cold?" he asked. With another person, or if Morgan had been a different person, she might have said yes, might have snuggled against him to show how cold she was. But Morgan could not do that. She could only shake her head, and wonder if ever he'd notice she was someone except Ned's sister. We're so darned *friendly*, she thought bitterly.

"Look," he said. "Let me put the charm on your bracelet." She held her wrist out, unsteadily, and he fumbled with the clasp, pulling it back with his thumbnail, and losing it. "Hold still, Morgy," he said, and slowly, with determination, fitted the little car to the silver chain. Morgan felt as though she were filled with warm pulsing wool. *Tom*, she cried silently, *please*, Tom . . . But, of course, said nothing and leaned back wearily when he'd finished.

"I suppose we should get back," he said, making no move to start the car. He stared through the tear-spattered windshield at the warships across the river, and shook his head slowly. "There they are," he said. "There they wait."

"What?" Morgan asked, looking across too, but unable to select from the view what it was that held him. "What waits, Tom?"

"The war. Its ships and its purpose. See those destroyers? Put in for repairs. The men'll get a few days off, and if they live around here they'll be home long enough to make people miss them more. Then off they go, ships, men. Ho for the battle. What do you think we're doing?"

"Us?"

"Not us. Well, us too. But everyone. What have we arranged for ourselves, Morgan? What have they arranged for us? You can't plan anything, anymore. Can't figure, even somewhat, what you'll be doing in a year, in ten years. My father says the depression was hard on young people then, and it was, all right. But at least they could count on *being* somewhere in those days. The guys I know, most of them don't count on a thing. We go to school, or get jobs, but it's all just contingencies. All just waiting, you see?"

She nodded, and then what he was saying crystallized. "Tom, are you going to be drafted?" she cried.

He seemed moved at her desperate indifference to all fates except his. But he seemed, also, and rather thoughtfully, surprised. "It's not just me—I—you know. It's everyone."

"I know, I know, but you're what I care about," she said frantically, not stopping to think how she sounded, what she was giving away. "I don't *want* you to be a soldier, to be killed . . ."

"Morgan," he said urgently. "Don't, please don't talk this way." He looked at her sternly, then softly, then perplexedly. "To begin with, I probably won't be drafted. Not till I've finished school."

"How do you know?"

"Well, I don't *know*. It's what I'm told, for what the Army's word is worth. I took that exam last summer, and the people who got the—who got good marks, are deferred. Some of them. Till they finish school. I have two years to go. I wasn't really talking about myself. It's just—I was trying to make you understand . . ."

Morgan dropped her eyes, and sighed. "I know. Pop tries to make me understand, too. I guess I'm just not bright."

"Don't *say* things like that. You are intelligent, and that's why it's wrong that you don't seem to know how important it is to understand what's happening in the world. If you were dumb, I wouldn't give a hoot what you understood. But people *have* to care, Morgy. They have to see that what happens in—Korea or Israel happens to them. Not to a few soldiers and the people of another country. We're *in* this. All of us."

"I guess we are," she said dully. Her face was hot with the recollection of what she'd told him in her fear of having him go. They were, apparently, to go on, pretending she hadn't showed her love, pretending nothing had been said of that at all. It hadn't in so many words. But she'd said it, and they both knew it, and it was almost worse to have it overlooked than it would have been to have him speak of it. "Let's go back," she said.

"In a minute. Look, Morgan, don't be sad."

"I'm not."

"Yes, you are. And I don't want you to be. Not because of me." She didn't reply, so he leaned over and took her hands in his. The bracelet jangled softly. Morgan, with the sort of prescience she had for Ned's feelings, realized that Tom was trying to say he loved her, and could not. She knew a moment of distaste for herself. He was dear and kind and honest. He was Tom, trying his darnedest to help her, and she wasn't helping either of them. Well, she thought, I'll wait. Maybe, some day . . . She looked up and gave him a very respectable smile. "I'll start reading newspapers," she said. "Tomorrow. Not today, because it's my birthday."

He released her hands with a lightened expression, as though she had delivered them both from torment. Even that made her happy, which certainly proved she was in love. As they drove off the pier, the hollow wooden floor rumbling under their tires, the street lights went on. They looked like huge floating dandelions in the rain and the mist from the river.

Julie was at Anna Marie's, where they'd spent the afternoon doing homework. "I guess I'd better go," she said, closing her books. She looked out the window. "There's certainly no prospect that pleases this afternoon."

"How's that?"

"It's raining."

"Oh, sure. It's been raining all afternoon." Anna Marie, softly blonde, looked at her thin friend. "You know, Julie, if you go on frowning that way, you'll get creases in your forehead."

"So what?"

"So then you won't be pretty."

"I won't be anyway. What difference does it make?"

"It will sometime. Besides, you'll probably be pretty in a few years. One of those coltish girls. Some boys like them."

"Are you going to start that too?"

"Start which?"

"The boy, boy, boy thing. It honestly seems to be all I hear anymore. Since when have you begun?"

"Well, Julie. You reach a certain age, you know. It's sort of unavoidable, I'm told. Do you want to be a girl Peter Pan?"

"Hardly," Julie said stiffly.

"Oh now, don't get mad. I was fooling, sort of." Anna Marie studied Julie, added, "*Do* you have a sense of humor, Julie?"

"I'm not sure. Probably I don't. I laugh at things, but that's not the same. It's more," she said with careful unoriginality, "being able to laugh at yourself, I suppose, that gives you a sense of humor."

"I think it's subnormal not to like boys."

"Abnormal. Maybe it is. Maybe I will, later on." Julie looked rather sadly around, back to Anna Marie. "Of course, if you do, start liking them, I mean, that'll be sort of hard on me. I'll have to catch up, I suppose. Or just not see you."

"In the first place, liking them and getting to go out with them are two different things," Anna Marie said soothingly. "And in the second place, what would it have to do with us and homework and all?"

"I'm not sure. But it isn't the same. Girls who like boys have to be talking about it all the time. And I don't feel like talking about it—about them. I don't propose to be one of those girls giggling in groups and sending anonymous valentines and calling boys on the phone and then hanging up when they answer."

"That's a very confused sentence."

"Well, I'm a very confused person."

Anna Marie laughed. "You know what my father says?"

"What?" asked Julie, who liked Anna Marie's German father.

"That the eleventh commandment is, 'Thou shalt not take thyself too seriously.' "

"Did he say it about me?"

"No, but that's a perfect example of what he meant."

Julie, reluctantly, had to smile. But the smile meant little. She was allowing Anna Marie to rebuke her, even to make fun of her in a friendly way. I'm awfully humble with some people, she thought. What a thing to recognize in yourself. "I have to go," she repeated. "It's Morgy's birthday, and Pop said he'd buy her a cake and candles before he left. I have to fix them."

In the street, she put up her shabby umbrella, clutched her books beneath the other arm, and started home. There was no search today for the face that might separate itself from other faces in the street, for the voice that might say, ". . . I've been looking for you." Behind the thin tent of her umbrella, she walked quickly, without thinking.

Amy came to the door when she entered the apartment. The kitten skittered over slippery linoleum on her small wide pads, then sat at Julie's feet, her pink mouth open in a series of mewings that might have meant anything. Julie took them to mean dismay over a long separation. She shed her dripping clothes, accidentally sprinkled Amy, who retreated.

"Come on," Julie said, kneeling. "Here puss, Amy . . ." The kitten advanced delicately, a smoke of fur and whiskers. She came almost within reach of Julie's fingers, then turned and ran up the back of a chair. It was manifest that Amy was not born for domination, but Julie did not feed alley cats to no purpose. She coaxed and wheedled, and eventually Amy, through some vagary of her own, succumbed and spent a few minutes kneading and purring in Julie's lap. She even followed when Julie, some minutes later, went into the kitchen to stick candles in the store cake.

"You're my little fur love," Julie told her aloud, and Amy made some answer to the low voice.

When Ned came in, Julie was getting dinner. "For Pete's sake," he said, "what are you doing?"

"Leaping from branch to branch of a young oak tree."

Ned recognized the reference and said without rancor, "That's a good story. Really, Julie, why are *you* doing this?"

"Because it's Morgan's birthday, and I thought I'd surprise her."

"That's nice. Can I help?"

"You can set the table."

"Okay. Say, do you have a flashlight?"

"Oh, sure, right here in my pocket. I always carry one for just this sort of emergency. Or maybe it went to the cleaners in my French lace overalls."

"What are you talking about? I just asked if you had a flashlight."

"No, I don't."

"I want to make a hut in the closet. The flashlight is for a lantern."

"In what closet?"

"Well, in the hall, maybe."

"No, you don't. There isn't any hut room in this apartment."

"Could I make one under the table?"

"I don't see where you can make one at all. Why should you anyway?"

"No reason. I just want to."

"Well, wait till Morgan comes and ask her. Where do you think she is, Ned?"

"She's out with Tom. In his new car." Ned stopped impressively. He'd been up at the Millers and had heard about the wonderful purchase and that Morgan was going to be the first to see it. He waited now for Julie's exclamation of astonishment.

Julie said, "Oh. Well, that's probably why she's late."

"Honestly, Julie, you're the most peculiar girl."

But she still was not interested. "Set the table, will you, Ned? I'm trying to figure out when to put the meat on. Don't you think the cake is pretty?" She took the meat from the refrigerator and looked at it curiously while Ned assured her that the cake was gorgeous. "I guess you just put it in the frying pan. The meat, I mean."

"You should learn to cook, Julie."

"Why?"

"Because all girls should. What'll you do when you grow up if you can't cook? Your family will starve, poor things."

"No they won't. Because I'm never going to get married."

"You aren't?" Ned, who didn't want Morgan to marry ever, was perfectly willing to have Julie do so at any time. "Why not?"

Julie shrugged. "I don't believe in marriage."

"That's crazy. If people didn't get married, there wouldn't be any children."

"So?"

Ned looked clearly nonplused. "If there weren't any children," he said tentatively, "there wouldn't be a world at all, after a while, would there?"

"I think," Julie said, "that the only real kindness people can do their children is not to have them in the first place."

"You want to *die*?" Ned asked in confusion.

"If you mean am I going to commit suicide, no, I'm not. But if I'd ever been given a choice, to be born or not born . . . Well, I just don't think there's *any* choice, that's all."

"Neither do I," Ned said emphatically.

They regarded each other sombrely for a moment, and then Julie laughed. "Anyway, here we are, so we'll have to make the best of it. If you don't do the table pretty soon, Morgan will be in."

Ned began to collect silver from the drawer. As he moved from the kitchen to the living room, he eyed Julie speculatively. Peculiar girl.

Chapter Ten

> April is the cruellest month, breeding
> Lilacs out of the dead land, mixing
> Memory and desire, stirring
> Dull roots with spring rain.

Ah yes, thought Dan, leaning his head on the heel of his hand. Memory and desire and the spring rain. The land, for all he knew, might be dead beneath the pavements here. There were no lilacs. He thought of lilacs in Indiana, growing wild beside the highways, along the country roads, in yards and gardens. Bursting white and purple, and somehow, in his memory, always wet with rain. Or was that the poem's picture, not memory's at all?

Strange to forget what you remember, he thought. It didn't matter. His roots were down, but would not stir again, and lilacs remembered or read of were not true lilacs.

"Hello, Mr. Connor."

He looked up, frowning near-sightedly through the grill of his cage as a quarter slid toward him, a voice greeted. "Oh . . . ah, hello," he said uncertainly to the girl with the long face and thick hair. One of Morgan's friends, he decided.

"You don't remember me." She smiled hesitantly. "I'm Verna Herzog."

"Oh, surely. How are you, Verna? Just for the moment I was preoccupied. What brings you to my station?"

"I've been shopping. Things for the party." She lingered as no train approached to drown their voices.

"Funny," he said, "you'd think I'd see a lot of people I knew, sitting here in the middle of town in the most-used transport system. But I never see a soul. It's been years."

"Maybe because you're always so busy reading."

"That could be. What party, did you say?"

"We're having a party, sort of. Didn't you know?"

"Did I? I don't recall. Seems to me you just had one, didn't you? Or a dance, or something?"

"Oh, Mr. Connor . . . that was last fall." The girl looked as though she might be going to laugh.

He shook his head. "Time slips by," he offered as the subway neared in unlovely crescendo. She wiggled her fingers at him and ran. Dan looked after her as she moved through the train and sat down. He had no thoughts about her at all, and as the train took her past his vision, it took her out of his mind. He started to glance back at his book as Maurice Vogel, a guard, came up to him.

"Hi, Dan," he said, pulling a battered newspaper from his hip pocket.

"Hello, Morry. What's new?"

"Little of this, little of that. Wife's rheumatics are bad."

"Sorry to hear it."

"That's the way it goes. I see here the Giants are in Florida for spring training. Boy, what I'd give—"

"Pretty soft, I guess." Dan managed pretty well to conceal his lack of interest in baseball. After all, you had to get along with your fellow men, and he sometimes thought that in baseball the common social denominator had at last been

found. Rich man, poor man, everyone loved baseball, ev.
one talked about it, everyone responded.

"Would you ever believe that I had a chance to pitch for
them?" Vogel went on. "Back in twenty-four, that was. If it
hadn't been for this bum leg of mine, I'd probably've been in.
Man!"

"Bad break, Morry."

"One of the worst. Oh, well. You hear Porter died?"

"Porter?"

"Guard up at Forty-second. You know, big guy. Never
would've thought he'd conk out like that. Just walking up
the stairs, they tell me. Alive one minute, stiff the next.
Funny thing."

"Yeah."

"Hear he had four kids, too."

"His wife alive?"

"Oh, sure." They suspended conversation as another train
arrived and departed. "Thing like that makes you think,
though. I mean, suppose *I* was walkin' up the stairs and
just—" He spread his hands. "Miriam'd have to go out and
get a job. That ain't easy, even these times, for a woman."

"No, it isn't."

"And after all these years of practically doing nothing, and
her rheumatics . . . well, I just don't know."

"Nothing? I thought you had three children of your own."

"Sure I have. But what the heck, a woman sits around
doing nothing but watch a few kids, how can she go out and
really work? They have it easy, let me tell you. Wonder if
Porter left his family fixed good."

"I hope so."

"A woman like that ain't gonna find it easy. Like I was
tellin' Miriam last night, you'd better be glad, old girl, that
you still got me around. Told her all about Porter. Way I
figure, it don't hurt to throw a scare into them now and then.

nk, know what I mean? I said to her how she's
mplainin' about her back, but what if she had
ly to worry about, huh?"
ıe say?"
she say?"
ᶴ head.

...en, I'll be goin'. Sure been a rotten winter. Kids've had
colds the whole time, and my knee ain't any too good. *But—*
I guess we're lucky to be eatin', eh, Dan? Think of the poor
starving Armenians, that's what I always say. You gotta look
on the bright side or go nuts. Well, keep your chin up. And
say, don't take any wooden dimes . . ." He walked away,
chuckling, pushing the paper back in his pocket.

Dan rubbed the back of his neck, made change for two or
three people. "You take the next train up to Forty-second,"
he replied to a woman's question, "and follow the green
lights to the Shuttle."

He pulled a piece of paper toward him, and between small-
change transactions tried to figure out how much his insur-
ance and his pension together would make for the kids, if
anything should happen. As Morry said, a thing like that
made a fellow think.

Verna, on the wicker subway seat, balanced her packages
and thought briefly that Mr. Connor looked sort of yellow.
Or maybe it was just the light in that booth. Of course he
practically lived underground, and nobody could look very
good under those circumstances. But he was awfully nice.
Polite and friendly, after she'd told him who she was. Morgan was lucky.

The train idled to a standstill, between stations, while another train went slowly, almost not moving, past it. Verna
glanced over, met the eyes of a young man in a pearl-gray

snap brim. She looked quickly away, back again. He pursed his mouth in a whistle and eyed her from under lowered lids. Verna, safe in a separate train, looked archly, boldly back. She smiled, and then the other train picked up speed and left them behind. She'd never have done that, flirted that way, with anyone who was in the same train. But this way it was fun. A chance encounter, like in the movies. Maybe he'd go home tonight and think about her. About how pretty she'd been, how dashing. She looked across the aisle, found a woman's disapproving eyes upon her. The old creep had probably been watching. Verna flushed, but she repeated to herself, *the old creep.* She clutched her packages and moved down the car.

As she let herself in the apartment with her key, she heard footsteps in the living room. That was funny. Emma was at work. Her mother and father were supposed to be spending the day, and the night, at her uncle's. She walked warily down the hall. Had Emma come home early?

Her parents were in the living room. Mrs. Herzog looked up apologetically as Verna, with the flimsy paper packages, entered. "Hello, dear," she said, looking with a warning eye toward her husband.

Verna was too surprised, too perturbed, to catch the signal. "But . . . I thought you were going to Uncle's," she said bleakly. "Aren't you?"

Her father turned his head from the radio dial. "No. We're not. You got anything to say about it?"

She stood silent.

"Well?" he demanded. "What the blazes had you planned that you don't want your parents around?"

Verna swallowed. "I had sort of . . . that is, we were . . ." She half-turned away, biting her mouth, turned back quickly at her father's impatient movement. "I was going to give a party," she said flatly.

"Oh. You were. A party. And since when do you plan things like this the minute my back is turned? What sort of a family is this, where the daughters sneak around behind people's backs planning parties? Well, miss, you can just forget the whole thing, see?"

"I know."

"What do you mean, *you know?*"

"Well—I just meant, I know. That's all, Pa."

Mr. Herzog turned the radio up high. "I suppose you're ashamed of us," he bellowed over it. "Can't give a party for your highfalutin friends if your folks are around, that it?"

"No, it isn't that. I just thought—you wouldn't want me to."

"Well, for once in your life, you're right." He looked at her for a long minute. "I suppose there were going to be *boys* at this—party?"

Verna breathed deeply and nodded.

"*You're* a nice sort of girl, aren't you?" he said.

"I'm all right," She met his eyes steadily. "Perfectly all right."

Her father looked away first, changed the subject. "Not that you're interested, but the reason we aren't going is because your uncle's sick."

"I'm sorry."

"I'll bet you're sorry."

Verna looked at her mother, who rose. "I'll just help you put away your things." Her husband had sunk to a chair, his attention on the radio. "We can go to your room now." She followed Verna down the hall, shut the bedroom door behind them. "I'm sorry, Vern darling," she said. "There wasn't anything I could do."

"I know." Verna dropped the packages. A hard, harsh sob pressed at her throat. "I hate him."

"Don't. Please."

"But I do, don't you see? I really, truly, hate him." She wanted desperately to cry. "Don't worry," she said to her mother. "I won't cry. Not for him, I won't." She sat on the bed, pulled out the paper tablecloth, the napkins. There were yellow and green spring flowers painted on them. There were paper cups and dishes to match, and little favors. "What am I going to do with all this stuff? I'll have to call Morgy. And walk over to Betty's—you'd think she'd get a phone. What'll he say when he sees the cold cuts and things in the icebox?"

" 'Make me a sandwich,' probably," her mother answered, trying to smile.

Verna put her hands over her face.

"Vern . . . maybe you could have the party at one of the other girls' houses." She hurried on when her daughter looked up. "Wouldn't Morgan or Betty let you take the stuff over to their place? I'd help you walk over with it, and get things arranged."

"What would he say?" Verna asked, indicating the living room with her head.

"Oh, he won't mind if you go *out*."

"You know, Mom, sometimes I think he's crazy. No. really. One time it's all right for me to do something, and another time he raises cain. I mean, he didn't say a word the night Morgan stayed here. And Betty did once. So what's wrong with a party?"

Mrs. Herzog sighed heavily. "Maybe because it's longer, or makes more noise. I think he's angry because we planned it for when he was away, without telling him."

"But that *is* crazy. He doesn't want to be told things."

"No. But he doesn't want things kept from him, either. Honey, *don't* ask me. I do what I can."

Verna began to put the things back in the bags. "You think it'll be all right? He won't say anything?"

"It'll be all right," her mother said firmly. "Only go out now, and see what the girls say. I'm sure one of them . . ."

"I suppose so. It makes me look—funny." Her voice faltered, and some of the repressed tears spilled out. "It's okay, Mom. I'll be fine, in a second." She took a long, steadying breath. "I'll call Morgy first, and then if she can't, I'll walk over to Betty's. Be back in a bit." She grabbed her purse and ran out of the apartment.

Morgan said how awful it was, but she couldn't have the party at her place, because Ned was having what he called the "chicken pops." "He isn't awfully sick, really. Just a few dainty spots and a terrible amount of energy that we have to keep in bed. But I still don't think it would be . . ."

"Of course not," Verna interrupted. "I'm awfully sorry. About Ned, I mean. If Betty can have us, can you still come?"

"Oh sure. He really is perfectly all right, and Julie will be here. I can't stay late, but I couldn't have at your house either. Oh, Verna, honestly it's an awful shame." Verna had only indirectly referred to her father, and Morgan did not refer to him at all. But his presence was solid between them, and there was no question of who had made the change in plans. "Are you going over to Betty's now?"

"Yes. I'll walk over. And then if she says yes I'll call you back."

"Are you home?"

"No. I thought . . . I'm calling from a booth. I'll let you know, either way. By, Morgy."

"Who was that?" Julie asked. She didn't care, really, but asked. "I wonder," she said, before Morgan could reply, "why people have this compulsion to talk? It's as if everyone was afraid if he didn't *say* something, and get an answer, he wouldn't be sure he was there at all, or anybody else was. I imagine that's the real difference between the human and the animal. The talking."

"Somebody said it was thumbs," Morgan replied. "Only, of course, monkeys have those. Or laughing. I once heard it was that people can laugh, but animals can't."

"Hyenas can," Ned said from his bed.

"But not *at* something," Morgan said. "Oh well, Julie's probably right." She went over to Ned, sank to the edge of his cot, and patted his leg. "How do you feel, love?"

"Itchy." He scowled. "Julie says I look like a cannibal."

"Caliban," Julie corrected.

"It's the same thing, isn't it?" Morgan asked absently, straightening the covers. She didn't see Julie's expression, but looked up at the tone of her voice.

"Honestly," Julie was saying, "I think it's amazing to have such hideous gaps in anybody's information. How could you not know who Caliban was?"

Morgan exhaled a long breath into the air above her. "It seems to me that all I hear on all sides is how ignorant I am." She looked at Julie pensively. "How in the world can I start learning all these things now? It's too late . . ."

"You could begin," Julie said, "by resisting that sort of reading." She indicated Morgan's love story with her head.

Morgan smiled and shrugged her shoulders. "Some other time, Julie. My resistance is low today." The three of them laughed. But Morgan, looking at Ned's afflicted face, thought, I'll never be good enough, or smart enough, or anything enough for Tom. I just can't begin reading, and caring about all the things he cares about. After their first ride in Bluebird, she had tried, really tried. She'd sat down with her father's *Times* and looked from one headline to the next, one important dispatch to another. But the paper was so sprawly, and by the time she'd got inside to finish one story, it seemed hopeless to go back to the front page and start another. She'd tried reading the editorials, which had, at least, the virtue of being all in the same place. But she was bored. None of this meant anything to her. She hadn't heard of half the people, didn't know what the references were, didn't care what these people thought about anything. Only what Tom thought . . . that was all.

She was housecleaning. A rag wrapped around her hair, an old cotton dress and a thin sweater, another rag in her hand. She left Ned, with a final pinch at his toes, and returned to the kitchen where she was scrubbing down the shelves. Julie was "turning out" the bedroom. That was a nice expression, used by housemaids in the movies. ("We're turning out the mistress' sitting room, sir." "Thunderation," says the master in a clipped voice, "isn't there any place a man can have a quiet brandy and cigar?" "I'm sure I don't know, sir," giggles the housemaid. Wasn't he the *one*?) Morgan wiped tickly perspiration from her neck, reached to the back of the low closet shelves. She wondered if she could bring Colin back. Suppose she were . . . Well, suppose she went downstairs, in a little while, with the laundry to put in one of the Bendixes. She'd be sitting on one of those benches they had, reading a book— What book? Why would she be reading one? Reading a—well, not reading. She'd just be sitting there, rather pale and pensive, her eyes fixed on the wall. And then in would come this tall young man, helping his aunt, who would live in one of the penthouses, because she liked to be . . . she'd be living in one of the penthouses. "My word, Aunty," he'd say, "why in the world don't you have Hulda do this sort of thing?" But his aunt, one of those peppery old characters with a sharp tongue (and, of course, a weakness for this charming scapegrace nephew) would snort, "Mind your manners, Colin. I'll do my own housekeeping till I'm too old to manage. Or do you think I'm too old now, eh?" But Colin would not reply. He'd have spied Morgan, leaning wearily against the whitewashed walls. . . .

"Morgy?"

Morgan looked around, conscious that she hadn't, for a moment, really lost herself in this dream. It had been carefully built up. In the old days, the days before Tom, all she had to do was start and then the dream took over, and an interruption, like Julie's voice, took moments to penetrate. Now she said, "What is it, Julie?" and let the half-dream go. It really wouldn't work. Colin wasn't anybody. She tried not to let herself dream about Tom, though he remained in her mind all the time. ("People *have* to care, Morgy. We're *in* this, all of us.") In what? In a big war just past, a lot of little ones going on? Of course, no war was little, because people died, and you die just as hard for a small cause as you do for a big one. She did care. Terribly. And she also cared that everything cost so much, that Ned was ill, that Julie grew more and more withdrawn. She cared that Tom would some day have to be a soldier, and that her father could not be home more. *Caring* was easy enough. But understanding . . . she didn't know how to begin that. She sat back on her heels to wring out the rag over a pail of soapy water.

Julie, her face smudged and frowning, came into the kitchen, perched on a little stepladder stool that was Ned's treasure. "My head is full of dust. It feels like an old attic. Not the kind with trunks full of glamor, the kind with bats. Dead bats."

"Well, sit for a bit."

"You're going to be awfully tired for that party tonight."

"If there is one."

Julie lifted her eyebrows. "What's the matter?"

"Oh, Verna's father. I guess he didn't go away or something. Poor Verna."

"What a crumb he must be," Julie said crossly. "Spoils everything. I'm glad we don't have that to put up with." For a moment they thought lovingly of their own father. "Is this our spring housecleaning, I hope?" Julie went on. "I'd sure hate to do it again very soon. You do pick the silliest times to clean, with Ned sick and a date tonight, if it works. Why don't we stop, and do the rest some other time? I'll have dust fever, or something."

Morgan continued to rub her rag in languid circles over the shelf. "We could, I guess. I'll finish this and stop. Can you think of anything for dinner?"

"Broiled mushrooms and tangerine pie."

"Pretty." Morgan smiled and stood up. "There. Now I'll put the stuff back and that's that." She began collecting pots and pans from around her. "Frankfurters and baked beans, I guess. And string beans. I wonder if Neddy wants anything."

"He's asleep," Julie said. "Let him. It's very strengthening, and keeps him quiet." She leaned her head back against the window jamb, closing her eyes. Morgan looked for a moment at the delicate curve of her sister's cheek and neck, the thickness of the lowered lashes. Why, she's lovely right now, Morgan thought. Perfectly lovely. Julie opened her eyes then, and the familiar, faintly discontented, faintly puzzled expression with which she faced the world returned. "Morgan," she said, "tell me something. What was—Mother like?"

"You don't remember?"

"Not enough."

"She was . . . she loved us a lot." Morgan paused, but Julie did not appear to have been told anything yet. "She was very thin. And excitable, you know? I remember she used to get all upset if one of us was sick or anything."

"Yes, I remember that too. What else?"

"Well, she was fun. Funny. She'd say terribly funny things." Morgan tried to recall some, but couldn't. "You and Ned laughed an awful lot at the things she said."

"Didn't you?"

"Sometimes. I didn't always know what she was getting at. And—" She hesitated. "And it seemed, once in a while, as though what she was saying *was* funny, but—unkind, too. Pop got a new suit once, a Palm Beach suit, very light colored. It was almost white and he was proud of it." She broke off.

"Go on."

"Oh . . . it wasn't anything, really. She said, 'Oh, darling, you look gorgeous. You look like a Good Humor man.' "

"Poor Pop. His new suit."

"She loved him, too. But I got the feeling, somehow, with her, that none of it . . . Pop and us and the way we lived . . . was what she'd planned. She loved us, though."

"Why do you keep saying that?"

"Because I don't seem to be saying the right things."

"I think it's very interesting that what you really remember of her is the unloving part," Julie said. "Almost as if you resented her."

"Do you think so?" Morgan said unhappily. "I don't mean to."

"Nobody ever means to." Julie got up. "You know what I remember?"

"What?"

"One time when it was raining like the devil, and Pop had lost that other job he had. Not the last one, the one before that. He came in, in those overalls, with his fists opening and shutting in his pockets, and he leaned against the table, looking at us. Then he threw a brown envelope on the table and said, 'I've been canned. There's two weeks' pay.' And Mother said, 'It was that organizer, wasn't it? That fellow from the union. You people lose your jobs because some windbag comes along offering heaven on a platter. He doesn't lose his job, does he, this organizer, if things go wrong? Oh no, he just goes off and gets a lot of other poor fools in trouble, stirring them up, promising things . . .' And then Pop yelled, 'Whose side are you on? Sure everything isn't blueprinted for Utopia in the unions, but we're a lot righter on that side than we'll ever be toadying up to the other, or putting our necks meekly on the solid gold chopping block.' 'Did they give you a reason?' she said. 'Reorganization,' says Pop. 'And you're reorganized out, with the other malcontents? Ah, you're a very Mars of malcontents, aren't you?' That's what Mother said."

"You *remember* all this?" Morgan breathed.

"I have a good memory. But I'm not finished, Morgy. Then, with poor Pop standing there, and Ned yelling, and—I don't know where you were—all of a sudden Mother went over and threw her arms around him and laughed. 'Oh, Mars, my love,' she said, 'let's not worry about it. Let's take the children out for dinner.' And that's what they did."

"They took us to Chinatown, and we had egg rolls and something very good that wasn't chop suey."

"You do remember."

"I remember the dinner part, and that it was the day Pop got fired. But not all those sentences and everything. How *can* you?"

"Some things stick in your mind. And it's funny, but I don't seem to be able to picture her, only hear what she said, and what her voice was like. Breathless, sort of."

"Yes, that's the way she sounded, always."

The phone rang and Morgan ran for it before Ned should waken. "Oh, fine," she said softly. "Can I help? Well—all right—it's probably better anyway, because I have Ned to—yes, we will. See you tonight, Verna." She glanced over at Ned, who slept in a curve beneath the blanket, one hand under his cheek. He hadn't moved.

She started water running in the tub, then went into the bedroom where Julie was stretched on the bed. "Well, the party's at Betty's. Wish I could care at all."

Julie shrugged her indifference to the party and Betty both. She rubbed Amy's small soft chin and wondered, am I brave? For instance, if a truck should be just about to run down Amy, *would* she have the courage to dive in front and save her kitten? She pictured the immensity of the truck, the horrified face of the driver, the terrible crashing of brakes. Would she? There was no way to tell. The picture remained at that paralyzing point . . . Amy before the wheels, Julie on the curb, the truck coming on but never, somehow, getting anywhere. Well, suppose it were Ned being run down? Surely then . . . ? But its being Ned rather than Amy did not make the scene more urgent. She twisted uneasily, rumpling the bedcovers.

Morgan moved about the room in her soft slippers. They did not refer to their mother again.

Tom and Morgan drove in Bluebird through the navy-blue April night. Morgan wore her winter coat, Tom his leather jacket. It was dark, and not warm. But it was April, and the wind prowled softly, flinging papers over the streets, clouds over the sky, bringing (from what distant place?) a scent of buds and roots and wet ripening branches. Morgan ran her window down and sniffed deeply, letting her hair tangle (though she'd spent an hour fixing it to look like somebody else's), letting the spring air flow against her face. Spring was coming into the city like a lover . . . the most capricious, most adored and unselective lover, taking all hearts at once, saying, "See, you must love me for myself, and I'll promise—oh, I'll promise many things . . . before I leave you." And this year, as in every other, Morgan agreed to love, to believe all the promises until they were broken, and then not to know that they had been.

Verna and her mother had used the Gilmans' "library table" on which to spread the yellow and green sprigged paper cloth, the matching napkins, the cups and dishes. They had piled the paper favors at one side, and hung three balloons on a string from the center light fixture. A large platter was laden with slices of pink baloney, gray liverwurst, salami starred with fat. There were two plates piled with sliced white bread, a dish of oleo, another of mayonnaise. There were cookies with icing on them, and cokes and cold tea. All the lights were on, and Betty met Morgan and Tom at the door.

Betty wore a close-fitting navy dress, with white at the neck and wrists. Her hair was caught high at the back with a huge barrette. She smiled and held out her hand. "I'm so glad you could *come*," she said, and repeated, looking Tom over, "So glad."

Morgan looked past her to where Verna stood hesitantly, unhappily, watching Betty play hostess. Verna, in a bright red dress. Morgan scowled at Betty, took Tom's hand and led him to Verna. "Tom, this is Verna. I mean, this is Tom, Verna. Verna's *giving* this party."

Betty glided alongside. "Of course. It's Verna's party. Only it *is* my home, so naturally I meet the . . . newcomers." She smiled at Tom. More introductions were ineptly performed, Morgan once again failing to hear the last name of Pete, here for Verna. There was a faintly familiar boy, a Phil Dunning, who seemed to be Betty's date, a blonde girl, Miriam something, with her date, Corney something else, and a couple of kids from school. By the end of the evening, first names were established. Morgan thought briefly that it was awfully muddled, that it could have been handled much much better, but who was going to see to that?

"The table looks so pretty, Verna," she said.

Verna smiled and ran her tongue over her lips. "Yes, we thought everyone sort of likes cold cuts, don't you think? And this way we can have a buffay, all of us getting our own. Or the boys serving the girls," she added unhopefully. She put her hands behind her back and grew silent, looking at the floor. As hostess, no one could deny Betty's superiority.

"*Now*," Betty said, "that we have all these *strong* arms," (the boys regarded each other suspiciously) "we can just roll this old rug back, and get ready for the dancing." She directed the removal of the rug, with little cries of, "Look *out*, Phil, that's a really priceless vase." (Phil looked up to laugh, but encountered her grave expression. He studied the vase with puzzled respect and moved it tenderly into the kitchen.) "*That's* right, Tom, just ease it into the corner, oh that's *fine*, Tom." (She talked more to Tom than to the others. Obviously, Morgan thought.) "Well, there's one thing we can say for having it here instead of at Vern's. *Here* we don't have a maiden-sister chaperon. If there's one thing I like less than a chaperon, it's—it's *two* chaperons," she said with so convincing an air of wit that the boys laughed.

"Where's your grandmother?" Morgan said. "Isn't she here?"

"Oh yes. The poor darling was exhausted, really exhausted, after today's session with the specialists. We had two of them," Betty said, turning her hands slightly. "They simply *insisted* that she go right to bed."

They began to mill about, sitting on all the available upholstered furniture and on the rolled-up rug, letting their glances slide over each other's faces, over the food. Miriam whispered to the impassive Corney beside her, Verna smiled and fiddled with things on the table, Morgan, looking around, felt depressed. Parties were stupid things. There was that Pete, cleaning his fingernails and whistling, tapping his feet, not making an effort to assist Verna, nor even to act pleased that he was here. Perhaps he wasn't, perhaps no one was, but the least you can do for a party is pretend you're glad it happened. Phil was saying, "No kidding, don't give me that stuff," though in answer to what, or to whom spoken,

Morgan couldn't tell. Tom, leaning against a wall, hands in his pocket, looked a little cross. Of course, he wasn't very keen on parties, especially high-school parties, and he'd only come at all to please her, but he could behave a little better than that Pete character, couldn't he? She hardened a bit toward him.

Betty was saying, "Look gang," (Tom winced) "let's sort of get better acquainted, shall we? I mean, I for one don't intend to let this poor party expire at my *feet*. That is," she glanced at Verna, "at Verna's feet. Let's put this show on the road. . . ."

She's incredible, Morgan thought. I've never seen her act this way before. Or, really, she had. Only not at such close quarters. Betty was a cheerleader (oh, how wonderful to wear the little flaring skirt, the white woolly sweater, to twirl the silver baton! But Morgan was too shy, far too shy, to attempt *that*) and she was trying to drive the old football spirit into this room of goons. Because we are, Morgan insisted to herself. All of us. Even Tom. Standing around saying practically nothing, avoiding each other's eyes, letting all the fun leak like air out of a balloon. You, she reminded herself, are not being any better, and you're criticizing yourself in everyone else. She smiled brightly at Betty and moved across the room.

"We could put names in a hat," she said, "and then whatever name somebody draws, they dance with that person?"

"Suppose two girls draw each other?" Pete said, deserting his fingernails in order to carp without distraction.

At least he's talking, Morgan thought. A little progress. "I only meant to put the girls' names in," she said. By now, people had arisen and were moving about. Conversation, painfully prodded, slowly gathered enough drive to continue on its own.

"I'll write my name twice, then I'm sure to get a choice of partners . . ."

"Hey, what's your name? Miriam? Hey, Miriam, if Pete gets you, how about a trade, you don't wanna dance with him . . ."

"Pete's a pretty good . . ."

"When's the chow is what I want to know . . ."

The hat was produced, the paper slips fluttered in. "Super," said Betty. She held the hat to Tom first, with, "Be careful what you draw," and a quivering smile. Tom smiled back, thrust his hand in the hat, examined the slip, close to his chest, like a poker player.

And suddenly everything was fine. The girls began to laugh, as girls at a party should. The boys addressed each other by last names and fell to strutting. The records wound round and round the phonograph and the silky sinewy jitterbugging couples went round and round the floor.

There was a hammered clamor on the radiators, and everyone stood frozen.

"Looks like downstairs is peeved," Phil Dunning said. His foot slid back and forth slowly.

Betty looked disapprovingly at the floor, through the floor. "A couple of sleep-creeps."

"Do we heed them?" Pete asked. "Or do we dis-heed them?"

"Oh well." Betty pulled out of Corney's arms. "Let's eat. Then we can start again."

"After they've been lulled good," one of the boys said.

"That's the idea, boy," Pete agreed. He walked to the table, began to pile a plate for himself.

"Want me to get you something?" Tom asked, coming over to Morgan. But she shook her head, glanced at Verna. "Too obvious," she whispered. They secured their food separately, settled on the rug.

"Hey, you know," Pete said, plumping down on the other side of her. "Roy ast about you the other day."

"Did he?"

"Surest thing you know. Said where's that cooky can't swim?"

"Well, he certainly did remember me," Morgan said sweetly.

"Sure thing. Why not? Boy, is that guy smart."

"Is he?"

"Surest thing you know. Why one year, when we were studying for those, you know, scholastic appitude tests in our school, he made a coupla dollars an hour, coaching people. Lot of guys studied with him. He cleaned up."

"You can't study for scholastic aptitude tests," Tom said. "They aren't like regular examinations. They're designed to get the potential capacity for study, not how much has already been studied."

Pete shrugged. "Can't help that. He did, and we did, that's all I know. Why that guy, any time at all, can get a job out at Sperry, two hundred bucks a week."

"So why doesn't he?" Verna asked.

Pete shrugged again. "Temperament. He's lousy with it." He shook his head admiringly.

Betty, stepping lightly through the clutter of people, settled beside Tom. She reached back, turning up the radio, so that now everyone could talk in undertones, with privacy. She turned to Tom and said softly, "Morgy says you go to college. Not that I wouldn't have known anyway."

"How?" he asked. After all, Betty was a pretty girl, the sort in whom silly remarks are not only forgivable, but charming.

"Oh, *you* know. You look—different."

Tom nodded, not in agreement, but because she'd said what he expected her to. She was young. Another couple of years and she'd have more finesse. With that, and her looks, she'd get along just fine. He began to wonder when he and

Morgan could leave. He hadn't stopped wondering why they'd come. This didn't seem like her sort of thing at all. Probably, he decided, it was because of Verna. He felt an exciting rush of affection for this girl, this lovely Morgan who seemed to wander through life in a dream, and at the same time managed school, housework, and the care of a family in which every member leaned upon her constantly. Dan Connor, as much as the kids. More than Julie, probably. He could sense now Morgan's quick uncertain glances at Betty (who was pressing rather close to him), he could hear her short distracted answers to the conversation of that square. Ah, Morgan, he thought. Morgan, my love. And the thoughts that came to his mind surprised him. Sure, he'd liked her from the day they met, when she hadn't seemed much taken with him. He'd even, in a way, loved her. It would be practically impossible to know Morgan and not love her. But in a different way . . . he'd thought. Because she was dear, and fun to be with. In a way somehow connected with Ned, that swell, competent, but sort of lonely kid he'd encountered in the playground last year. Morgan was Ned's sister. Wasn't that, hadn't that been, about the size of it? But—what now? What he'd been thinking these last few minutes had little to do with Ned. He edged slightly away from the soft pressure of Betty's body.

"Nervous?" she asked, in a low, intimate tone.

"Nope. Just crowded." At her expression, he relented. She looked stricken, and the blood flushed her white skin. She was, he repeated to himself, very young. "Morgan tells me you're a cheerleader. I bet you look terrific in one of those getups." She relaxed a little, the blush receding, but made no attempt to cozy up again. Just as well, he thought. Won't hurt her to get a comeuppance now and then.

"Poor Morgy," she said, with a return of confidence at his words and his smile.

"Why that?"

"Oh well. She's so practically—lazy, you know. *Darling*, and I absolutely adore her, but just the most unathletic girl. She tells me you're a cross-country runner. I just adore track meets. A man I was engaged to took me to several. We had the best seats. . . ."

"Engaged?"

She turned a hand over negligently. "Oh yes, but that's all *too* past for words. I couldn't bear—certain aspects of his character. You know what I mean?"

"I can guess."

"It isn't what you're thinking at all," she said primly.

"Nor what you're thinking either," he grinned. "Anyway, Morgy's not lazy. She's . . ." He broke off, his perplexed mind going back to Morgan and what he was beginning to think she was.

"She's what?" Betty insisted softly.

"Huh? Oh, what I was going to say was, you're the grey-hound type—" Betty looked pleased and acquiescent. "And some people like that fine. Tell me more about this engagement," he said hastily, as her face resumed its uncertain shade. He thought, she's not nearly so confident as she'd like us all to think. It made him a little sorry. He listened attentively while she spun an incredible tale of her wealthy but unacceptable suitor.

They played Twenty-one Questions, using easily guessable movie and baseball characters. They continued to nibble at the food, listen to the radio, gather in groups, shift into others. Now and then a couple would disappear to the kitchen, emerge looking smudged and stealthy. Pete picked bits of lint off the floor, dropped them in his empty glass. The air became a low cloud of smoke that spiraled and swung when a window was opened, but seemed not to dissolve. Verna grew bright at the attentions of Corney, while Miriam solaced herself with Phil, who kept looking at Betty. Morgan and Betty remained sitting on the rug beside Tom.

Anyway, Morgan thought, she can't outstay me, because I'm going home with him. She decided they could leave now, and turned to say so. It was then she heard the faint cry from the bedroom at the end of the apartment. A cry that carried with it an impression of repetition. Morgan leaned across Tom. "Betty? Look, Betty, I think your grandmother is calling you."

The pain made her think of trees. It was having a tree within, raddled leaves trembling in wrists and fingers, twisted trunk driving up her back, tortured roots in legs and feet. A tree, bent and crumpled out of shape, dying, tormented by time. She lay with the branching pain, listening to the music, the voices muffled through the closed door, the sawlike sound of feet on the bare floor. She faced the window. Black bones of the fire escape, drawn blinds of apartments still lit here and there in the building across the alley. She could detect, in this room she shared with Betty, darkness that had shape where furniture stood, and darkness that was space. She pushed at the blanket with fingers that had once been comely and praised, that now were twisted painful twigs, and wondered how long the party would last, how long it would be before Betty thought to come in and help her to another position. She lay, trying to will Betty to the bedroom. Calling out would be so hard, would take so long, would feel so desperate. The lights in the building across the way began to go out, the pain began to burn in her back until she knew that if she couldn't be moved a little way to one side or the other, she'd scream. She began to call her granddaughter, trying to pierce the closed door, the series of rooms, the music and the voices. When the door did open, she was not aware of it, and went on calling in her old despairing tremolo. "Betty, Betty . . ." The music snapped off, and her plea, "*Help me . . .*" was sharp and thin in the sudden silence.

"For heaven's sake, Gram," Betty said in a loud whisper, "do you have to make such a racket?" She turned on the light and its glare brought tears to Mrs. Metzger's eyes. She didn't answer. She waited, in a torture of anticipation, for Betty's strength to bring her relief.

In the living room, the cry and the abrupt silence sliced the party off as coldly as the shears of Atropos cutting a life thread. One moment it was whole and spinning out to apparently endless length, the next it lay severed, and there was no thought of picking up the thread and going on.

When Betty came back people were beginning to glance at each other, at their coats, at the door. "Well," they said. And, "I suppose we should . . ."

"Don't *go*," Betty said automatically, but she was disturbed, not truly unwilling to see the end of them, of the evening. She smiled and said she was so glad, as people thanked her for the party. Verna, pulling on her coat, said, "Yes, thanks a lot, Betty."

Betty began to say how nice it had been to have her. She frowned suddenly, looking at the rumpled rug, the scattered food-spattered paper dishes, the string of balloons subsiding into wrinkles overhead. "Hey," she said. "After all, Verna, this was *your* party, even if I did lend my place. Can't you help clear up this mess?"

Verna turned at the door. "I did the first part. And you know perfectly well it hasn't been my party. So suppose you take over now." She and Pete went out with Corney, the blonde, and another couple. Betty was left, with Morgan and Tom and the party flotsam. "How do you like that?" Betty demanded. "If she doesn't have the most stupefying gall."

Morgan looked at Tom. "We can help," she said coolly,

and began to pick napkins off the floor. "But Verna doesn't have a corner on the gall by any means."

"And what's that supposed to mean?"

"What I say. Didn't you take the party over? Did anybody say good night Verna it's been a lovely evening thanks so much? I don't blame her a bit. Could you pull the rug back, Tom?"

He did, as Betty carried a cardboard carton in from the kitchen and began to dump paper plates and cups in it. She looked tired and uninterested, even in Tom. She was wondering when her mother would get in, thinking of what her grandmother had said. . . .

She had turned her grandmother's light body toward the wall, straightened the sheets, stood there wondering if they'd all heard that old voice cry out. "You okay, now? Gram?" The old woman's breathing was loud in the dark room. For a moment, Betty thought she wasn't going to answer. In the living room there was a shuffling undertone of movement. Betty took a step away from the bed, hesitated, heard her grandmother's caught breath and the thin words. "Betty, how did I get so old? I keep wondering . . ." The voice trailed away.

Betty stared down at the small flat figure, barely discernible in the shadows. "Don't you feel good, Gram?"

"No," Mrs. Metzger whispered. "No, Betty. Not good—at all."

Betty leaned over, touching the flaccid arm. "I have to— I'll be back soon," she said, and hurried away to her departing guests. Now she looked up from the brimming carton. "Morgan. I think—that is, I'm worried about my grandmother. She's—funny. Maybe . . . do you think I should get a doctor? Her voice is so peculiar, and there's a—I don't know—a funny *feeling* . . ."

"Who's your doctor?" Tom said. "I could round him up for you, I guess."

"I don't know. I mean, we don't have one, really." Betty bit her lip. "Maybe I'm just imagining." She was suddenly impatient to have them gone. "Yes, I'm probably just nervous. Anyway, Angie will be in soon. You two just go along, and I'll clean up here . . ." She tried to urge them through the door with her voice.

"Well, don't you think we should wait with you, till Angie gets here?" Morgan said.

"No, I don't. I mean, I'm sorry . . . I'm tired, and Angie'll be in in no time. You go along—"

Driving home in Bluebird, Morgan and Tom were silent till he'd parked the car, turned off the headlights and leaned back. "I never did like parties," he said at last.

"I hope Mrs. Metzger gets better. Or isn't worse."

"Nice for her, having to lie back there while we reveled."

"What's Betty to do? We don't all live in spacious apartments like yours, with no inconvenient invalids on hand."

"Don't, Morgy."

"All right. But it's hard, just the same. Betty's a funny girl," she added thoughtfully.

"It's a funny world. This country's got a youth complex anyway. The Mrs. Metzgers don't have a chance."

"Why?"

"Oh, we're all—not us, because we don't have to yet, but we as people—trying to stay young and beautiful, which is to say happy. Mrs. Metzger is a disquieting presence at our frolic. Just look at the ads, and the books that get put out. 'How To Hide Wrinkles and Live.' 'Your Age Won't Show If You Don't.' That sort of thing. There isn't any real reverence except reverence for a youthful appearance. And all the time the old guys, the ones who pay us and tell us what to do and where to live and how to die, are sitting on their steel and gold behinds and descending once a year for the old Reunion. Staying young, you know. Maybe they use up all the youthfulness, and that's why people who aren't youthful, but just aren't old, haven't got much of the bounce left. The fellows I know are trying like the devil to age so that they can get past the Service deal and find jobs with good pensions. Then they can start getting the know-how and shaving with yogurt." He shrugged. "No more. Your turn."

Morgan shook her head. "I have nothing to say. You're right, I guess. I know I wonder sometimes why we aren't gayer. You, me, the people at school. Julie. She's very—nervous—for a girl her age. Not light, you know, or interested in—oh, the things you'd think she would be."

"Julie's different. Perhaps she's decided to think her way through life, not feel."

"But isn't that sort of sad?"

"It might be if her thoughts stay sad. Maybe they won't. I was like that, sort of, as a kid. Spent my time reading and pondering the significance of the sun casting shadows, that sort of stuff." She looked uncomprehending. "That if you have sun, you have shadows. One presupposes the other. It seemed darned symbolic then. Don't look so impressed," he grinned.

"I'm not. I mean, not by the sun and the shadows."

"By what, then?"

"You," she said softly. "I've never known anyone like you." She stared down the street, almost empty now. The street lamps glowed quietly, the darkened doorways and windows seemed meant forever to be empty. A wind moved over the river, trifling with papers in the gutter. "And I love you," she added. "I suppose I shouldn't say it, but I've wanted to so much."

"Me too," he said in a quiet voice.

Morgan sat utterly still, knowing what she'd heard him

say, not able to believe it, brimming with a turbulent emotion that nothing she'd ever known had prepared her for. And yet almost afraid that if she made a gesture, spoke a word, the words he had said would be brushed away, would not have been spoken at all.

He put his hand on her cheek, turned her face toward his. This was how she'd dreamed it once—their eyes close and searching, his arms tight around her and his beautiful mouth swiftly, softly against hers.

"It isn't a dream, is it?" she said wonderingly.

"Why should it be a dream, darling?" he asked. "Morgan —" He kissed her ear, her hair. "Morgan, I do love you. I love you terribly."

She leaned against him, trembling with the dream that had made itself true, the one that she'd been dreaming toward all her life. *Tom, Tom, the Millers' son, stole my heart. . . .*

His mother was reading when he got in, and his father working the delicate angles of his model boat.

"How'd the party go?" Mrs. Miller asked. She glanced at the clock. "You're home early."

Tom looked too. "Only twelve?" he said. He hoped his voice was normal, he hoped it wasn't telling in its tone what he had said in words a little while ago. "The girl's grandmother got sick," he explained. "So the party broke up."

"Oh. That's too bad." His mother looked at him carefully, looked away. "How's the car running?"

"Like silk."

"You're careful, I hope?"

"Sure I'm careful. Think I'd take Morgan out and not be careful?" He added quickly, "Or anyone, for that matter. After all, when I'm driving, I'm respon—" He stopped, smiled a little, stretched. "Guess I'll get to bed."

"The Connors are nice children," his mother said slowly.

"Morgan's not a child. She's seventeen."

"All grown up, then," Mrs. Miller sighed, as her son went off to his room.

There comes a time when parents must recognize an adult being born in the child, must hear the new voice affirm itself. "Ready or not," this emerging person calls, "Ready or not, here I come."

But who is ever ready?

Chapter Eleven

Ned, when he had recovered from his chicken pox, got measles. He did not go back to school at all that year. For days he drifted in a hot oblivious sea of illness, unmindful of tending hands, of unhappy eyes fixed upon his tossings, or stricken ears receiving his cries. He sank and twisted and scuttled in his private dark sea, and those who stood at the surface, staring down, reaching with their love and care and fright to bring him up, sometimes thought the drowning shadow would elude them and sink away forever.

During those days, when he was most ill, Morgan never left the apartment. As she, Julie, and her father had all had measles, they were not quarantined, but a quarantine could not have kept her more firmly at her brother's side. She sat on a chair by the cot, holding his flame-like hand, running bits of ice over his whitened cracked lips, studying his marred, heavily flushed face. "Please, Neddy," she'd say gently. "Please, *dearest.*"

The doctor came daily for almost a week. There was something unreal about his visits. Each time she saw him there, Morgan would think, yes, he's here, all his implements, his bag snapping open, snapping shut, his voice. But which visit is this? Today's, yesterday's? He came and went, with his antiseptic odor, his unsurprised manner, his precise swiftness that could only leave her wondering if he'd been there, or had just flashed through her mind. She was quite too in awe of doctors to question him about Ned's progress, and nothing he ever said informed her clearly.

One day, just after her father had left, the doorbell rang. Morgan, blinking scratchy eyes, went to answer. He's early, she thought, and opened to Mrs. Miller. "Oh. I thought you were the doctor." She stepped back and began to laugh. "Did I ever tell you an awfully funny thing I did? Come in, sit down, it's awfully nice to see you." She went on laughing, wondering at herself, not stopping. "I answered the door, you see, just like now, thinking it was Ned. And I was going to surprise him, so I stooped down very low so that our faces would be level and I opened the door and said *Hi*! And there were a man's legs, in a green uniform, and I looked up, still stooping because I was so rattled, and the poor man's face was absolutely white, looking down at me. I couldn't even explain. He was the meter man. He still comes, and he always looks at me in the most suspicious way, and never says a word . . ." Her laughter subsided. She sank limply to a chair and sighed. "I guess I'm tired."

Mrs. Miller nodded. "I guess you must be. And it *is* a funny story." She looked at Ned, who was sleeping. "How is he?"

"I don't know, Mrs. Miller. I don't seem to be able to get the doctor to say much. He's very nice, and all, and a good doctor. But we aren't . . . understanding each other very well."

"How often it works out that way." She walked to Ned's cot. "He seems to be sleeping peacefully, Morgan." Morgan was at her side immediately. "Don't you think so?" They spoke in low voices, their eyes on Ned's face.

175

"He does," Morgan breathed. She put a light hand on his forehead, turned to Mrs. Miller. "He really does. Not so—hot and angry-colored." She wanted to go on, but her voice and her legs seemed abruptly weak. She went back to the chair and leaned her head on the arm. "Just a minute," she mumbled. "I'll be fine in a minute."

"Morgan," Mrs. Miller said. Her voice seemed distant, but piercing. "Morgan dear, get up and go into the bedroom. Sleep for a couple of hours and I'll watch Ned." Morgan swayed to her feet, inaudibly grateful, surprised at how suddenly, overpoweringly sleepy she was. It was a weight upon her, this desire to lie down. Mrs. Miller was walking with her to the bedroom, talking. "I'd have done this before, but Tom probably told you we were up at the lake, trying to get the cottage in order. I hurried down here the minute we got back and Tom's out now getting some fruit and things that we thought you might . . ." She went on and on. How kind she is, Morgan thought, and what a terrible lot of words she knows. The bed was before her and she plunged into its arms, sat up again to remove her shoes and skirt, lay down and felt the cover being drawn over her. "You're . . . nice to do this," she said thickly. "But . . . the doct . . ."

"I'll take care of the doctor," Mrs. Miller said, and Morgan heard nothing further.

She awoke to mauve-toned twilight at the open window, odors and sounds that indicated someone in the kitchen getting dinner. How beautiful, she thought. How wonderful to lie here, letting people work for me. She nestled under the cover, breathing the air that even now, with the sun gone, had something of its warm gold presence, its late spring softness. Amy, not a kitten any more, not quite a cat yet, was curled beside her, purring and indolent. "Aren't we a pretty pair?" Morgan whispered. Amy extended a languid paw, heard the icebox door open, and departed.

"Oh well," Morgan said to the vanishing tail, "I suppose I should too."

Ned was lying with his head propped up a little, a glass of ginger ale beside him, and a look of bright comprehension in his eyes that was glorious to Morgan's. *"Baby,"* she said happily, "what have you *done* in the last two hours?"

"Got better," he said huskily. "And don't call me baby, Morgan. There's people all over the house."

Morgan grinned at his petulance. "You certainly did," she said. "Get better, I mean. They tell me that a patient who's cross is on the mend." Ned smiled and sucked on his ginger ale, and Morgan went into the kitchen to Julie and Mrs. Miller. "It's incredible," she told them. "He was *sick* this morning. Really sick. And now look at him."

"And now listen to him," Julie said. She sounded pleased. "Did you have a good sleep?"

"Oh wonderful . . . marvelous. I just can't thank you," she began, but Mrs. Miller fluttered that away with her hands. "Anyway, it was wonderful, and I feel made over." She looked at the meatloaf being removed from the oven. "I'd have got dinner."

"I decided," Mrs. Miller said, "that you'd better really get a rest, or you'd be sick too. Tom and I have invited ourselves to eat with you. Oh, and the doctor says he won't be back again. He left some instructions for you to follow, but Ned will be all right."

"Only he isn't going to school any more this year," Julie interrupted, "so who's going to take care of him? You'll have to go back to school pretty soon yourself or you'll never graduate. But we can't leave him alone, can we?"

"Pop will be here most of the time. I'll get out earlier in the afternoon. We'll manage."

"Of course you will," Mrs. Miller said, and Julie, who accepted any word from that source as the ultimate opinion,

grew still. "Morgan," Mrs. Miller went on, "I have an idea
. . ." But she did not, just then, have a chance to say what it
was. Tom, who'd been up explaining to Geoff and his father
why they must eat alone, came in.

"It's marvelous out," he announced, with a quick look for
Morgan and a general one for the rest. "The air's like . . .
like . . . oh, marvelous. What do you think of our Ned,
Morgy? Take you off the case and he's better in minutes.
Mother, Geoff says he doesn't care if he eats or not. I think
he's in love."

"Again?" said Julie.

"Oh sure. Geoff is a weather vane in the wind of love, this
way, that way . . ."

I hope it doesn't run in the family, Morgan thought.

It was the first gay meal in a long time. "Ned's recovery
dinner," they called it, though Ned ate only ice cream.

"I thought," Tom said, "that after dinner, Morgan should
go to a movie, to relax. And I should go with her, in case she
gets lost."

"Excellent suggestion," his mother replied. She glanced at
Julie, who shook her head. "I don't like them, anyway," Julie
said. "I'll stay here with Ned."

"Oh, I'll stay too," Mrs. Miller said casually, and Julie
gave her a look of dedication. But haven't we been lucky,
Morgan thought, haven't we been awfully awfully lucky.

That was when Mrs. Miller said, "Now, about my idea . . ."

When she and Tom got to the street, Morgan said she
didn't really want to go to the movies. "I just wanted to get
out," she explained.

"With me?"

"Yes."

"I'm glad."

178

They walked along, not touching, not having any real direction, happy to be together, saying nothing. The warm May night, colored and sweet as dark grapes, had lured the sidewalk chair sitters out. They wore light sweaters now, and jockeyed for positions against the walls, but this was the beginning of their summer evenings in the air, sitting on their stone stoops, canvas chairs, old barrels, in places that would shortly become as reserved as theater seats. They all seemed, this evening, sweet-faced and dreamy-voiced, watching their children play on the pavements, eying benignly the pedestrians, the little dogs, the traffic that passed. The hard-faced handsome boys stood again at street lights, at corner drugstores, but now they glanced at Tom next to Morgan, and looked away. Music tumbled lightly through open windows, and it was all music—the purring auto wheels, the children calling, the voices saying, the night deepening.

"What do you want to do?"

"Walk."

"Where?"

"Anywhere. Where you say."

"We'll go over by the river."

"That would be nice."

The river was jet, shiny, like a beetle's back, streaked and stippled with gleams that slid across the surface, dived, reappeared. The river traffic, the little lighted cabins of tugs went past, their red and green lights floating around them. At the nearest pier, a freighter was tied up, lightless and stiller than stone. The bridges sprang from shore to shore, bright beads and black wire crossed back and forth with moving spears of yellow light.

It was the same pier they'd driven on during the rain and the first ride in Bluebird. Not cold now. A pier of purple air and intermittent lights from boats and cars going past. There were other people. A night fisherman, his small daughter beside him, sat with dangling legs and line at the farther end of the dock. A man leaned against a piling, reading by a flashlight. A couple sat, their dark shapes close, on the pier's wooden edge.

Morgan and Tom sat opposite the fisherman, next to a bulkhead. Morgan felt she could never breathe deeply enough the rapturous warm dark air. Spring was a time of long breaths, of smelling things, of wanting to swallow the air, or hold it, or fly into it. "I have spring fever," she said.

"It's practically summer."

"Even so." And perhaps it wasn't only spring. Perhaps it was Ned, no longer ill, or Mrs. Miller's kindness, or . . . It was Tom. Sitting beside him now, their shoulders touching gently, she did not feel the nearly frightening urgency of love she'd felt in the car that night . . . the urgency he'd felt too, so that they'd pulled apart, shaken and confused, and had gone quickly upstairs with scarcely a good night. But after that Ned had been ill, and until tonight she hadn't been alone with Tom again. And tonight she was tired, happy just to sit here quietly, being with him. She leaned her head against the brine-scented bulkhead, thinking about him. And about his mother. What would it be like, she wondered, to have that sort of generosity, that chance to indulge it? To invite the two children—well, herself too—away for weeks of the summer. To offer the country, with all the country must be, to people who had never known it. To be able to offer, and to want to. So often, Morgan thought, there is just one without the other.

"Your mother," she said. "She's so—"

"Isn't she? But she's crazy about Julie and Ned, and they'll be crazy about the lake. Good for them. And I don't see why you won't go along."

"Tom, you know why. Pop's here. I don't just go off and leave Pop."

"No. When's his vacation?"

"I don't know."

"Maybe you could then."

"I don't think so. Pop . . . It's the children I'm glad for. Tell me what it's like."

"Wonderful. The lake is wide, and there's a broad meadow behind the house, and a wood that's gradually coming to live with us. We're right on the water, so you only have to walk about four steps and you're wet. Geoff bought a canoe for taking his girls into romantic settings. If you'd come up, I'd take you."

"And your other girls?" she said, not sure if she teased or not.

"Stop it, Morgy. You know I've never given a darn about a girl except you." He turned to her in the dark, and his breath was fresh on her face. "You do know that, don't you?" he repeated.

"Well . . . Yes, I know. Only I don't know why," she whispered.

"Morgan—my love." He leaned over and kissed her cheek lightly. "Morgan, you're the last person in the world to feel —uncertain. So don't, please. Don't make me think I make you feel that. You don't love people because they read the same books you do. That's what you're thinking, isn't it?" She nodded. "You love people because . . . *Why*? Do *you* know why? Well, neither do I. I only know that I do, that I think about you all the time, and wonder what you're doing a million times a day, and want to be with you, and hold you, and . . ." He broke off. "And I love you so much it sort of scares me, Morgan. As if . . ." He looked down at the dark lifting water, up at the star-chalked sky. "Well, anyway, don't ever think that I don't."

Morgan's eyes were large and still on his, and her lips a little open. "*Morgy*," he said fiercely, and then had his arms around her, holding her tight, rubbing his cheek against hers and whispering her name. And Morgan, listening, kissing him, understood very well, though she'd never known before, what it was they were feeling. Not tired now, not content to sit peacefully together, but caught up in this terrifying daze of pleasure and yearning. I don't care, she thought, I don't care what happens . . . But she did, and when he said, "Please, Morgy?" she pulled away breathlessly.

"I'm sorry," he said in a little while.

"Don't be sorry. Please don't be. We love each other, and if people love each other, they just naturally—they just—" She sighed, and went on. "But we can't, Tom. You know that."

"Of course I know it. What do you think I've been telling myself, trying to tell you? I know what we can't do. But what I don't know is what we do *about* it. I tell myself over and over that it'll be perfectly all right. I'm a little gentleman, and you—you're a sweet—lovely—girl and I wouldn't do anything in the world to hurt you. I've explained this thing to myself more blasted ways. And yet, every once in a while, when I'm with you, like tonight . . ." His voice slackened, and he took her hand quietly. "I forget what I've told myself."

The fisherman across the way began to put away his tackle. Morgan and Tom waited in silence till he and his little girl had gone past. The other couple, they noticed, was gone too. Only the two of them and the flashlight reader remained on the shadow-steeped pier.

"What do you suppose people do?" Tom asked in a gentle, curious voice.

"They wait," she whispered.

He said quickly, "Sure they do. I frightened you, and I didn't mean to. But you understand, don't you?"

"I understand. And you didn't frighten me . . . anyway,

not more than I did myself. You aren't all alone, you know," she said, smiling a little.

"We are together, aren't we?"

She nodded.

"Morgan, look. I'll be out of school in two years, and then I suppose I'll have to play soldier for a while, and then get a job. Suppose it all takes four years . . . will you marry me in four years?"

Morgan, who hadn't cried in a long time, cried now. "Oh, I want to," she said with the hot tears streaming over her cheeks, easeful and easy. "I want to. I will . . ."

In the morning Julie burst in upon her father's sleep to tell him about the trip to the country. "Is it all right, Pop?" she asked. "You'll let us go?"

He smiled. "Tell me about this country retreat." He listened to Julie's rapturous detailed description of a place she'd never been, allowing his mind to stray now and then to the gracious donor of one richness after another. One gift following another gift. Give, give, and do, do. The world is so full of a number of things, courtesy of Mrs. Miller, sometimes known as Mother Nature. A cornucopia of nothing but the best. Genuine, hand-turned kindness, built to last. Make no mistake, he told himself, this is the real thing, and you'll never regret having had a share in it. Or, anyway, the children never will. And are you in a proper position to carp? Do you have something to replace a few weeks in the country, or the companionship, or any of the other undoubted riches they are offered from that source? You do not. Therefore rejoice—or at any rate try—in the good fortune that led your younger children into the arms of Mother Miller. And your elder daughter into the arms of her son, he reminded himself. Though this, of course, was nothing he'd ever discussed.

They think no one else can see, or understand, or remember, he thought. They think it's the first time ever, and that no one till now has had the secret of the heart. Oh well . . . he'd thought so too. And perhaps they were right, and each time was the first, though not the last.

". . . and I should think there'd be cows," Julie was saying. "At least, you would think so, wouldn't you? And buttercups and flies. Butterflies, I mean. I'll take a book along and keep notes on all I observe and feel. It could be valuable for next year's schoolwork . . ."

"How I Spent My Summer Vacation?" said her father.

"Well, they're bound to. They always do."

"I know. Even I got it."

"You did?" Julie said, as though this were using "always" in a broader sense than she'd intended. "And fields, and the lake, of course. I don't have a bathing suit, but I can swim a little, from going to the Y. I'm going to take some poetry with me."

"That'll be good," her father said. "Take a book some day, and go away by yourself and read, and then you'll find so many things, in poems you thought you knew, that are fresh and differently lighted. Oh, and you'd better buy a bathing suit."

"What is poetry?" Julie asked dreamily.

Her father irresistibly added, What is truth? But he said, "Not the same thing to any two people. To me . . . I think it's a cry against all the things we can't understand, nor accept, nor reason with."

"But poetry shouldn't be a cry against something."

"That's why I say it's different to each person who reads it. Just be glad you do, Julie. People who miss poetry miss a great deal."

"Even though they never know it? Can you miss something you don't know?"

"I think so. I know I've missed something," he said with puzzled slowness. "Not knowing what it is hasn't prevented the sense of it."

Julie did not, as Morgan might have, stir restlessly. She said in soft encouragement, "What do you think it is? What *do* you want, Pop?"

"Oh—" He smiled, lifted one eyebrow. "A united Ireland."

"Don't, Pop. Tell me."

"It's as if . . . Well, you know, Julie, in those old heraldic ballads, how the knights rode forth into the glimmer and darkness of the forests, to break the enchantments and deliver the castles? I feel like one of those knights—I do have some medieval sense in me, like Miniver Cheevy—but I arrived at my destined castle to find it . . . undeliverable. Deserted." He looked at Julie pensively. "Do you understand? Does that make any sense?"

"Oh, it does, Pop. And you know, you *are* sort of knightly. Like Don Quixote," she added innocently, and as her eyes were lowered she did not see the start of dismay, nor the following acquiescent smile that greeted this. "But, of course," she added, "you do have some things. I mean, the castle may be deserted, but look at all you've picked up on the way."

"My three heralds?"

"Yes."

"I'm prouder of them than I'd have been of the castle. Except that it would have been nice to present the castle to them."

"Oh, we'll take you as you are," Julie assured him warmly, so that once again he realized that true communion between them wasn't possible. Julie understood, to a point. But she did not (how could he expect her to?) really identify the undelivered castle with her father's unaccomplished dreams. Well, we have those, all of us, he told himself a bit

185

impatiently. And why should I assume that mine held something more richly enchanted than all the others scattered through the forests?

"Metaphor," he said suddenly, "is a treacherous thing. After a while it's better to forego it and do something objective, like eating breakfast or putting new laces in your shoes."

"I think you're very right," Julie said.

Dan thought how excellent it was to have a child like this. She was the most vulnerable of the three, and, possibly, the least attractive. But there was something there, some slender, springing, inquisitive spirit that Ned with his charm and poise, Morgan with her lazy grace, did not share. Oh, but they were grand, the three of them. "Why isn't Morgan going too?" he asked. "To Mrs. Miller's lake?"

"She said she didn't want to."

"Because of me?"

"Not altogether, maybe. She said she's going to get a job." Julie looked momentarily charmed by this idea. "If I could get a job, I'd work in the ten-cent store, at the goldfish counter."

"Why not at a pet shop?"

"Oh, I couldn't. I think a pet shop is the saddest place in the world." She wondered what would happen to her alley cats while she was gone. Would they, on Friday afternoons, come with their wandlike waving tails, their proud heads, their little feet, into the alley where liverwurst had been so unfailingly presented? Would they drift about, puzzled and waiting, while she didn't come? It seemed almost wrong to leave when so many cats were dependent on her. Only, truly, they were not. Cats were never truly dependent on anyone. And hadn't they all come back, after the three-week period before Christmas when she'd been saving for presents? And it would be summer. It was easier for cats in summer, easier for anything or anyone poor. The cats would be all right, she told herself. And she really, truly, *had* to go to the country. "I'm going to take Amy with me," she told her father.

Ned, who'd been asleep, woke and said, "She'll run away."

"That's silly," Julie answered calmly. She glanced at the clock. "I guess I woke you up pretty early at that, Pop," she apologized.

Her father said he'd never been so pleasantly awakened before.

Like an urchin on whose closed lids and slack limbs the sun shines as thickly gold as on a sleeping prince, the tattered little park across from the school was wakened and warmed by June. Trees feathered into leaf, the patches of grass flung up tiny shoots, the stone fountain a little spray. Squirrels with hectic tails fled madly along the branches, and robins found their way to this dowdy scrap of nature.

"Robins," Verna said. "Would you believe it?" She studied a ruddy bird who bounced about with all the relish he might have displayed on country lawns or meadows.

"Lost his road map," Betty said. "Or he's in hiding. There probably won't be half a dozen of his kind here all year, and he figures he's safe."

"If I were that robin," Verna said raptly, "I'd just lift up my wings and fly and fly."

"Till you got where?" Morgan asked.

"To some other part of the world."

"And another robin?" Betty said slyly.

"Don't you ever think of anything else?"

"No less than you, Verna dear."

They yawned, first Morgan, then the other two, and went on eating lunch out of paper bags.

"I had lunch in the drugstore last week," Betty said, wiping her fingers on a paper napkin. "Honestly, that sodajerk is a riot. Do you know what he said to me?"

"Gasping to," Morgan said.

"He put my tomato sandwich down and looked at me and said, 'Some tomatoes have all the luck.' "

"He probably meant you, because he was serving you," Morgan decided.

"Is that all you had? Just tomato?" Verna asked. "No lettuce or bacon or anything?"

Betty grinned. "You two are just jealous because you didn't eat there."

"I did, about a month ago," Verna mused. "You know what he said to me?"

"What?"

"He put my sandwich down and looked at me and said, 'Good luck.' "

Betty and Morgan rocked with laughter. They'd been, all three of them, laughing continuously since they'd come over at the lunch bell. They wore light blouses and skirts, bobby socks and hair ribbons. They felt free—freer than the robins at their feet or the sparrows overhead, lighter than the shimmering leaves, gayer than—oh, gayer than anything they saw around them.

"We could just skip this afternoon," Betty said. "We really don't have to go back at all."

"I know. That's why I'm going," Morgan said. "I adore doing things I don't have to."

"Or shouldn't."

"Who doesn't?"

"Search me." Betty stretched her arms high above her head. "No more, no more, no more," she crooned. "We're finished tomorrow, and we don't have to go to school any more."

"I never knew you hated school so much," Morgan said.

"It isn't as if you couldn't do the work, or anything. I mean, you get better marks than Verna or me."

"That's no standard," Betty grinned. Characteristically, Verna flushed and Morgan nodded vague agreement. "What I mean is," Betty continued, "we won't have to go to that crawly crypt over there any more. I swear there've been times when I expected to find a mummy wrapped up in shredding linen when I opened my locker. Look at the thing!" They all looked. "It's a grave, isn't it? There lie all my young aspirations, molding away because they couldn't grow in such an atmosphere."

"You mean you don't have any left?" Verna said.

"I mean I'll have to grow a whole new set, in different ground."

"Oh well," Morgan said. "I don't think school was so bad."

Betty giggled. "That Tom has certainly wrought curious changes in you."

"Maybe," Morgan said. "I guess he's made me understand that learning isn't something a lot of teachers are trying to trip you up with."

"I never thought it was," Betty said.

"We're talking about me," Morgan said mildly. "And I did. And now I don't."

"Now that you're practically through with it, you mean."

"Not necessarily. Just because you leave school doesn't mean you stop learning, does it?"

"I don't know. That is, I know for me, but not for you, and as you say, we're talking about you."

Verna, never quite at ease when Betty and Morgan talked this way, crumpled her paper lunch bag and moved impatiently, but the other two didn't notice.

"Did I tell you that I've decided to go to college?" Betty asked suddenly.

Morgan looked at her dubiously. "No. You didn't."

189

"Well, you don't have to use that tone of voice, because I am."

"Where?"

"Oh . . . somewhere."

Morgan shrugged, and then smiled. What if Betty did say things that everyone knew were silly, or not true. At least there was a sort of flair to Betty's lying, a masterly indifference to whether anyone believed or not, and a sort of point to what she lied about. Sure, Betty would like to go to college. Practically anyone would. Not me, Morgan realized glumly. I wouldn't like it at all. But most people would. Verna, she remembered, had once said she wanted to, though of course only to meet boys, and Verna wasn't saying anything about it now. But if it made Betty feel good to simply announce that she was going, who were they to laugh at her? Lying, she thought, might sometimes be the only defense Betty had against a life that had not yet given her anything beautiful. And didn't they all want that? So, if Betty had spent her years till now in an ugly place, having to take care of her dear but sick grandmother, having to watch her nice but giddy mother run around so much that she couldn't herself, who could blame her for trying to dress things up, somehow? Morgan had never felt so close, so understanding, with Betty before. Besides, she thought with surprise, some people lied for a living and made it pay. Actors did, and writers, and probably lots of others that she couldn't think of now, being somewhat amazed at having evolved the idea at all. Probably, in some way or other, everyone lied. Only most people managed to conceal it, or make it a profession, and either of those seemed more acceptable to the world than Betty's rather simple approach. "You know," she said, "you could go to college at night."

Betty, about to say grandly that she intended to go away to Cornell, or some other magnificently caparisoned campus where she could be a cheerleader and a sorority sister (at the movies, Betty superbly identified with the successful girls, the ones who were immediately "bid" to all the best "houses," and not with the unfortunates who had their lives ruined—often committing suicide—because unsuitable backgrounds or uneven hemlines barred entrance through the charmed portals), looked thoughtful. "I *had* considered it," she said slowly. "Only . . . it seems like such a . . . big thing. Do you really think so?"

"Lots of people do. I could ask Tom about it, if you wanted."

Betty hesitated. "All right," she said at last. "That would be nice of you. Not, of course, that I wouldn't have *preferred* . . ." She interrupted herself, repeated, "that would be nice. I wonder how much it costs?" she added with unusual candor.

"I'll have to ask that too."

"You could do it," Verna said. "If you worked, I mean."

"Oh, I'll have to get a job," Betty said, forgetting in her casual way that she'd just practically said she'd be away at school. "That's for sure."

"I've got one," Verna said suddenly.

The other two turned to stare at her.

"But—where? I mean, when?" Morgan said. "How did you do that?"

Verna moved her shoulders back as though they pained her. "I saw a sign in a window, and I just went in and asked, and they said yes. I start next week." She didn't seem proud or pleased, but rather sorry that she'd mentioned it at all.

"Where is it?" Betty persisted.

"It's in a cafeteria," Verna said flatly. "I'm going to dish out food from twelve to eight, half hour for dinner. The pay isn't bad," she added.

Betty and Morgan said nothing at first. Betty was being

191

personally revolted by the sound of the job, and relieved that it was none of hers (*she* intended to work in a swank department store on Fifth Avenue), and Morgan was wondering, for the first time, how you went about getting a job. It made her feel weak, as though all her muscles had slackened. They really were finishing school, the three of them. Ugly or not, that school had protected them all for four years, and now, tomorrow, it would cast them forth and the business of arranging their lives as working people would begin. I'm frightened, she thought. I feel almost the way I did when Mother died. What did you do when the place of refuge closed its doors, the person of refuge closed her eyes? What had she done when her mother died? She shivered in the sun, trying to remember, but her mind was glazed and darkened. She was here, but the past and the future were walled, and behind those walls her crowding future, the solutions of her past, gave no answer to questions, no help to weakness. She wound her fingers together and tried to think.

"We'd better get back, if we're going," Betty said, getting up. She tossed their lunch bags in an iron mesh garbage receptacle. "Last time for that, too."

"Oh, don't," Morgan said softly, but they didn't hear her.

Chapter Twelve

Dear Morgy and Pop: I like this place.
There is a lady who lives down the road
named Mrs. McCray and her husband is an awfully nice old
man, he has traveled all over the world and has a garden that
is swell he gets plants sent to him from everywhere and has
the littlest rosebush in the world, not even a foot high. He
has all kinds of other flowers that we've never seen before
and in the house he has a collection of different things, sea-
shells and crystels. I bet you wont believe it but he has two
little fishes that are 17 million years old, they are all dried
up and look like little round stones. The best thing of all is
he has a lot of arrow heads he has found around—stone—
that the indians used and he gave me one, its black. I wish
you were here. I miss you. Geff is teaching me to swim pretty
good. Love, Ned.

Dear Pop and Morgan: This is really the most wonderful
place in the world. The lake comes practically to the door
and Geoff takes us out in his canoe and has been teaching me
to dive and Ned to swim. His vacation will last two weeks
more and I'm glad. There are a couple of girls, a bit older
than me, who live up the road and I've gotten to know them

pretty well. They're like all the rest about boys but somehow that doesn't seem as silly as it used to.

I do not mean that I'm interested in a boy, but they're having some down over the week end and there'll be one for me, as there are three. I'm a little nervous about this, but not angry, you know, the way I used to be.

Amy is *crazy* about it here. I've put a bell on her neck, attached to a garter so she won't strangle if she gets caught on a bush. She looks rather wicked. My back and arms are all brown and I lie in the sun for hours every day, which is practically the nicest part of the country. Pop, I do read the poetry, and you were right, it's different from reading it in an apartment. Don't be hurt, and of course I miss you both and want to be with you, but I love this place more than anything I've ever known. Mrs. Miller won't let me do much to help her, because they have a woman who comes in every day and she says I'm too thin and should just relax. Isn't that nice of her?

And the fields are full of daisies and clover and flowers I don't know the names of. Wood sorrel sounds nice, doesn't it? Only I don't know which one it is. Mr. McCray's garden is like heaven. He has it decorated with rocks, minerals, crystals, coal. There's one big red crystal that is the most beautiful thing you ever saw. He said he's going to give me a piece of crystal. He made a fireplace out of different stones in his living room and you should see it at night. It shines. My room is very pretty and looks at the lake. I have it all alone, except for Amy, who doesn't always stay. It's strange, at night, to be alone, listening to the trees and the water. Is Tom happy at the camp? Don't you miss him? Love and kisses, Julie

Dear Pop: This letter is just for you, so don't show it to Morgy. She's very sweet, but sometimes I want to say things that I don't think she'd care about, so just explain that I'm writing you one for yourself. I'd like to try to explain something to you, or ask you something, I'm not sure which. It's a windy dark night, and I feel very old. I know you won't laugh. I do feel old, and I don't trust myself to become a good person, and it bothers me. Not always, but tonight it does. Do you know what I remind myself of? Those people who pinch all over a box of candy, trying to find a piece they like, and finally they've got nothing but these sort of squashed—rejections—with cracks top and bottom and the filling coming out the sides. That's what I do with my life, and what I want to know is, will I stop? I know we don't talk much about things in our family, but once in a while you and I talk a little and I get the feeling it could be more if we were ever alone. Like—I pray. I pray every night, and I have for years, though I didn't tell anyone. And I always say God Bless Mother. Now you know we aren't religious especially, but praying helps me. It's an outlet. It's a habit, really. You see, if someone knew that I prayed, they might think it was lovely and sincere of me, but I know it isn't, because I'm using it to help *me*, not for any other reason. Do you suppose I'm ever going to have any sort of character? Don't let all this bother you, Pop. It's just that it's dark and windy and I think too much—about myself, I guess. Love, J.

Dear Morgy: Since I sent my last letter to Pop, I'll send this to you. Those boys came on the week end. In the afternoon we—Jan and Barby and these boys and Ned and Geoff and I—oh well, might as well give the boys' names too—one is Percy, but he likes to be called Piggy. Isn't that ridiculous? The other two are Fred and Hank. Piggy's the one for me. I mean, he's the one I got, and he's really pretty nice. Tall and doesn't talk *too* much and dives divinely. Where was I? Oh yes, in the afternoon we all cleaned the barn, the back yard, and the back steps. It was fun, except that the dog, Plunder, killed a robin, which made us all, especially Ned and me, pretty sad. We buried it. And now, Morgan, the strangest part! I went *dancing*. I was scared to death when they said we were going to a roadhouse down the way and dance, but Piggy said he'd stay home too if I did, and that wasn't fair. So we went. It's a sort of old barny place with a juke box, where only young people go. That is, one old couple (not really old, you know, still in the dancing stage, but definitely not high school) came in and they left right away. And I danced. I just did, Morgy. Piggy says I'm very good, but I think it's really that he is.

Mrs. Miller says I'm putting on weight and she's pleased. I'm not really, because I get on the scales every morning, but I must look better. Mr. Miller comes every week end. Geoff has to leave tomorrow. His vacation is over, but he's coming up week ends too. Julie P.S. Plunder and Amy adore each other.

Dear Morgy and Pop: Its a lucky thing I broght these sneakers along. Its raining. In answer to your question I am quite sure it was a cow that chased Geff and my snake wasnt asleep he was walking. You never said if you like the things I stick in my letters, those pieces of leaf and all. The spider bites all gone now. The other day we were cleaning the yard and things and Plundor killed a baby robbin, one of the three little birds I told you about that were eggs when we got here. Well when we were all sure it was really dead we buried it with bird seed and gravel that was colored that Mr. McCray gave us and a penny to cross the River Sticks. Theres a lot of birds here, mockingbirds, goldfinshes, redwinged blackbirds, crows, robbins, and some called oven birds. In the morning they sing and at night but not much during the day. Julie is getting different, shes a bit nicer to be around and doesnt have those funny ideas so much or doesnt say so anyway, which is just as good. If you dont write to me I wont answer. Do you think you could send me 50¢. One day Mrs. Miller said shed like to have Julie and me live with her always. We talked about it after and we like her very much and this place but dont want to. Love, Ned

Dear Pop: Thank you for your letter. It was so funny, but so good, to have you know what I was talking about. I don't feel like that all the time. In fact, lately I am much better. It must be your letter, and the sunshine. Love, Julie

Chapter Thirteen

Morgan hadn't gone to the graduation exercises. "I'm too busy, Pop," she explained when he asked. "Anyway, it doesn't mean anything to me. I suppose it should, but it just doesn't. There're about three hundred people and nobody really cares about anyone but their own kids, so the noise and talk is awful, and it's too long, and . . . Oh well."

She had to pack for the two children, do some mending of clothes, some inescapable shopping. And she had, too, to prepare herself for finding a job. Betty was constantly around, talking of the advisability of wearing navy blue with white collar and cuffs for job hunting.

"It's the appearance, that's what counts," she told Morgan. "Crisp white collars make all the difference."

"I don't have a navy-blue dress."

"Then maybe you'd better get one."

"I can't afford a dress till I've got a job."

Betty could see the reasoning in this, but was privately convinced that her own navy blue with white would be a talisman to put her behind the perfume counter in the finest shop imaginable.

Morgan had bought a school yearbook, a thick, glossy-papered memento, inscribed here and there by students or teachers, which would shortly be relegated to the bookcase and forgotten. There were small pictures, twenty to a page, of this graduating class, with italicized mottoes, brief biographies, young faces.

"Morgan Connor. *Dream Girl*."

Now how in the world, Morgan wondered, did they figure that out? She'd never been curious enough even to wonder who got the yearbook together, and was astonished to find this percipience with respect to herself.

"Oh, that," Betty explained. "They just ask your teachers and some of the kids in your class. They certainly taped you, didn't they?"

They hadn't, Morgan thought, taped everyone. Verna's picture, not a very good one, with a sober expression and an exaggeration to the long face, was captioned, "*Is't not fine to dance and sing?*"

Morgan frowned. "What does *that* mean?"

Betty thought it meant they didn't know what to say about Verna. "They always use something like that when they can't figure a person."

Next to Betty's own picture was the provocative, "*Oh call it by some other name, for friendship sounds so cold.*" Morgan wasn't sure it was complimentary, but Betty was charmed. Betty, also, was the only one of the three who had a couple of clubs and a nickname included in her biography. " 'Bets' is one of our most popular cheerleaders, and you can check with 'Phil' Dunning on that. She admits adoring radishes, Van Johnson, and late sleeping. Her pet 'peeves' are cold water and people who say 'What's cookin'?' Like her ambition, her future alma mater is subject to change without notice. Gold Masque Players, Cheerleader, Basketball Varsity."

"Where'd they get all this goofy stuff about you?" Morgan asked.

Betty looked bland. "Can't imagine."

Morgan had, on an impulse not entirely explainable, since she was scarcely an interested or applied English student, asked Mrs. Reinholt to sign her book. She didn't understand the quotation Mrs. Reinholt had given her. *"For we, which now behold these present days, Have eyes to wonder, but lack tongues to praise."*

"That is," she told Betty, "I expect I understand what it means. But what's it got to do with me?"

"Did I tell you what she wrote in mine? *'Success in circuit lies.'* I think it's a crack of some kind."

It was the last time in either of their lives that they mentioned or thought of Mrs. Rheinholt. Like the yearbook itself, she was remarked briefly, with little comprehension, and put aside.

"*Have* you thought any more about college?" Morgan asked Betty, who shrugged and said she didn't know. She'd *thought* about it, but the excitement of having a job to consider seemed more important now.

"If you are going to go, you should start applying or something."

But Betty continued vague. "Angie says I'm changing my mind so often she's in danger of losing hers."

Morgan lost interest. "How's your grandmother?"

"She seems better. Or as better as she'll ever be." The words were heartless, but possibly the tone was not.

Morgan decided not to look for a job until the children were packed off to their presumed three weeks at the lake. If Ned, suddenly stricken with homesickness before he left, had known that the three weeks would prove to be all summer, he might not have gone at all, but once he arrived at the lake he promptly fell in love, in his gay darting way, with everything around him.

They drove to the lake. Not in Bluebird, for Tom was to take that next day and head for the Catskills and his summer camp. "Do you actually expect that contrivance to take you 150 miles?" his mother asked. "It isn't as if it were all level ground. You're going into hills." But Tom defended his auto with aplomb. "She's not, perhaps, the most fashionable car on the road, but she has a sound mind in a sound body." At Geoff's snort he added, "I don't think you're the one to speak, my boy, since you've never managed anything more advanced in the way of locomotion than your own feet." Tom was enormously complacent over having got a car of his own before his older brother had. ".Well, at least my feet don't rattle," Geoff said imperturbably.

The morning they left was high and spacious, as though summer required more air than winter, as though it ranged lightly space that winter, pressed with cold, could never reach. Morgan and Mr. Connor, waiting on the sidewalk for a last farewell, a last gesture of the arm, wondered if they never would get started, if Geoff would never have done with shifting the luggage, Mr. Miller would never cease inspecting the tires and the seating arrangements. Finally, when Morgan was sure she'd never hold back her tears another minute, the motor sounded, the wheels began their slow initial revolution, the Miller car swung gently from the curb, and Ned, who had wished to be underprivileged for just such a privilege as this, was waving shakily out the back window as he went toward his summer in the country. The car going around the corner was a reprieve.

Morgan and her father looked at each other, sighed, turned back to the development, to their apartment.

"I don't think he wanted to go," Morgan said.

"They both looked a little uncertain. The charm of the

unknown has a way of evaporating when you're actually on the point of getting into it. They'll be all right," he decided wearily, standing beside his daughter in the apartment that thronged with emptiness. It had been, the whole enterprise, tiring and saddening. The children had vacillated between ebullience and total refusal to go at all. Morgan had looked more and more drawn, though whether that was because of Ned, or Tom, or her sudden tense withdrawal on the subject of jobs, Mr. Connor didn't know. Dan, himself, had simply submitted, and submission, he sometimes thought, presented the hardest role of all. Surrendering what you couldn't possibly keep seemed like logic, but felt like a forecast of Hell. *"When last I died, and dear, I die As often as from thee I go. . . ."* was not, he thought, written solely of lovers, but of all who love and leave each other. *Parting.* What we're born through, live and die through, and everything else just a waiting between. He was, for a moment, nearly wrenched into clarity by this latest parting, and then the blessed smoke that stood between him and reality drifted to his defense. "I think I'll lie down for a while," he said to Morgan. "I'm tired today, for some reason."

Morgan thought the reason plain enough, but merely answered in the uneasy tone that her father's emotions seemed so often to summon, that if he didn't mind, she was supposed to see Tom. "He's going tomorrow, you know, and we thought . . ." She broke off as her father turned away, removing his coat.

"It's all right, Morgy," he said. "I really do want to lie down, and you have nothing to do." He looked back, smiling a little. "I'm glad you'll be here this summer. I wanted you to go, and yet—"

"I know, Pop," she said, embarrassed by the tremor in her voice. "To tell the truth, I don't think I'd make much of a country girl. I *like* the city."

Now her father seemed unable to continue any conversation at all. They smiled at each other once more, placatingly, and she went out to meet Tom.

They spent the entire afternoon and evening together, and there were times when Morgan wished it were tomorrow, and he'd already gone. Like the parting from Ned on the curb, this was going on too long. They took a ride in Bluebird, up the East Side Drive, across town to the Park, where they fed squirrels and pigeons, sitting on a sundusted bench and not talking for minutes at a time. They had dinner in a downtown diner. They went to a movie. The hours went by, and Tom carefully kept their words on trivialities, on baseball and space travel and the likelihood that Bluebird would be intact ten years hence. Morgan felt strangeness filling her, like water slowly filling a jar, until, when they left the movie, it spilled over and she spoke to him frantically.

"I don't know what you think, or what you've been meaning all day," she said in a low voice, looking straight ahead as they walked, "but I don't wish to hear any more of either. I might just as well have stayed home, or you gone out with anyone. We've done nothing but talk about nothing the whole horrible time and I'm tired of it . . ." Her eyes smarted, her heels hit the sidewalk with hard little slaps, and still Tom said nothing. "If you . . . if you have something important to say, like . . . like not . . . caring about me any more, then for goodness sakes *say* it. Don't go on and on like a radio commercial or something, just using up your voice and using up our time. What am I supposed to think about it, or do about it, or anything about it?" she asked miserably. Her voice suddenly shaping the fright and uncertainty that had grown all afternoon now made them realer than ever, and she wanted, for the first time in months, to throw herself on the bed and cry. It was just too much. "Everybody's *leaving*," she said plaintively. "And nobody cares except me." That, of course, wasn't true. "Ned cares, I guess."

"*Morgan.*" Tom said her name, said nothing further for the length of a city block, but Morgan relaxed. Actually, he needn't have said more at all. The torment in his voice uttering one word was enough to quiet the dreadful unsureness this day had brought.

"I'm sorry," she said softly. "I should understand better." And yet, she thought, if ever I doubted I loved him, now I am sure I do. To give up so easily a chance to be wronged, to wring contrite words and passionate denials was a gesture possible only to love, and Morgan, without putting words to it, felt what her gesture meant. For what can be more delicious than to wound and draw back and distort meanings, knowing that the moment of submission and reconciliation can be arrived at whenever you wish . . . a gambit, almost a policy, known to the feminine and not easily relinquished. Morgan relinquished it now, unable to bear the pain in Tom's voice. "It's all right," she said. "I'm just sort of . . . upset, today."

"Upset?" he said. "Well, that's a word for it."

They were at her apartment door. Morgan leaned against the wall, and there flashed through her mind the memory of Marty and a shadowed hallway. She looked at Tom, standing, hands in his pockets, eyes on the floor, a little away from her. If he were Marty, he'd be right in front of her, hands on the wall beside her, pressing close . . . She shook her head a little, and Tom looked up inquiringly. "I was just thinking," she said, "how different you are from other people."

"I'm not, really," he said slowly. "That's the whole point, Morgy. It's what I've been trying to say, in a not very bright way. And why I had to take this job. Don't you think I'd like to stay here this summer, and see you? Do you think I *want* to go up to the Catskills and play games? Only," he added with a trace of a smile, "better there than here." Morgan blushed. "Well," he burst out, "I'm sorry. But there it is. I grabbed this job before I could get a chance to think it over, because if I *had* thought it over—" He took a step toward her, then leaned forward and rubbed his cheek against hers. "There now," he said, "I'm leaving. Immediately. I love you, Morgan." He kissed her lightly and went down the hall, through the stairway door. Morgan entered the dark apartment. It was funny that she didn't feel anything at all, except tired.

The day after Tom left, Verna came to see Morgan. "How do I look?" she said gaily.

"You look fine," Morgan answered. Verna did. Bright-eyed, excited, in a cotton dress that was new and pretty. "What's it all about?"

"I'm going away."

"Away? How do you mean?"

"I mean I'm going to get on a bus tomorrow and go away. I have a suitcase all packed, and Mom's and Emma's blessing. Not my father's, need I add. As if I cared."

"Where are you going?"

"Back up to that hotel where I worked last summer."

"But you said you'd never go back there."

"I know. But I got a letter from the manager and he asked if I'd come back. They liked me, I think. I'm going to be a waitress, instead of a maid, and that's nicer." And maybe . . . just maybe . . . she told herself, that boy would be back, and perhaps this year he'd see a change in her. She'd be calmer this year. Not talk so much, or care so much. She'd be very dignified and reserved, and maybe. . . .

"What about the other job you had? The one in the cafeteria?"

"Well, that's what I came to see you about. I mean, besides saying good-by and all. Do you want it?" Morgan hesitated. "We could go over there together," Verna went on, "and I'd explain, and tell that man, Mr. Krebble, who hired me, that you're going to take it instead. I'm sure he wouldn't care. I mean," she broke off, "if you wanted to. I just thought perhaps it'd be better than looking . . ."

A cafeteria, Morgan was thinking. It wasn't the sort of job she'd thought of. She didn't, actually, know what she had thought of, except in terms of alarm about finding it. A cafeteria. Betty would scoff, and the others would probably think she was spineless. But the thing was, she *was* spineless. When the really big job had come, the taking over of a family, in a role too old for her, she had managed. Managed pretty well, too, she thought. Maybe it had used all her courage to pick up the dropped pieces of her mother's job and put them together, hold them together. Maybe that was why she'd been, these past weeks, so frightened of trying another. She didn't especially want to work in a cafeteria, but she didn't want to work anywhere else, either. "What did you say you were going to do there?" she asked. "Dish up food, or something?"

When Verna came in with Morgan and a confused explanation of their plan, Mr. Krebble considered having a tantrum. The heat was distressing him so that a word was a rock in his mouth. Miserably he decided it was too hot to be angry. He looked at Morgan and found her clean and calm, splendidly healthy-looking. For a moment he wanted to ask why she would take a job here, and then was afraid she wouldn't. It would be like having a bright cold brook, a willow tree, in this place of fat-brindled soup, limp spaghetti, fried fish, this room of food where the mashed potatoes took on a carving consistency, the firm gravy looked like lava, and all the flavor was in the steam. He looked at the black menu overhead, where little white letters spelled out, "Today's Soup du Jour—Chicken Noodle," and said, "I'll be very glad if you take the—the position, Miss, uh . . ."

She waited up for her father that night, and told him. After she'd explained the change, and that Mr. Krebble had been agreeable, she thought her father wasn't even going to answer. Finally she said, "Is something wrong, Pop?"

Mr. Connor sighed. "Oh no. I suppose nothing's wrong. A job's a job, and I've always maintained that any honest job is nothing to be ashamed of." But was that true? He was ashamed of his own job, not because there was anything wrong with it, but because he knew—thought—he was capable of something better. Shouldn't we, each of us, he wondered, work to the best of our capacity? Was dishing vegetables the best Morgan could manage? He felt a moment of icy rage and humiliation that he was afraid to direct against Morgan or himself, and so must aim at the world. What stupid circumstance would put this beautiful, gracious, in some ways very intelligent girl behind a pot of peas and carrots in a cafeteria under an El? It's money, he thought viciously, money. Because I can't send her to college, or even to a decent business school, all that she is has to be lost in the few things she isn't. Not trained for something better. And not, he thought with an abrupt weariness, not, in the way of the world, resourceful or independent. She could go out on her own and get a better job than this, but because she had a chance to take something already secured, she did. The sins of the father, the weakness of the father, is visited on his child. Julie wouldn't do this, he thought. Julie would *never* . . . Julie, also, would never have run this household, no matter what her age. Poor Morgy, he thought. She was destined, from the start, to be a mother and a wife. Not anything daring, or glimmering. Not a Morgan le Fay, ever. What a pity she can't marry that kid. Dan was acutely startled at the thought. But it was right. It was a pity they were so young, with so many stages to get through before they'd ever be able to marry, if they still wanted to when the time came. Morgan could never leave them . . . Julie, Ned, himself . . . now. And the boy had school, the Army . . . What a washout I am, he cried soundlessly. The very thought of Morgan's leaving alarmed him so that he said, hastily, as if in fear, "It'll probably work out fine, Morgan. You go to it." But he couldn't look at her, couldn't meet her grave glance which would, he knew, be quite undeceived. They avoided each other's eyes, as though they shared a shameful secret. Our mutual frailty, Dan thought, with resignation that was not calm, but bitter.

Chatham's was a large cafeteria under an El station. It was furnished with marble tables for four, chairs with worn wooden seats, and, in the center of each table, a lazy susan bearing catsup, salt, pepper and sugar and mustard. The plate-glass window, with "Chatham Cafeteria" in gold lettering and paper stickers advertising Specials, was at no time really dirty, and the floor, an expanse of small tile lozenges, at no time clean. Three large fans, fastened to the ceiling, stirred the air. Streamers of flypaper, successfully dotted black, swayed lazily in the currents.

Mr. Krebble, manager and cashier, was a wanly thin man harassed by undefined health problems. From nine in the morning till nine at night he sat behind the cashier's booth, head held in the palm of his hand, belching sadly. He stayed there except for occasional tours of the kitchen and serving areas. Twice a day he sat down at the table nearest his booth and ate meagerly. Morgan couldn't bear to watch him. He chewed slowly, with a strained expression and a full-looking chin, like a child who thinks this stuff may make him sick but has been told to eat it and like it. Morgan wondered why he bothered at all. If I were him, she thought, I'd go out of here mealtimes. I'd eat somewhere else. Or I'd just walk and not eat at all. She got her own hot dinner with the job, but had little appetite for it. After a week or so, standing over the steam table, ladling, spooning, tonging the slick gravied food into endless thrusting dishes, she'd close her eyes a moment and think that if she could face food after this, the only possible thing would be a cold green cucumber. A cucumber, crisp and chilly, with no taint of the cooking process.

Now and then, Mr. Krebble would be driven out of silence by anxieties too difficult to bear alone. "How do I look?" he'd ask Morgan, or Cora, or Mick, the big cook. "How do you think I'm looking?" He'd wait, breathing quickly, while they scrutinized his face. With kindness, they didn't answer too promptly, gave a moment's consideration before telling him he looked, "Fine, just fine. Seems like you've put on a little weight, too." He'd sigh deeply, content for the moment. But presently his eyes would begin to flicker as new apprehensions rose. Were people just being kind? Or bored with him? Were they telling the truth, or brushing him off? He'd put a few soda mints in his mouth, and make change for diners, and worry.

The fans curled, distributing sluggish air. There was always the rattle of silver, the flat ring of metal trays, the voices lifting and falling. Always the unpleasant pitch of the cash register, the advancing and receding roar of the El. Morgan shoved a well of gravy into a heap of mashed potatoes. "Veg?" she asked the plate.

A voice beyond the hand that held the thick dish said, "String beans."

She supplied string beans, released the plate, reached for another that hovered in air. "Meat or fish?"

209

She worked afternoons from twelve to eight. The usual five to seven peak of diners was well under way, and Morgan's vision was preempted by the passage of plates, her hearing by selections of heavy food. How *could* people eat this way in hot weather? Her hair was covered with a white cap made of cheesecloth, and perspiration misted her upper lip. She was aware of Mr. Krebble glancing at her now and then with the same hopeful devotion he gave his bottle of soda mints. But most of the time he just sat behind the cashier's desk, staring down, making change without a word. Some of the people who waited while he poked the register and caught the sliding drawer as it flew at him had been eating in the Chatham for years. Cora and Morgan had a word for familiar faces, but Mr. Krebble recognized no one.

"How're you doin', kid?" Cora asked. She was on salads, breads and desserts today. They alternated, by their own arrangement, sharing the steam.

"Fine," Morgan said. She smiled at Cora, who was stout and sometimes cross, but never with Morgan. "Just dandy." And she couldn't help recalling the importance she used to put upon catsup in a little blue bowl. How could anyone who really liked things to be nice work in the Chatham? Morgan didn't know the answer. She enjoyed Cora and Mick, was sorry for Mr. Krebble, and disliked the job. But the pay was, as Verna had said, pretty good. Anyway, did it really make a difference, what you worked at? After only two weeks, Morgan was unprepared to say. "There's one thing," she told Cora. "I'm losing weight." Then she was sorry she'd said it, as Cora obviously was not losing any. "Meat or fish?" she asked the plate before her.

The mail came about nine in the morning. Morgan would let herself quietly out of the apartment, hoping not to waken her father, and run downstairs with the little mailbox key. She'd abstract Tom's almost daily letter (Dan considered that practically psychopathic fealty, but as in so many other matters was judging from his own viewpoint) and carry the rest up for the two of them to share at breakfast.

"Place sounds like the Garden of Eden," Dan said, wiping off his fingers and picking up Ned's letter to reread. He smiled, "And Mr. McCray is its keeper."

"He sounds like an awfully nice man."

"Certainly does. Seventeen million years old, eh? These fish of his. Have you ever seen a fossil?"

"I don't know if I have or not. Isn't it nice that Julie has a room of her own?"

They came to know all the people, the places, to feel the sunshine and the cool lake water, to wonder how Geoff made out with the cow, to sorrow over the murdered robin. ("Not murdered," Dan said when Morgan called it that. "Animals don't murder, they kill." "Is there a difference?" "Of course. Killing is a barbarism." "And murder?" "A pure product of civilization.") They sent forgotten clothing, money when they could, and letters of their own, Morgan far more often than her father. They breakfasted together, spoke lightly, and somehow the weeks passed. Mrs. Miller wrote and asked to keep the two children for the remainder of the summer, and what, as Dan said, could they reply but yes? "It's good for them," he explained, as though Morgan had disagreed. "If they came home we'd probably all be miserable, with them thinking about the lake and us thinking we'd deprived them of something."

"I know," Morgan said. But she was disappointed. The summer was lonely, her father more withdrawn than ever, and she had no one to talk to. Betty had got a job in a Fifth Avenue department store, just as she had said she would. She said she was on the "Flying Squad," a group being especially groomed for better positions and usually limited to college girls. Morgan hoped she really was. In any case, Betty had made a lot of new friends to keep her busy. "I don't ever ask them to my house," she explained to Morgan, on one of their infrequent meetings. "I mean, it's all right, and I don't mind some people seeing the sort of place I live in. But these people are, oh you know . . ."

"I know," Morgan said.

And I do know, she thought, lying on her bed one evening after her bath. I know, more or less, what Pop means and what Betty means. I know, truly, what Tom means. She pressed his last letter against her cheek. It was almost worth having him away, to get his letters. But what I'd like to know is, what do I mean?

"Here's one from Julie, just for you," she said to her father one morning, handing him the envelope.

"Oh?" He turned it around. "That's funny."

"Not especially. Why shouldn't she want to write just you now and then?"

Privately, Dan was pleased. "I'll read it later," he said, trying to think of some good explanation for that, failing, and deciding it didn't matter, as Morgan was already deep in the daily clarion from Tom Miller. After a while she put her letter away with smoothing gestures, as though it were a little life, and rose. "Pop, I have to go shopping, so I'd better do it now. If I bring the stuff up, you'll have time to put it away, won't you?"

Dan looked up absently. "Oh, sure. Isn't it funny, Morgan, how we ask things we know the answers to perfectly well? All of us, I mean. I imagine half the exchange of conversation in the world would stop if none of us asked what we knew was already answered."

Morgan nearly yawned. "You mean like saying 'what?' when you really heard. I suppose it's to fill time. People have to talk to each other, don't they? And you can't always have something important to say."

" 'I gotta use words when I talk to you. . . .' "

"What?"

They both smiled. "Well," Morgan said. "I *didn't* understand that."

"It's a poem. A line from a poem."

"It certainly doesn't sound very poetic."

"Nevertheless, it is."

"I guess I'd better go."

When she'd gone, Dan took a clean knife and carefully slit open his letter. He lit a cigarette, sat beside the window, opened the pages and began to read. "Dear Pop: This letter is just for you. . . ."

The room was warm, the air from the river a little fetid, and hot. But Dan's fingers, holding the letter, grew cold, and something within, like a seed of ice, spread and numbed him. "Can you tell me? . . . It's just that it's dark and windy. . . ." Dan put his head in his hands. The cigarette twisted in his fingers and he had to get up, to put it out.

When do you begin to fail your children, if you love them? If you do not, of course, the failure begins at conception. But no children had been more loved than his and Sarah's. Where then did his failure begin to lay out the path of uncertainty which led to this letter? Or how, he thought painfully, at what time did I give her the security which would lead her to send it to me? Tribute and remonstrance both, and both would have to be answered.

Morgan, coming in with the groceries, found her father sitting at the window, the letter in his drooping hand. "Anything wrong?" she asked nervously.

He looked up and shook his head. "No." He rubbed his hand across his chin. "No. I was just thinking."

Morgan nodded. She was used to that. For a moment she'd been frightened by his expression, but Pop's thinking was a process she respected and, generally, avoided. "I'm just going to dump the groceries in the kitchen, Pop. If you can, remember to put them away. Some of the stuff has to go in the icebox."

"I'll do it, dear."

"Well . . . all right. You don't mind if I go now?"

"I suppose you must." He hesitated. I just can't ask about that job now, he thought. I have too much to deal with. He got up with a brisk air and started for the kitchen. "Might as well take care of this little job right now."

"Okay," Morgan said. She glanced at the letter in his hand, turned away. "See you," she told him.

He stored their provisions with competence, keeping the neat alignment of Morgan's shelves undisturbed, remarking to himself on the immaculate air of the kitchen, of the whole apartment. But how did she manage it? That girl works all the time, he thought. He wished she could have got a job as . . . as what? What job would fit Morgan, till she arrived at the obviously predestined wedding? Well . . . she'd make a splendid figurehead for a boat. She'd be ravishingly perfect as a princess sleeping till her bridegroom came. A dairymaid, he thought. What a bonny dairymaid she'd be. Only not in this country. In Ireland. Oh, she could be almost anything Irish, legendary or real. Deirdre, dairymaid, warrior queen. Without disloyalty to Morgan, he wondered what their lives would be, hers and Tom's, should they actually marry. Many a man had wed a lovely face, a sweet temper, and then found himself wondering what to talk about. On the other hand, many a man had wed a brain and then found himself wondering how to endure it. Tom and Morgan and all the other young ones, they took their chances. Time would tell them what they'd have to know.

The letter lay on the cot where he had dropped it. It was no use to think of anything else. "It's no go the groceries, and no go the auld sod," he muttered, picking the letter up, re-reading its cryingly sincere message in the affected hand-writing. Little circles over the i's, strangely contoured e's and m's. He found a sheet of paper, a pen, and sat at the table, not writing. Elbow on the window sill, he leaned over, look-ing out. There were the women spanking their baby buggies away and back again. There the waifish tan dog who seemed to be on any city street, any time of day, running along with his head lower than his bony shoulders. There the sidewalk children playing jacks and games less innocent. Julie, he thought. What about Julie. She should, perhaps, have had a family life. The sort we like to represent as typically Ameri-can. A house outside the city, steady loving father, wise but playful mother. A rumpus room. If she had had all that, she might not have read poetry, might not be following this cir-cuitous thinking path to reach herself. Would it have been better for her? Was it better to have values and a background which put questions to sleep and convinced you that not only had you found yourself but that the "you" found was just what the doctor ordered? There was much to be said for stable rearing, with the proper number of parents and or-derly attention to reading matter, associates and orthodontia. Wasn't there, also, a redeeming feature to the life Julie had so far known? Something to say for the lack of fetters, the freedom to choose, the freedom, even, to make mistakes? Would a carefully guided, suburban Julie have written that letter, or carried a battered volume of modern poetry to the country? When she'd been a little girl, Julie had been tor-mentingly persistent with hypothetical questions. If she'd been born a year later, a day later, would she have been the same person? If Pop had married someone else, or mother had, would there be a Julie at all? And if there were, would it be Julie in her own self, or some other girl, or a little bit of each? If she'd been a boy instead of a girl, how much of what she was would still be living? Dan had sometimes smiled, sometimes evaded, once in a while tried to give a vestige of reply. "How can we tell, Julie? How do we know what would happen if we'd taken the other road? I can't imagine your being anyone but Julie, and I'm sure you can't. But if you had been, that other girl might be asking just your question now. Why don't you assume for a while that the other girl *is* asking, and you're the answer?" He'd said that once, and intrigued her into silence. But no such facility would satisfy the girl who had written this letter, the girl Julie had become. If there's an instance in the world of demand exceeding supply, Dan thought, it's here. There will always be more questions than answers. And if it were not so, he reflected, we might very well cease to question at all We might not even wish to live.

Slowly he unscrewed the cap of his pen. Perhaps he could answer . . . a little, tell her part of what he'd just been thinking. He wrote slowly, for a long time. It was painful, this effort to communicate with a mind and heart outside his own. It had been so long that the vulture, the creature he'd created, had been feeding on his heart in privacy and silence.

"Well, what do you think of Julie?" Morgan asked about a week later.

"Think of her?" Dan repeated cautiously. That morning the mail had brought a letter each for Morgan and him from Julie. Had Julie said something of what she'd told him to Morgan, too? He was aware of disappointment. Aware of Julie's new power to wake in him feelings he'd thought were

216

put by for the rest of his life. The brief, almost flip little note he held in his hand had hurt him . . . before he forced himself to remember the strange quality of correspondence. The hand and the mind may burn with emotion as the words are shaped, the letter written, and anxious thoughts follow the message on its course (Is it there? Can it have arrived?), but between the writing and the reading some diversion, some alteration, must occur, and though the reader now burns with the hurt, the passion, the confusion or triumph of the words, the writer must be, at that moment, eating a peach, or wondering if it will rain, or answering someone's comments in a tone quite unlike that of the letter he'd written a few days before. If we are going to write each other letters, Dan thought, any of us, we must be prepared always for contradiction and cross-purpose, must always be prepared for the answer that misinterprets or falls short.

But *had* Julie spoken to Morgan as she had to him? It would be, unlike the note in his hand which was merely alteration of mood, a sort of betrayal. "What about her?"

"Oh, the dates and the dancing, and the long list of things to be sent. Here." She handed him her letter.

Dan relaxed, reading it. "She certainly does need a lot of stuff, for a girl who never paid much attention to *things*."

"I couldn't be happier. That letter sounds absolutely girlish. Cute."

"She sounds very gay," he said. Well, perhaps it was his letter, or the sunshine. Perhaps not. That poem ". . . *and only the snow can begin to explain how children are apt to forget to remember. . . .*"

The letters came faithfully, though with longer intervals between as the summer went on. Dan and Morgan agreed to let the children stay away all summer, and they both became

lonesomer. They recognized names, pondered over the walking snake, discovered that Ned wanted to take a bee home
for honey making, that Julie and Amy took long walks together. They met each other over these letters, at breakfast.
Now and then Morgan told him a little of what Tom was
doing.

But with them, unremarked upon and never forgotten,
was the fact of Morgan's job.

Chapter Fourteen

On a Sunday in August, Morgan and Betty took the train and went to Jones Beach. "Don't take a thing but your towel and bathing suit," Betty said firmly. "This is one time I won't eat from a sack on the sand. We'll buy hot dogs and pop." Morgan hesitated, agreed. After all, she was making enough money to manage a small treat for herself now and then.

The ride was overlong, perspiry, hot. Morgan thought surely she'd have to go to sleep. Her arms and fingers had a numb, drifty disproportion, her lids weighed down, blotting out the flat Long Island landscape that went past in a wavering series of jerks as they stopped at, departed from, the frequent dingy stations. Now isn't it an interesting thing, Morgan thought, that if you are hot and sleepy it's difficult to remember what else you are. Like in love. I'm in love, she told herself. Tom, Tom is far away. When's he coming back to stay? She couldn't, for a moment, remember where he was, or . . . where she was . . .

"Morgy, for Pete's sake," Betty said. "Stop falling on me."

"Huh? Oh, sure. Sorry," she mumbled. She wanted so desperately to sleep . . .

"Here we are," Betty said, as though she'd won a point.

Morgan pressed her eyes shut, opened them, followed Betty from the car.

But on the beach, with the great breakers racing against the South Shore, she was awake, crisp and light as the beading foam on the combers. Betty could swim, but she stayed close to the shore with Morgan, playing in the riotous cool waves that surged around them and trailed away. "You couldn't swim, anyway, in this," she said, and dived into an approaching wall of water.

Morgan simply stood, or sat like a child and patted the water, or dipped her face in the salty swells, letting her tan hair swirl and cling like a drenched plant. There were ships, far out, and opalescent gulls in the air above them. Thousands of people leaped in the water, lay on the beach, and yet when the two girls left the waves there was room for them to lie on the burning flaxen sand and feel apart. They dried their hair, tossing it in the sun, and shook their heads till the little warm rush of water cleared their ears. Carefully they spread thin bathtowels and lay, face down. Now their smooth backs and limbs courted the sun, relaxed beneath its warm response. Nearby, a little portable radio presented the sea and the sky and the sand with a dance tune, and a couple, a boy and girl in their teens, danced in bare feet. The girl was little and hard-looking. Her complexion in the bright air was coarse. The boy was beautifully formed, brown-bronze, with a curling lip and half-closed eyes that little could please and nothing surprise. Their stamping feet sent the sand spitting in all directions, but the dancers ignored the irritated glances around them, and no one was bold enough to protest. Morgan shuddered to think what words would come from that boy's lips if anyone spoke up against his radio, his dancing. She turned her head away, resting it on her arms, and after a while could tell by the absence of little sand particles flying that the two had subsided to their blanket. I know what they're doing now, she thought, but curiosity made her look. And, of course, they were twisted round each other in oblivious embrace, their heads close to the radio.

"Some animals need more privacy than that," she muttered.

"Oh well," Betty said, following her glance. "Live and let live. You don't have to do it, or look at them."

"No. I just wish they were somewhere else. It sort of spoils things."

"Don't be such a prude."

"I don't think it's prudish to dislike ugly things."

Betty looked again. "Well, they certainly aren't pretty," she agreed indifferently. "But lots of things aren't. I should think anyone who worked where you do would know that."

"When," Morgan asked in an access of irritation, "are you gong to develop a little tact?"

"Tact? You mean you're that ashamed of the job? Why don't you quit it?"

"Oh, I give up," Morgan said and closed her eyes.

Betty went on talking. It really was a pity Morgan wouldn't try to get a job in her department store. Well, she hesitated, in *some* department store, perhaps it wouldn't be too good for them to be in the same one. She means, Morgan thought, it wouldn't be too good for me to find out she isn't on the Sailing Team or whatever she calls it, at all. Betty thought Morgan would be grand at selling. Maybe not costume jewelry, which Betty was on at the moment, but something . . . heartier. "Ironing boards," Morgan suggested. "Double boilers." Yes, that was what Betty meant. But really, didn't she see it would make all the difference? A job with nice surroundings, even probably just as good pay, or practically, and how could that creepy cafeteria afford such wages anyway?

"I'd like to work in a pretty place," Morgan said.

"You could. There's no reason why not. They're hiring

girls at all the stores, I think. Or anyway, someone like you, who's attractive and sort of capable shouldn't have trouble."

"I don't know what's the matter with me," Morgan said in a low voice. "I never would have gone looking for this job. I wouldn't even have gone in if I'd seen the sign in the window, like Verna. But when it was just . . . handed to me, it was so much easier than looking. And the pay's not bad." How many times have I advanced that as a reason? she wondered.

"You sound just like Verna."

"Is that supposed to be a slam?"

"No. But she *is* sort of wishy-washy, you know. And you aren't. At least you never used to be."

I know it, I know it, Morgan thought, her stomach squeezing with despair. I didn't used to be, and I am now. But why? Must I trudge over this worn-out ground forever? Or work in that stinking cafeteria forever? But what was she saying? Forever? That hole? She rolled over on her back, lifting her head a bit and closing her lids against the gold burning of the sun. Voices rang over the water, and laughter, and the little radio, and under them all the steady-paced booming of waves hitting the shore. I'm afraid to look for a job, she thought. And I'm sick of staying where I am. I want to go backward. To take care of the children, work in the house, pretend to work at school. But let Pop do the job part. Not me. I don't want it, I don't want it. I'd rather scrub floors, as the saying goes. But I practically do, what I do is not much better. I want to scrub floors at home, like a lady. She began to giggle.

"Now what?" Betty said suspiciously.

"What do you mean, now what? Can't I laugh if I want to?"

"Not in that tone of voice."

Wouldn't you think, she asked herself, that now I'd really

be brave and gay? Now, with Tom loving me, what more do I want? That, of course, was the trouble. She did want more, and so did Tom, and perhaps if they hadn't met, if Tom hadn't said . . . hadn't said that some day they'd marry . . . she would have gone out, like Betty, and found a nice job, and thought it fun. It's just that I'm waiting now, she thought. I've started waiting for something else, something really rather like what I've been doing all along, only this time with Tom, and I can't stand the part in between. She had to. There would be years yet . . . years of waiting. She wondered for a moment if she would tell Betty about Tom, about getting married . . . but knew she wouldn't. Not Betty. Not Verna. The only person she might have told was Kitty McMahon, and Kitty was far away. Even if they met now, she probably wouldn't tell about Tom. And so there was no one to talk to. I want him back, she thought painfully. I want him where I can see his face, and listen to his voice. Even if we had to sit in a room full of people and never touch, I want to be where he is. She wondered what he was doing, now, while she lay on the sand and missed him. What was he saying, or thinking? What person was so lucky as to be listening this moment to Tom's voice, looking at Tom's face? And probably doesn't appreciate it, either, she thought. The darn fool. There were people all over that camp who could stand beside him, glance over and meet his eyes, ask, "What do you think, Tom?" and hear his voice respond. Not me, she thought. All those people, but not me. She turned her head, encountering the pair beside the radio. They lay very still, thighs and shoulders touching. Well, perhaps they had no other place to go, no other way to be near each other.

"You hear anything from Verna?" Betty asked.

Morgan blinked with surprise. "Oh . . . I had a postcard that didn't say much."

"That'd be the first time for our Vern," Betty laughed.

"She seems to like it up there."

"I met Emma, her sister, on the street the other day. She says Mr. Herzog nearly pulled the place apart when he heard Verna was leaving. And Verna says she isn't coming back in the fall, either."

"Isn't coming back? What can she do except come back?"

"If that man were my father, I'd go anywhere to get away from him. Or my husband, either," she added. "Although how in the world anyone could have married him to begin with—" Betty frowned. "You know, I get that feeling about practically everybody. I look at people in the street, or in the store, and I know most of them must be married, but how did the other people bring themselves to do it?"

"I guess the awful ones marry each other, so it sort of cancels out."

"Cancels out nothing. They have children and add more awfulness." She lifted her shoulders with distaste, shook her head slowly, with lowered eyes. "Morgan, I swear I will never marry at all before I'll grab at some grisly straw like Mr. Herzog. She must have been *desperate*."

"Maybe he was different when he was young," Morgan said without conviction, and agreed with the scorn in Betty's eyes. "But what did Verna say she was going to do?"

"Emma says all she says is she isn't coming back. After all, Verna's practically twenty. She should be able to support herself. She could join a Service. That'd be sort of fun. Loads of men."

"You just finished saying you hated them."

"Oh, I did *not*," Betty laughed. "I'm crazy about them. I was talking about old men, the sort who are married and have families. Soldiers are darling. The young ones, anyway. Some of them."

"They'll get old too."

"I meant I'm going to be *very* careful who I marry. Too

many girls grab the first dope that asks them, just to keep from being left. How do they know something better won't come along?"

I'm going to marry the first one who asked me, Morgan thought, with a secret delight tilting through her, an exhilarated sensibility to the summer and the waves and the happiness that she'd attained. She thought, a bit faintly, of what it would be like when she saw him again. When he stood, really there, back with her again. It was almost worth having him away . . . Not really. But now she smiled peacefully. There were moments like this, when she just cozied up in the thought of him, and was content.

"Let's go back in the water," Betty said.

Morgan sat up. "What sort of man *do* you want to marry?"

Betty looked over the waves. "I want my marriage to be . . . absolutely not like the ones I've seen. Not like our parents'. I want to have a nice house in the suburbs and a car, and belong to a country club where they have waiters in white jackets. I will *not* live in some flat in the city, growing plants out of sweet potatoes and taking care of a lot of kids."

"You don't want any children?"

"Well, maybe one or two. But clean ones, you know. Not those awful runny-nose brats and six to a family. Twins, maybe, a boy and a girl. And I want a garden, with a low wall around it and lawn furniture and people to drop in for tea." She sighed. "A sort of Colonial house, like the model on the sixth floor . . . at the store."

"Well, it sounds very grand," Morgan said, getting up. They ran toward the water, and neither noticed that Betty had described a home, not a husband.

They got back to the city in the late afternoon. Walking through the crowded streets toward home, their bodies taut and languid with salt and sun, they had little more to say. Once Betty mentioned that it was a good thing they'd stayed in the hot-dog place for a while. "I'm going to have a sunburn as it is."

"Me too. I adore it."

"Do you?" Betty asked lazily.

"Mmm. It feels so healthy, and so clean."

"I hope I don't peel. That'd be fine at the store."

She's in love with that store, Morgan thought. She seems to think about it as much as I do about Tom. And I talk less about him. It was strange, to go along these littered streets and remember the ocean rolling its long, lace-wreathed waves toward the wide pale beach. There was a breeze out there. It lifted their hair as they ran, and flung white spume, tossed sand in tiny gusts. Here was no stir of air. Here were the groceries, dry goods, gritty-looking bakeries. Their combined odors hung and mingled with those other city summer odors, gasoline and sweat. Flies spun over the pavements, children and dogs dashed in the mouth of the heat, men and women went from where they'd been to somewhere else, always crossing each other, never meeting other eyes. They walked under the thick webbing of the El, and at swift intervals a dull rumble would gather overhead, to be followed by the turbulent swaying of a train that blocked off the sun as it passed.

They paused a moment at a side street, where firemen with wrenches had opened a hydrant for the kids. Morgan smiled, wishing she could put her feet in the clear strong gush of water that sprang at the children, flooding the tarred street and the sidewalk. Screams, hoarse with exuberance, burst from the children as they threw their drenched bodies into the fountain, makeshift bathing suits clinging in soaked folds and furrows. Last year Ned had leaped and screamed in these fountains of delight. Morgan noticed, before the children

226

did, a fireman reluctantly pick up his wrench. "C'mon," she said. "Let's go." Betty, protesting, quickened her steps.

When they were around the corner from Betty's, they became aware of the siren.

"That thing's awfully close," Betty said. "I hate them. They frighten me."

"I know. Like a warning of some kind."

"Well, of course," Betty said in a tight, nervous voice that was too loud, as though she hoped the siren might have sped into silence when she stopped speaking, "they are warnings. To get out of the way."

"I meant the other kind. It doesn't toll for someone else, it tolls for you, or whatever that fellow said. Ernest Hemingway."

"It's stopping, Morgy." Betty turned her head, an expression of alarm in her eyes. She went around the corner rapidly, halting with such abruptness that Morgan collided against her. "That's our house it's in front of," she whispered. "Oh my God . . ." She turned to Morgan, eyes staring, hands clasped in front of her. She swallowed, but no words came through her open lips.

"My gosh, Betty. It could be anybody. That's a big apartment building." Morgan was feeling alternately hot and cold with fright herself as Betty's fear communicated itself. "Why do you have to think right away it's . . . for your place?"

"I don't know," Betty moaned. "I just . . . Come with me? Please?"

"Sure I will," Morgan said. "We . . . I guess we'd better go in."

They began to walk slowly toward the building, clutching their wet towels and bathing suits, breathing with nervous haste. Betty was trembling. "I don't know why I'm so scared," she repeated. "It's probably perfectly all right." But suddenly she was running, and Morgan after her.

Two men, rolling a rubber-wheeled stretcher followed them in the doors that Betty held back. "Where . . . where are you going?" she asked huskily of the nearer one, who looked at her quickly and said, "Take it easy, sister. No reason to get panicked."

"Isn't there? What apartment are you . . ." She broke off. The man looked at his companion, at Morgan, back to Betty. "Look, sis," he said. "You just go along to your place, and we'll take care of our job. Go on, like a good girl," he urged. He looked again to Morgan for assistance.

"Yes," she said. "Come on, Betty. We'll go up." But why this awful hollowness within her? They went up the three flights of stairs running, and down the narrow ringing hallway. The Gilmans' door stood open.

"Oh no," Betty breathed, leaning against the wall. "Please. No."

Angie came out and walked toward them waveringly. Her eyes were blurry, her face puffed, her usually careful curls twisted oddly. She took Betty's hand, glanced at Morgan, and the three of them went back to the apartment as the men with the stretcher appeared at the head of the stairs.

There was a great deal to be done, by Angie, by Betty. But Mrs. Metzger was dead, and past all that.

She was buried on Tuesday. That evening, alone in the apartment, Morgan sat quietly in a chair, searching the room with restless eyes, listening to the traffic, and the clock, though she didn't know what time it was, twisting the charm bracelet round and round her arm. Once she turned on the radio, but the sudden swirl of dance music reminded her of Mrs. Metzger, sitting close to the swing bands and the soap operas. She turned it off. What were Angie and Betty thinking of, in the apartment where the chair beside the radio would cry out its emptiness, unchangeable now forever? Betty, for two days, had been sickening over memories of all she'd done and left undone. Angie recalling the many kindnesses, Morgan repeating the old woman's occasional words of praise . . . it went past Betty's hearing. It was rather rough for Angie, Morgan thought, that Betty swept all the sorrow and the self-recrimination into her own arms, leaving Angie with little to do but attempt comfort. She wondered if it was always this way, when someone died, that the first person to break prevented all the others from taking whatever solace that would give. Maybe Angie preferred it that way. Perhaps her own consciousness of having often neglected her mother and daughter would be eased now by having to support Betty and remain firmly upright herself. At least, that was what Dan had said. And probably he should know, Morgan thought with peculiar detachment, since he broke first when Mother died.

She clasped her elbows in an attitude of chill, yet the night was hot, as hot as it had been Sunday when they came home from the beach.

"You're going to the funeral?" Dan had said. "You don't have to do that, do you?"

"No."

"But then . . ."

"There won't be anyone there, only Betty and Angie and me. I'm going."

"Yes." Dan bit his lip, stared over his daughter's head. "I'm sorry about it."

"Well, she was going to die sometime," Morgan said, almost impassively. "But you're never ready for anyone to die, are you?"

"No. You never are."

It isn't Mrs. Metzger, she thought now, leaning forward, slowly, till her body was in a curve, till she was in a curled,

229

defensive position. It's the dying . . . Though Mrs. Metzger was very sweet and probably wished to live a long time yet with her pain and her blindness. It was the dying. What if Ned . . . ? She hunched her shoulders. She loved so many people . . . Pop and Tom and Julie and Ned. And all of them had to die. How do we stand it, she wondered. How do people *stand* it? What do you do? How do the days ever pass, or the nights, the nights? Mother . . . *how did we stand it?* I hope I die first, she thought. Before all of them. She closed her eyes and suddenly lay back in the chair. Some day I'm going to die, she told herself carefully. Some day we will all be dead. It was nothing believable, but it was true. There was an actual day waiting for each of them, wherever the future waited for people to catch up with it, and on that day, for them, the world would end. Against the rough frieze of the chair arm she could feel the tiny beating pulse in her wrist. How could a heart go on beating at all? Mrs. Metzger's had stopped so suddenly. How could this soft hammer tap away steadily for so many years? There's a moment ready to stop that beating, she thought. There will be the moment before, and then the one for me, and then nothing will beat here in my wrist again. Only . . . me first, she thought. Me first.

She got up and walked across the room, back again. It was seven o'clock. Still light out. She thought about Mrs. Metzger's gray curls showing over the edge of the coffin while the minister spoke and they three, Angie, Betty and herself, sat in the little room off the chapel. In the chapel there'd been only the bier and the minister, since no mourners came to sit there. The organ . . . she didn't know where the organ music had come from. She had not gone up to the coffin, and neither had Betty. Only Angie, who'd stood a long while, looking down at her mother. Angie's back had looked thin in the black dress, her ankles bony, her shoulders sharp. She had been, Morgan thought, a figure of grief. Grief was a terrible word. It should only be used for mourners. But I wish, she thought, turning her head from side to side, very slowly, I wish that the curls hadn't showed over the edge of the coffin.

She was frightened. She hadn't been till this moment, but she was now, terribly frightened. Isn't there anyone, she wondered as the throbbing fear rose, anyone I could see? Or go to? You'd think she'd know somebody, even if it wasn't a friend especially, but *somebody* she could be with till her father came home? She began to cry in harsh jerky sobs, realizing that tonight she was quite alone. Unless she went to Angie? But that, of course, she couldn't do . . .

Her crying turned to whimpers as she looked at the phone. Beside it in a second, she swallowed over and over, trying to steady her voice enough to speak to the long-distance operator. He'll be there, she told herself, as the call was being put through. Tom, you *will* be there, won't you? And then she heard his voice, and leaned her head against the wall. "Tom?" she said. "Tom, talk to me for a minute. . . ."

She went back to work the next day. There'd been a thunderstorm earlier and the air had a washed sparkle overhead that made the cafeteria's slumped gloom even more oppressive. Mr. Krebble, in his wan way, brightened a bit when she came in. "Well, here's a girl we're glad to see back, eh, Cora?" he said in a tone obviously meant to be jolly. Cora said sure thing, but the moment of glee had passed for Mr. Krebble. He sighed and settled in his customary folds behind the cashier's desk.

"Get *him*," Cora said, with a wink for Morgan. "First time I ever seen the old boy notice anyone."

"Poor thing," Morgan said in a low voice. "You shouldn't make fun of him."

"Come off it. I'm not making fun of him. In fact, if there's one thing doesn't get made in this dump, it's fun."

"Probably because you can't eat it. Do you suppose we could make it look like meatballs?"

Cora grinned at this caprice. "Well, did you get the body stashed away? If you was somebody else, we'da thought you went to a ball game, but I said to Mick, if that kid says funeral, you can bet your molars it's funeral. Honest as the day is too long, I said." Morgan was looking at her with stunned immobility, but Cora talked on, never knowing when she'd said something crude or cruel and always aiming at kindness, in an unvarnished way, of course. "You gotta face facts," she said often. "No use pouring perfume on a bad smell. If things is tough, so then they're tough. Face it," she'd say robustly. "Look it in the eye!"

Morgan turned away, hoping Cora wouldn't notice, but not wanting to hear any more. She put on her white butcher apron, her cheesecloth cap, took her station above the steam.

There were just a few customers (coffee and Danish) at this hour. Like most of the people who ate in the cafeteria, their clothes looked hard-used. Their eyes at this mid-afternoon time were vacant, their postures fatigued. Spoons stirring pallid coffee set a low jangle in the air, the fans whirred untiringly, a few iridescent greeny horseflies banged against the window and whined.

Oh, well, Morgan thought, I'm finished here. It was no conscious triumph over her shrinking distrust of the world where people sought jobs. She had not arrived at a painfully firm decision, nor taken heed of what everyone had been saying against the Chatham. It was surfeit. Perhaps the knowledge of bright air somewhere, or recollection of Ned's clean young smell. She neither looked for the reason, nor thought of changing her mind. The Chatham was simply a place not to be endured any longer.

She told Mr. Krebble during the dinner half-hour, when she'd finished her salad and tea.

"You are?" he said in his voice that always seemed to be falling down. "I suppose I shouldn't be surprised. Is there any reason . . . any particular reason?"

"Well, I don't know, Mr. Krebble," Morgan answered uneasily. "Maybe . . . I think partly because of the old lady who died." She wondered at the words as they were spoken. But it was, in a way, true. Mr. Krebble would probably think she was crazy. He didn't seem to, when she looked in his face. He looked weary, but quite willing to think that was an answer. "You see," she added, "I've been . . . it's sort of made me think. Look, Mr. Krebble, I don't like to leave you all of a sudden, but after all it doesn't really matter, does it? You can get someone else. And somehow . . . her dying . . . it's made me think how awfully much you only have one life. I'd sort of like to . . . oh, find a job . . . in a pretty place," she concluded, using Betty's word.

He nodded. "I see. Well—do you think you could stay till I replace you?"

Morgan looked faintly shocked. "Of course. I wouldn't ever just walk out on any kind of job." But she hoped it would be soon that they replaced her.

That night, when the last customer had left and the large gray mop had made its final gray swirl over the tiled floor, Mr. Krebble pulled the sign out of a drawer in the cashier's desk. With Scotch tape he stuck it in the window, to the side, approximately halfway up. Then he locked up, leaving one bulb alight over the serving area and desk. Outside, he stood a moment, looking at the shadowed interior, the tables topped with stacked chairs, the ashen gleam of coffee urns. He looked at the sign in the window. *Help Wanted.* The

233

street under the El was lighted and dim in a patchwork, red, green, black, yellow. Evening traffic buzzed and stumbled past. A child laughed and stopped abruptly, as though fright, or a hand, had cut him off. Mr. Krebble sighed and loosened his tie. He'd thought, in a moment of strange sentiment, that the Connor girl was rather like a strayed willow tree. He'd been surprised to have a willow in the cafeteria at all, and should hardly have expected it to take root.

When Morgan let herself in the apartment, slightly after eight o'clock, Tom rose from the cot and came toward her. For a swift second, she was alarmed. "W-What?" she stammered, then laughed as the bright truth came. "*Tom . . .* when did you come? What are you doing?"

He stood, smiling a little, rather shy and very brown, very deeply glad to see her. "What I'll always be doing. Looking for you."

He took a step forward, Morgan took several, and they leaned against each other, tight-clasped, wordless, trembling a little. "I was worried about you," he whispered at last. "You sounded so . . . so alone and miserable, and I got to thinking about it till I just couldn't stand it. I have to go back tomorrow."

"You do? Why do you?"

"Oh . . . work. I told them I had to have two days off, but they couldn't give me any more. It's . . . wonderful to see you."

"More than wonderful," she said in a voice like cream. "It's all there is."

They sat together, on the cot, gravely holding hands and smiling at each other now and then. If heaven could be a moment in your life, Morgan thought, I'd want my heaven to be this.

Still the loud clock put that moment behind them, and the ones that came after, and boats brayed on the river as night came and in a while they had to speak.

"I stopped at the subway station," he told her, "and your father gave me the key. I'm a surprise," he added. "That's why I didn't go up to that restaurant for you."

"I know. And you are a surprise. It's nicer this way." She twined her fingers in his. "I'm leaving there, anyway."

"You are? That's the best news yet," he grinned.

She began to smile, a smile that was tremulous, and her blood quickened with what she was about to say. "You . . . don't seem to mind now, being . . . alone with me."

He turned toward her, and his eyes fixed on her face in a long, absorbed, unsmiling gaze. "I mind," he said at last. "I love it, but I mind . . . and I'm aware of where it could lead. Except that it won't, Morgan. We're going to spend the rest of our lives together, and not hash it up in the beginning." His eyes left her face, dwelt on their locked hands.

"That's what it would be? A hash?"

He shook his head. "You know what I mean. For us, it would be . . ." He broke off shakily, took a deep breath. "For us, nothing but wonderful, and right. Unfortunately, there isn't just us. And for everybody else concerned, a hash about describes it."

"I love you."

After a while, Morgan made coffee and sandwiches. They sat in the living room, he on the cot and she in a chair, talking. But not of themselves.

"I'm glad you're quitting that job."

"Me too."

"Are you going to get another, or what?"

"Oh, I have to. But it doesn't worry me any more. And now I have a navy-blue dress." Tom frowned and she laughed. "Betty says you can't get a job without one."

sorry about her grandmother, Morgan. It's . . . too

: funeral was terribly sad. Nobody came, nobody
to care, except us. Pop sent some flowers, and a bunch
hen from Angie's office did, but that's all. I . . . hated
it," she whispered. "For a while . . . while we were sitting
there, listening to the minister, I got the most peculiar feeling. As though—" She lifted her hands, lowered them to her
lap, "As though nothing really mattered at all. Even you or
Ned. What difference does it make, if we're all going to die
anyway? I've never felt like that in my life. And I don't now,"
she added, with a low laugh of relief. "It's all gone, and
everything matters more than ever. Do you ever get the feeling that it's *marvelous*? Just to walk around and feel things
and want things? Just to be alive?"

"Sure I do. Especially—" He interrupted himself. "Did
that guy, Krebs, the fellow at the restaurant, mind that
you're leaving?"

Morgan looked up in surprise. "No. Why should he? Oh,
he hoped I'd stay till they got a replacement, that's all."

They leaned back, their store of talk diminished for the
moment. The smiles were left, and the long glances, and the
heavy beating of their hearts, and in all that the breathless
reality of their love.

Chapter Fifteen

The great elm in the middle of the meadow was like a giant, Julie thought. A mother giant with tawny flocks, who leaned over girl and grasses and said in a hoarse entrancing voice, "Oh, *there,* the summer's long . . . it comes again."

But will it for me? Julie asked, unanswered. Will it come again for me? Because if she were not here, summer would not come again for her. I love it, she thought, sinking down in the rough warm grass, out of the tree's shade. I love it, I can't bear not to come back again. Arms on her knees she looked as far as she could in all directions with a fierce devotion in her eyes. The meadow was warm and slightly hilly. It lazed away behind the house and you couldn't see the highway on its farther side unless you walked far past the rise where the elm tree stood. Julie had, once or twice, walked all the way, just to know she needn't care for highways yet. There was a low stone wall at the road's edge. Wild bean and bind weed wandered across it. There were holes where black-and-gold chipmunks, perhaps even little snakes, had their homes. Julie had walked along, flicking at the berry bushes, darting her hand through the briers to pick a berry, feeling the small stones press through her soft moccasins. Then she'd turned away from the highway that led to the city and walked back to the house. Today, so close to leaving, the highway seemed to run across her heart. She looked toward the wood, where even now she could hear that wood-wind call. Mr. McCray said it was the song of the oven bird. She memorized the barn, the beehive beside it. Could she really see the bees from here, or was it just spangles in the bright air? A large green grasshopper sprang to her knee, poised on slender angled legs, seemed to study her face with his big opaque eyes. He darted off to a waving perch of grass. Below him the insects brawled in their tin and glass voices, above him fan-winged butterflies dreamed past. Amy ran scatter legged in pursuit.

"Can I look you up, sometime this winter?" Piggy had said, before he left last time. He'd been up, with Fred and Hank, many times since the first, that week end when they'd cleaned the barn and buried the robin. She'd got used to him. In a way, rather liked him. Piggy was slight and tall, and, like Julie, given to hypothesis.

"Suppose you were in the Navy," he'd say to Hank, "in the submarine corps. And suppose the sub sank. Wouldn't you hate to be one of those guys at the bottom? No way to get up, food running out, nothing to do but wait."

"They play cards," Hank said. "They're usually terribly brave about it. Of course, you'd have to be tough to go in the subs to start with."

"But if I were going in one of them, a sub, I'd take along a gun or a pill or something, just in case."

"Seems like lousy psychology," Fred offered. "Starting a trip with a bullet and a bottle of cyanide."

"I know an easier way out," Hank said.

"What?"

"Miss the boat."

These boys were all about sixteen.

"I don't know, Piggy," Julie had answered when he asked about seeing her in the winter. She really didn't know. He was nice. It was fun to dance with him, and swim, and watch him dive. Fun to race around with, with the others, at twilight, playing hide and seek. But it would be different in the city. Dressed-up clothes, movies, she supposed, and sodas afterward. It wasn't anything she could get interested in. "Couldn't you just wait, and see me next summer?" she asked.

"Well heck, how do I know you'll be here next summer?" He'd gone on talking, but Julie didn't know what she'd answered. It was the first time she'd even considered that this summer's invitation might be the last. The thought of not seeing this lake, this barn and meadow again made anything Piggy had to say insignificant. To call or not to call when the frost was on the city—she couldn't, now, sitting on the hillside, remember what their decision had been.

"But, my beautiful," she whispered to the trees and the water and the fox-colored barn, "my beautiful." On the lake a sailboat skimmed past with upflung white-sleeved arms. At the water's edge were blue spiked pickerel weeds, and scarlet swinging lances of the cardinal flower. She was filled with that passionate love which comes so close to being pain. I have to come back, she said to herself, I *must.* . . .

"Julie!" That was Ned, coming up the hill to get her. "Julie, it's lunchtime!"

"I'm coming."

"We're having lemon meringue pie."

"That's nice."

"You don't sound especially pleased," he complained, waiting for her to come up beside him.

"O Pie!" she caroled. "How I love thee . . . how I *dote* on thee, Pie!"

"Oh, you're nuts."

"I think you've grown, Ned."

"Yeah? A lot?" he said with pleasure.

"Quite a lot. At least a quarter of an inch."

"Julie," he said, turning to face her. "You have a terrible disposition."

"No, I don't. It only seems that way."

"Not much to choose, if you ask me. Why are you cross?" he asked curiously.

"I don't know, Ned. Maybe I just don't want to leave here."

He slowed his steps. "Well, neither do I. But in a way I'll be sort of glad. I miss Morgan." Julie said nothing and he added suspiciously, "Don't you miss Pop and Morgy?"

"Naturally. Only . . . It's too hard to explain, I guess. It's just that I've loved it here more than anywhere else I've ever been. And I get scared maybe Mrs. Miller won't ask us back."

"She will," Ned said confidently.

"You can't *know* that."

"Sure I do. I asked her."

"*Ned!*"

"If you wanna know something, you ask."

Julie didn't answer. She was wondering whether to allow herself to fly into the rapture Ned's words offered, or to hold off, for fear they should be a snare. His own anxiety (and he was nearly as fond of the place as she was) might have misinformed him. And anyway, she thought, who can tell a thing about next year at all? Time was the strangest thing. She could remember—it was not too long ago—when time had seemed interminable, yet anything had seemed possible. Ned was still at that age. The stretch from one Christmas to the next appalled him, but he believed the next would come. Her father, she knew, paid no attention at all to time, but none to possibilities either. And she . . . well, time was endless, and she wasn't at all sure that next Christmas, or next summer, would come. Like religion, she thought, coming back to the question that had been with her now for months. I'm like a person who believes in Hell, but not in Heaven. Even for Julie, this seemed a little too dramatic. She embarrassed herself. To disguise that, she began to talk about the city in a casual way. She wondered if that man across the street still kept pigeons, and whether Mr. Rasche, the grocer, would remember them, and if everything would look the same.

"You talk like we'd been gone ten years."

Julie flushed. "Well, I'm glad I have my crystal," she said softly.

"You scared to start high school?" Ned asked bluntly.

His sister looked surprised. "Isn't that funny? I never thought of it at all." She considered, shook her head. "No, I don't think I am."

"That's good. You've always been such a chicken heart about new schools," Ned said with the lack of feeling his own confidence gave him.

Julie agreed carelessly. "I know. I'm not now, though." She wasn't. One school, another school, it made no difference. The people made no difference. Wherever I am, she told herself, my thoughts will be here. It would be a refuge among strangers, would provide her with armor.

The night before they left, the last night in her little room, Julie sat by the window and thought of that armor again. The truth was, she needed one, had always needed one. It was easier, now that she knew. In a way, Pop had tried to tell her in the letter that was his answer to her desperate one earlier this summer. He'd called it escape. "You see, dear," he'd written, "we all need an escape sometime. Morgan used to get away from us (people, that is) by daydreaming. Now, of course, she *plans*, which is escape in its way, though perhaps

241

more enterprising than daydreams. I read. You are still searching. Squeezing the chocolates, to use your metaphor. Wherever you find your escape, don't be ashamed of the need." There'd been a change in the color of the ink here, as though he'd sat long, thinking, and the ink had paled in his pen. "How," he'd said in a final paragraph, "could we live at all if we didn't have this? Sleep to rest the body, and escape, dreams, call it what you will, to rest the spirit? How fine it must be, Julie, to have a room all your own, and the wind, and the trees. . . ."

She looked around the room now. She didn't have her lamp on. Chamois-colored moonlight touched the bedspread, the hooked rug, the Boston rocker. It gleamed gently in the old mirror above the bureau, sparkled on the round refractive eyes of Amy, who lay across the sill beside her.

Armor, escape, dreams. As Pop said, call it what you will. Sometimes, lately, her heart had felt bruised by the love—the tender altered love—she had for Pop. Even as she read his letter, she knew he put too strong a case for escape, and knew why he had to. She thought the best, the strongest thing Pop had ever done for her was write that letter. She knew at what cost he'd have pulled out of his own private world to send a message into hers. Pop's escape, she thought, must be rather like a prison, since he can never get out of it. She told herself proudly that hers would not be like that, nor her armor too heavy to wear, too tight to cast off if she wished. She felt, suddenly, a superb strength. She was even, for a while, sure that next summer would come and she be here.

"Hey, Julie!"

She leaned out the window. "Hi, Geoff. When did you get here?"

"A bit ago. I came up to drive everyone back tomorrow." Julie smiled tremulously. The words hadn't frightened her. She felt a little sad at them, but not anguished. "Come on down," Geoff said. "We're going to have a game of hide and seek in the moonlight."

"Oh. Okay, I'll be there."

Ned was It. They all stood round while he pondered a moment, scattered as he leaned his arm and his head against a tree. Julie hid behind a rosebush from which the roses had long disappeared.

". . . ninety-eight . . . ninety-nine . . . a *hundred!* Ready or not!" came Ned's warning in the moony dark. "Ready or not, here I come!"